The Spectre of Hawthorne Manor

An Utterly Addictive Historical Cozy Mystery

Anna Elliott and Charles Veley

Contents

Epigraph

"Murder will out."

—Geoffrey Chaucer, "The Prioress's Tale,"
The Canterbury Tales (1386)

Prologue

In the lively village of Crofter's Green, under the looming shadow of the grand and brooding Hawthorne Manor, whispers still stir about what happened in June of 1908.

That was the summer when American millionaire Gerald Wentworth swept into town with his young wife Gwendolyn, a duke's daughter, on his arm.

Wentworth hadn't come for the scenery—everyone knew that. He came to parade his beautiful young wife right under the nose of his old school rival, Lord Hawthorne. Their rivalry, brewing ever since their Cambridge days, was as obvious as a thundercloud on the horizon.

Yet rivalry was only part of the story. The locals often murmured that Gwendolyn, for all her grace and charm, had grown weary of Wentworth's heavy drinking and his jealous temper. Her gaze, they said, sometimes lingered a little too long on Lord Hawthorne—a glance that held more than courtesy.

Whether Wentworth noticed or simply sensed an unspoken bond, what happened next remains a mystery. One hot afternoon, tempers flared behind the manor's heavy oak doors, and Wentworth stormed from the house, his expression dark. That night, alone in his room at the inn, he scrawled a note—a cryptic message that's been the subject of speculation ever since.

Going to make it easy for the two of you to be together, my dear. A sip of Dutch courage and then I'll make all the arrangements.

Presented at the inquest as key evidence, the note stirred as much suspicion as it did pity. Some claimed it hinted at a self-inflicted tragedy, his final act a twisted gesture of release. Gwendolyn's own account was more chilling: she believed Wentworth intended to take both her and Lord Hawthorne with him, ending what he saw as a betrayal in a darkly fitting way. She'd long insisted Wentworth was a man with powerful, dangerous connections.

Yet the constable had his facts. The note had been found next to Wentworth's body, a whisky flask drained beside it. Inside his suitcase lay a vial of cyanide. The medical examiner was unequivocal: the flask had contained enough cyanide to kill within moments.

Lord Hawthorne himself offered another perspective, suggesting Wentworth's act was one of self-sacrifice, to free Gwendolyn to remarry.

The coroner ruled it a suicide, and life moved on.

Soon after, Gwendolyn became Lady Hawthorne.

Chapter One

Evie

E vie Harris didn't believe in ghosts. Which was fortunate, because she'd just awakened to find a pale, spectral figure peering in at her through her bedroom window.

She blinked, her mind momentarily trying to sort out whether she was awake or still asleep and dreaming. Her subconscious generally speaking tended towards more fact-based nightmares— smoke-filled visions of the nightly bombings in London, for example, or the occasional dream of Paul.

The figure refused to vanish, though, even after both her brain and her vision had cleared. Outside, the night sky was just beginning to lighten to the grey of early dawn. The spring air was cool but not cold, which was why Evie had left the window partly cracked open and once she'd put out her bedroom lights hadn't bothered to draw the blackout curtains. Against the pearly sky, the ghostly figure seemed to hang suspended in the air, a human-shaped form that fluttered as though wrapped in transparent and yet somehow eerily luminous gauze.

The face was blank, and yet the gauzy folds were moulded somehow to suggest hollow eyes and a mouth open in a silent scream.

Evie jolted upright, fumbling for the Luger P08 pistol that she kept under her pillow. She had her own reasons for worrying about unwanted visitors to her cottage, and those had nothing to do with ghosts.

She crept towards the window, her eyes on the glowing figure. Her bedroom was still dark, the antique dresser and bookshelf and washstand little more than hulking shadows, but she had long ago learned to move skilfully and silently without the advantage of light.

Or rather, she used to be able to move silently in the darkness. As she crossed the room, her ankle gave a sudden fiery twinge of pain that caused her to stumble and bite her lip to hold back a catch of breath.

Instantly, the ghostly figure whisked out of sight.

Evie had inherited the cottage and everything in it from her grandmother, and Gran's personality permeated everything, from the china cups in the tea shop that Evie had restored and re-opened downstairs to the big black cooking range and polished linoleum in the kitchen. But it was always here, in the bedroom, with its patchwork quilts and hand-hooked rugs, that Evie seemed to feel her grandmother's memory most strongly.

Now that sense of Gran's lingering presence saved her from uttering a word of which her grandmother probably wouldn't have approved. Evie's ankle, broken during a German air-raid in which the roof of her house had caved in on her, had very nearly healed, but it still tended to give out at inopportune moments.

She allowed herself exactly one and a half seconds to grit her teeth through the fiercest wave of pain, then she spun, caught up her dressing gown from the back of the chair, and raced out of the bedroom. She struggled into one sleeve of the dressing gown as she lurched down the narrow flight of stairs, clinging one-handed to the bannister so that she wouldn't top the broken ankle by breaking her neck, as well.

She ran through the kitchen without pausing and burst out into the garden, which was covered with early-morning mist.

Empty. The neat vegetable beds in her back garden lay quiet and undisturbed.

In this, the second spring of what was beginning to feel like an endless war, food rationing was growing ever more stringent. Evie had decided to try growing her own vegetables and had spent an entire day last week hoeing the earth and planting potatoes and peas.

Now she finished putting on her dressing gown and picked her way around them, wishing that she'd also taken a moment to put on shoes as the chilly morning dew from the grass soaked her bare feet. Still no one in sight. No sign of an intruder.

Evie wasn't surprised.

Anyone capable of fashioning as elaborate a prank as this one would surely have planned a ready escape route to avoid capture.

If prank was the right word. Crofter's Green had its eccentrics and chronic grouches among the residents, just like anywhere else. Some of them frequented her tea shop.

But Evie couldn't think of anyone who would have had either the resources or the motive to play such an elaborate practical joke. So far as she knew, she didn't have any enemies.

Not in Crofter's Green, at any rate.

"Out for an early morning stroll, Mrs Harris?"

Evie spun around to see Inspector Nigel Brewster looking at her from over her garden gate.

A tall man, the local police inspector was lean and broad-shouldered, with a hard-featured, humourless type of face.

Or maybe it was his disposition that was perpetually grim and humourless, and his expression merely reflected that. He had chiseled features, reddish-brown hair, and extremely observant brown eyes that were currently watching Evie with a look she couldn't entirely interpret.

She actually liked Nigel's uncle, Harry Jenkins, who was a retired Scotland Yard Inspector and lived in a small cottage just up the lane from her own. A few months ago, thanks to Harry, she had assisted in solving a murder and, at least temporarily, protecting Crofter's Green from a London-based gang called the Iron Dukes that dealt in black market goods and looted valuables.

By now, she viewed Harry— burly, grey-haired, and slightly bear-like— as almost an honourary uncle.

His nephew Nigel was an entirely different story.

"I thought I saw an intruder out here," she said.

Given that she was still clutching the Luger pistol, she could hardly claim that this early-morning excursion was purely for pleasure.

"An intruder," Nigel repeated.

He didn't put any inflection into the words at all, nor did his expression change. And yet he managed to make Evie feel not only as if he didn't believe her, but also as if she were guilty of some unnamed crime or folly.

It was a trick that probably stood him in good stead in the interrogation room, but was distinctly less welcome now, at five o'clock on a chilly May morning while Evie was acutely conscious of being barefoot and clad only in her nightgown and robe.

More importantly, she was also silently and furiously debating how much of her own theory about the ghostly apparition she could afford to reveal, even to a member of the local police force.

On the theory that the best defence was a good offence, she asked, "What are you doing here?"

Nigel continued to look at her with the same calmly flat gaze, and she gave it even odds that he would simply refuse to answer.

In a way, she would have loved to suspect him of having orchestrated the ghostly apparition. But for one thing, he wasn't in the slightest degree out of breath, which whoever had been operating the gauzy spectre would be, after having to beat such a hasty retreat from her back garden.

For another, no matter how much she disliked Nigel Brewster personally, Evie would be hard put to think of anyone in Crofter's Green who was less likely to be playing tricks with false spirits.

Or— to give him his due—less likely to be mixed up with German spies.

"I had a case out near Ashford," he said at last. "Local man lost his temper and went after his wife with a tyre iron."

"Is she all right?" Evie asked.

"For now." Nigel went on, almost without a pause, "That's a German make of gun, isn't it?"

The abruptness of the question was clearly designed to throw her off-balance. Evie smiled pleasantly. He'd made a mistake in skewing the tone of this conversation towards the adversarial.

She'd been interrogated by far more frightening men than Nigel Brewster, and with far worse potential consequences if she were caught out in a lie. A small, buried part of her had enjoyed it, too. Not the threat of the consequences, per se. But she had relished the complete immersion in the present moment, the knowledge that her life hung on the balance of her ability to convincingly answer any questions that were asked.

Now that part of her, the one that she'd buried deeply along with all thoughts of her old life, woke up.

"This?" She looked down at the Luger and said smoothly, "Oh, yes. My husband brought it back from a mission. He was shot down behind enemy lines and took it off the body of a dead German soldier."

Her answer even had the benefit of being true. She just didn't mention that she had been with Paul at the time, or that it was her own shot that had prevented the German soldier from killing both of them with this same Luger.

"I keep it with me now since I'm on my own here. It makes me feel safer at night to have some protection," Evie finished.

She'd been hoping that Nigel might be softened slightly by the reminder that she was a war widow living on her own. Policemen were trained to be considerate and protective of the weak and vulnerable.

But no. He folded his arms on the top of the garden gate and asked, "Do you know how to shoot it?"

Evie gave him another pleasant smile. "It wouldn't be very much use to me if I didn't."

Nigel was silent a moment, then he said, "That's not your only area of surprising competence, is it? During the blackout murder affair, when we were facing that German agent in the barn, you managed to disarm and disable a man who was probably close to twice your weight."

Evie didn't allow herself to show it, but she winced inwardly. In the moment, she hadn't had any choice but to tackle the extremely unpleasant man who'd been threatening to shoot both Nigel and his uncle. But she'd been hoping that Nigel either hadn't noticed her close combat technique or had forgotten.

"Before my marriage, I was a games mistress at a girl's school in France," she said. "I taught physical education to all the students, which included a course in self-defence."

"I see." Again, Nigel's completely neutral tone managed to convey the impression that he didn't believe a word of her story.

"You never entirely explained how your return trip from Ashford managed to include a detour into my back garden," she said.

Nigel, still leaning on the gate between them, didn't answer at once. Then he said, "I'm fond of my uncle Harry."

This time, he did manage to catch Evie off-guard with the abrupt change of subject. She blinked. "So am I. He's a good friend."

Nigel's level stare didn't alter, exactly, and yet it somehow intensified as he peered at her through the lightening shadows of early dawn. "Do you know, I'd swear you're telling the truth about that."

"I am. Whether you believe it or not."

"My uncle is a good man," Nigel said. "And he likes you, which is why I'm giving you this warning: if you put him in danger or betray him in any way, you'll have me to answer to."

The grimness of his expression had Evie revising her earlier estimation of his character: under the right circumstances, Nigel Brewster might be every bit as dangerous as any Nazi officer she'd faced.

"Do you think I would?" she asked.

"I think"— Nigel laid slight emphasis on the word— "you're a woman who's clearly not quite who she appears to be. And this morning, I happened to see a figure— just a shadow— come running out through this gate here." He smacked the gate lightly with the flat of his hand. "I came in to investigate, and found you out here with a gun."

"I told you I'd seen an intruder."

"You did. And rather than staying inside and telephoning to the police like most civilians would have done, you came running out here without even bothering to put on shoes first."

His glance flicked to her bare feet.

"What exactly is it that you suspect me of?" she asked. "Spying for the Germans?"

Nigel didn't answer that. "Is there anything you'd like to tell me about why an intruder would be targeting you?" he asked.

"I've no idea. Maybe it was one of the Iron Dukes or the Black Briars, either out for distraction or revenge after the Blackout murder affair."

That was a genuine possibility, and frankly, Evie would be delighted to think that it was the right explanation. But if it wasn't— if this morning's ghostly apparition was a sign that her old life had somehow caught up with her—

Nigel looked at her another long moment, then tipped his head in a brief nod. "Good day, Mrs Harris. I'm sure I'll be seeing you around the village."

It sounded far more like a threat than a simple goodbye.

Hands in the pockets of his overcoat, he turned and walked away.

Evie went quickly back into the kitchen, locked the door behind her, and then, shivering, set the tea kettle on the stove to boil. This morning's spectral visitor was troubling.

But Nigel Brewster had the potential to become an even greater problem.

Chapter Two

Harry

Harry Jenkins walked down the corridor of the Ashford police station house, his boots echoing off the tiled floors. He'd been asked to stop by Superintendent Miles Sedgwick's office for a chat—an informal check-in, Sedgwick had called it. Since arriving in Crofter's Green, Harry had kept his detective instincts sharp and his ear to the ground, and he'd grown a bit of a reputation after his help with the recent Iron Dukes case. It seemed Sedgwick had taken a liking to him, or at least found him useful.

When he reached the office, Sedgwick waved him in, a broad smile breaking across his face. The superintendent leaned back in his chair, hands clasped across his middle. "Ah, Jenkins. Good of you to come by," he said. "Sit, sit. I thought we'd go over that business with the Iron Dukes and Black Briars. Can't tell you how much it helped to have an experienced copper like yourself poking around."

Harry nodded politely and took a seat. "Glad to have been of service, sir," he replied, though he could feel the faint tug of unease settling in his gut. He'd worked the Iron Dukes case with Nigel—Inspector Nigel Brewster, his nephew—and while Sedgwick had praised him, it hadn't escaped Harry's notice that Nigel's contributions were rarely mentioned.

"And it's not just the Iron Dukes business," Sedgwick continued, clearly warming up. "Your instincts are sharp, Jenkins. Made all the difference. Without your help, I daresay we'd still be fumbling around with that mess."

Harry felt his jaw tighten slightly, but he kept his face impassive. Nigel had worked tirelessly on that case, digging up leads and connecting dots in ways that had left the whole department impressed—well, everyone but Sedgwick, it seemed.

As Sedgwick rambled on, a young man stepped through the door, interrupting. He was tall and broad shouldered, with a shock of dark hair and an easy confidence that seemed almost too big for the room. His left arm was in a sling.

"Ah, Barkley Robbins!" Sedgwick greeted him, his voice hearty. "The son of Mayor Robbins himself." He clapped the young man on his uninjured shoulder. "Harry Jenkins, meet Barkley. Took a blow during one of the air raids in London, didn't you, lad?"

Barkley nodded, smiling modestly, though his eyes were sharp and calculating as he looked Harry over. "Yes, sir. Not the kind of experience one forgets in a hurry," he said, glancing down at his arm.

Sedgwick beamed. "Once that shoulder's healed, we'll have you fit for police work in no time, eh?"

"Looking forward to it, sir," Barkley replied smoothly, his tone carrying the kind of entitlement that set Harry's instincts on edge.

Harry managed a polite nod but felt a flicker of unease. He'd seen types like Barkley before—sons of men in high places who assumed they'd coast into positions of authority. He'd also seen how easily men like Sedgwick were impressed by a well-connected name. In his mind, he could already see the inevitable outcome: Barkley being set up as a rising star, quietly edging out the competition. And he had a sinking feeling he knew who the competition was.

"Fine lad, that one," Sedgwick said, after Barkley had exited. "With his father's connections and the experience he's picked up, I wouldn't be surprised if we see him rise quickly through the ranks. A natural fit for leadership, don't you think?"

Harry kept his voice neutral, though he felt his suspicions solidify. "Aye, could be," he replied. But as he left the superintendent's office, the weight of it settled heavy in his chest. Sedgwick's focus on Barkley's "promise" felt like a dark omen for Nigel. His nephew had worked his way up through hard-earned experience and countless hours in the field, but that kind of determination didn't always win out against connections and a polished surname.

As he stepped out into the cool afternoon air, Harry couldn't shake the feeling that this new lad was more than just another recruit. He was the first step in a shift that could easily push Nigel out of the picture. *I'll be keeping an eye on this,* Harry thought grimly, his fists clenched in his pockets as he walked away from the station.

Chapter Three

Evie

"Did you just say, *Haunted*?" Evie Harris asked.

She looked up from the tray of tea cakes she'd been arranging on a Wedgwood blue serving platter, wondering whether the experience with her early morning spectral visitor was somehow warping her hearing.

She had spent the last two months restoring her grandmother's tea shop and re-opening the place for business. The roof still leaked occasionally, and Evie had at best an uneasy truce with the big, temperamental cooking range. But all in all, Evie's Cozy Cup was on its way to becoming a modest success, even though sugar was in scarcer supply than it had ever been. As were butter and flour and eggs and— as Evie found herself reflecting on particularly trying days— nearly every other ingredient that it took to run a successful tea and baked goods shop.

Today's recipe for walnut cakes with lemon icing relied mostly on nuts for moisture and richness, and now Evie was adding half of a shelled walnut to the top of each cake to distract attention from just how thinly the icing was spread.

She had exactly ten minutes before she had to leave for Hawthorne Manor, the seat of the Hawthorne family.

Which— unless her ears were in fact playing tricks— her assistant Dorothy Baker had just claimed was haunted.

Dorothy turned away from the sink full of dirty dishes she'd been washing.   A pretty, young woman with rosy cheeks and blue eyes, Dorothy wore a red and white print apron over her blue cotton dress.   Her blonde hair curled around her face.

"Well, that's the rumour going around," she told Evie. "Alfred Travers was in for a pint at the King's Arms last night.   I'm not sure if you'll have met him before, but he's the groundskeeper up at Hawthorne Manor.   And he said that Lord Hawthorne's suddenly afraid of his own shadow and swears that the manor's haunted."

Evie set another tea cake on the tray while she weighed that information.   She didn't believe in coincidences any more than she believed in ghosts, and two incidents of spectral sightings in one week in the same village were unlikely to be unrelated to each other.   But she didn't want to tell Dorothy about the glowing figure outside her own window.

As far as Dorothy and the rest of Crofter's Green knew, Evie's past life was an open book: she'd grown up in America, worked as a schoolteacher in France, met and married her husband Paul, and then moved to London to do her part for the war effort as an air raid warden until Paul's plane was shot down and he was killed.

Filling in other details— like the reason Evie slept with a loaded pistol under her pillow— would only put Dorothy in danger.

"So is this just a recent fancy of Lord Hawthorne?" Evie asked after a moment's pause. "Not some sort of a local legend going back centuries?"

Crofter's Green was a beautiful, old-fashioned village in Kent, not far from the coast.   Even the war and all it entailed: rationing, blackouts, and the planes— both German and British— that flew overhead hadn't been able to destroy the peace and beauty of the place. The streets were paved with cobblestones, many of the cottages still had thatched roofs, and all in all, Evie would have been prepared to bet that even the local ghost stories had a kind of quaint and cozy charm.

Dorothy shook her head, though.   "I grew up here, and I never heard any stories about the manor house being haunted.   I don't suppose Lady Hawthorne mentioned it when she telephoned to put in her order?"

"No, she didn't say anything about her husband at all. All she told me was that she was planning to host a charity tea at Hawthorne Manor to benefit wounded servicemen and was wondering whether I could bring her a tray of some of our baked goods up to the manor so that she could sample them. She said she might hire us to do the catering."

Which was why Evie was currently scrambling to assemble walnut tea cakes with lemon icing. She glanced at the clock that hung over the pinewood Welsh dresser where she stored her grandmother's dishes. Eight minutes, now, until she had to—

The front doorbell of the cottage jangled.

Evie's pulse instantly kicked into higher gear, although she kept her voice calm as she said, "That's strange."

Evie's Cozy Cup didn't open for business until eleven o'clock, when housewives out shopping were likely to drop in for a restorative cup of tea after braving the endless wartime queues in the stores. And any of her neighbours wanting to speak to her would have just come around back to the kitchen door.

"I'll go." Dorothy stopped washing dishes and reached for a towel to dry her hands, but Evie moved quickly past her, abandoning the tray of tea cakes.

"No, it's all right, I'll go."

Evie pushed open the swinging door that led from the kitchen into the tea room.

The front entrance to the tea shop was set with a long rectangular window in which she could hang a sign that either read open or closed. The sign was flipped to closed, now. But behind it, she could still see the figure of a thin teenage boy standing on the stoop outside. He was wearing the uniform of a telegram office messenger.

"They said Mrs Dorothy Baker would be here," the boy said. "At the inn, I mean. It's sixpence."

Evie's first, brief reaction of relief was transformed into dread that pooled in the pit of her stomach. She turned around instinctively, one hand up as though to try to stop Dorothy from coming out of the kitchen, even though that would accomplish nothing except to delay the inevitable.

But Dorothy had already come to the kitchen doorway and seen the messenger, too. She froze, her mouth open in a low, despairing moan. "No."

Dorothy sagged and might have fallen if Evie hadn't stepped quickly to put an arm around her. She was still shaking her head and moaning. "No, no, no."

Evie helped her to one of the tables that dotted the tea room and gently lowered her into a chintz-covered chair, but she didn't say anything. What could she say?

Dorothy's husband Tom was away fighting with the army, which meant that any unexpected telegram was quite literally the stuff of nightmares. There wasn't a single word of reassurance that Evie could offer in this moment. The thought of Dorothy being left a widow with an eight-year-old son to bring up on her own might make Evie feel as though the world was broken, fundamentally *wrong*. But Evie also knew firsthand that the world was in fact broken, and that life sometimes could be exactly that cruel.

"Do you want me to . . ." she began.

Dorothy nodded wordlessly. Her hands were braced under her ribcage and tears were already starting to stream down her face.

Evie fished in her pocket and exchanged a sixpence for the message that the telegram office boy clutched. The boy tipped the brim of his hat without a word and hopped back on his bicycle to pedal swiftly back up the lane.

Evie couldn't blame him for not lingering; he'd probably witnessed more scenes of wrenching grief in the past few months than most people did in an entire lifetime.

With another sick, sinking feeling of dread, Evie turned the telegram over. Then her breath went out in a rush.

"He's not dead," she told Dorothy. "The message is to tell you that Tom has been wounded, but he's still alive."

For a moment, Dorothy just stared at her, seeming to scarcely even be able to comprehend the words. Or maybe it was just that she didn't dare to believe them. Then at last she faltered, "Tom's . . . alive?"

"Yes." Evie crossed to squeeze her hand and offer her the telegram. "You can see for yourself. He's wounded, but he's recovering at a hospital in London."

Dorothy looked from Evie to the telegram, her expression dazed. "Alive," she said again. She squeezed her eyes shut a long moment. Then she looked up at Dorothy with a start. "I have to go to him," she said. "But Tommy . . . and Mum—"

"Don't worry about anything except catching the next train to Dover," Evie told her firmly. "I can visit your mother on my way up to the manor and let her know you've been called away, and Alice can easily go and fetch Tommy home from school this afternoon."

Her nearest neighbour Alice Greenleaf was an older but still vigorous woman who ran the local apothecary shop and contributed herbs for Evie's homemade blends of tea.

"You know he always loves playing at Alice's house," Evie told Dorothy.

Dorothy stood up shakily, but then stopped. "Are you sure?" she began. "Your meeting with Lady Hawthorne—"

"Will just have to be a bit delayed."

Dorothy's husband might be alive, but no one knew how long he would remain so.   The telegram didn't specify anything about how serious his wounds were.   Evie certainly wasn't going to point out as much to Dorothy, though, so all she said was, "I'll telephone and let Lady Hawthorne know what's happened, I'm sure she'll understand."

And while she was there, she would also find out everything that she could about the sudden appearance of Lord Hawthorne's ghosts.

Chapter Four

Dorothy

It had only been about nine months since Dorothy had last been in London, but the city was still so changed that she scarcely recognized it. The day was warm with the bright spring sunshine, the sky overhead bright blue, but even that couldn't take away the sombre feeling in the air.

On nearly every street, there were buildings that had been scarred or reduced to heaps of broken concrete and wood by a bomb. On some streets, nearly every building was destroyed, and those buildings that were left looked lonely and vulnerable, standing out in the open alone, just waiting for the next bombing raid to strike them down, too.

Nearly everyone— men and women alike— was in some sort of uniform. Although a few housewives in headscarves were lined up at the ration shops, or hurrying home with string bags filled with tinned goods. Many of the London children had been evacuated to the country, so there were few to be seen.   But here and there, Dorothy saw a few boys playing in the rubble of a bombed house.

An ambulance tore by, sirens wailing, forcing them to wait at the corner of Lambeth Road behind what looked like a solid wall of other cars and army transport vehicles.   It was the third time that they'd been brought to a standstill this way, and Mr Murphy, the Hawthornes' chauffeur, glanced at Dorothy in the rear-view mirror.

"London traffic's something fierce.   Should be there soon, though."

He was a sprightly, grey-haired man with a thick Irish brogue, a cheerful face, and ears that stuck out slightly from under his driver's cap.   He was too old for military service, which was why he was still working up at the manor.

Growing up in Crofter's Green, Dorothy had known him all her life, and she was grateful that he was the one driving her— insofar as she could think about anything besides being worried about Tom.

Wounded.   The word felt like a spike being driven straight into her ears.   *Wounded.*

But the telegram hadn't said how badly Tom was hurt. What if he was dying?   What if he died before she could get there?

Her hands locked tightly together in her lap, she nodded in answer to Mr Murphy and said, "Thank you for driving me."

"That's all right, luv." Mr Murphy winked at her. "Beats staying at home and listening to his lordship maundering on about being haunted."

"Do you think he really is seeing anything?" Dorothy asked. Any distraction was better right now than thinking about all the cars in front of them and how many more times they might have to stop like this before she could get to Tom.

"Well, now, I don't know. Never seen a ghost, myself, up at the manor or otherwise," Mr Murphy said. "My old grandmother had the Second Sight, or so she always claimed. Although her predictions only came true about half the time. We kids used to joke that maybe her Sight needed a pair of spectacles." He winked again. "As for his lordship, that I don't know. I'd say it's all nonsense, but he looks like a man who's been scared almost to death. Whether or not the haunting's real, *he* believes it's real, I'll tell you that."

To Dorothy growing up, Lord and Lady Hawthorne had always been remote, awe-inspiring figures up at the manor house. You might see Lady Hawthorne riding by in the lane, dressed in a sable-trimmed riding habit, or Lord Hawthorne in a black top hat and kid gloves making a speech at the church fete. But otherwise they belonged to another world entirely from the simple farmhouse where Dorothy had been born.

"It's a rum business altogether," Mr Murphy went on. "If I weren't a sight too old to make a fresh start somewhere else, I'm not sure I'd stay."

"Really?" Dorothy always thought of Mr Murphy as being almost as much an institution as Lord and Lady Hawthorne. Stiff and correct in his chauffeur's livery, driving the big black Daimler to church on Sundays.

And now here she was in the back of that same Daimler car. It was a shame that Tommy couldn't be here, Dorothy thought. At eight, he was young enough that he might have been able to put aside worrying about his dad and be thrilled for a minute or two. She didn't want to think how he'd feel when he heard about his father being hurt.

Alice would look after him. She and Dorothy's mum had been friends since they were Tommy's age, and as such, Tommy thought of her as a great-aunt. But even still, Dorothy would have given almost anything to be the one to break the news.

"Ah, well, the manor's not the place it once was," Mr Murphy was saying. "The times we used to have in the servant's hall. But the staff's all gone, most of 'em. Or not worth their salt. Take Alf Travers. Supposed to be groundskeeper, but does he do the work he's paid for?" Mr Murphy snorted. "He does not. Skives off to Ashford every chance he gets to bet on the races."

The traffic ahead of them finally moved, and Mr Murphy put his foot back on the accelerator. The Daimler rolled forward.

"There, now." Mr Murphy pointed past a row of broken town homes that were being cleared away by a bulldozer. "You can see the roof of St. Thomas' just up ahead there."

Instantly, the sharp-edged lump of fear in Dorothy's throat was back. She nodded but couldn't speak.

Mr Murphy gave her another sympathetic glance. "Don't you be worrying, now. He'll be all right. Bound to be. Why, I remember your Tom when he was just a boy, the same as your little lad. Strong as a cart horse, even then. It'd take more than Hitler to bring him down."

Dorothy managed a small, mechanical smile.

The car made a turn, then another, and then St. Thomas' Hospital loomed up ahead of them, a huge brick building with white plasterwork and turrets on the corners. Some of the turrets had been damaged in the bombing raids, and Dorothy could see an area where workers were repairing a part of the roof that had caved in.

Being near the Thames as it was, the hospital was bound to be in added danger of being bombed. The German planes targeted the ships at anchor in the London ports, trying to stop supplies from coming into the country or weapons for the troops from going out.

Mr Murphy drew to a halt in front of the main entrance. "Good luck, luv.   I'll wait right here for you for when you want a ride back."

"Oh."   Dorothy hadn't even stopped to consider how she was going to get back to Crofter's Green.   She hadn't really thought about anything apart from getting to Tom, but of course they wouldn't let her stay in the hospital with him overnight.

She'd have to be getting back home to Mum and Tommy, too. They both needed her.   Mum's rheumatism was bad enough that she could hardly get around to make herself a cup of tea or boil an egg for supper.   And Dorothy always tucked Tommy into bed and told him a bedtime story before going downstairs to work at the King's Arms.   She couldn't skip their routine tonight, not when he'd just found out about his dad. "I can't ask you to stay," she protested.   "I don't even know how long I'll be."

"That's all right.   I've got the paper to read."   Mr Murphy nodded at the morning edition of the Times that lay on the front seat beside him.   "And I maybe can catch a bit of shut-eye if I get tired of reading the news of the day."

He gave her a shooing motion and a kindly smile.   "Tell your Tom I said hello.   And I'll be here waiting when you're done with your visiting."

Chapter Five

Evie

Evie had been running the Cozy Cup for a little under three months now, but she still felt a small thrill every time she crossed the tea room to turn the sign in the front door from closed to open.

The tea shop was always at its best first thing in the morning, when the sun slanted in through the lace curtains at the windows, making the polished wooden floor gleam and the shelves of homemade jams and jellies and marmalade glow with reds and purples and golds.

Today, though, she had the beginnings of a headache from having been awake for much of the night before. No visitors—ghostly or otherwise— had appeared outside her window, but she had stayed awake in tense expectation of another uninvited guest and had only dropped off to sleep in uneasy fits and starts.

The sight of the morning's first customer who was already waiting on the doorstep brought a fresh twinge behind Evie's eyes.

"Inspector Brewster." Evie unlocked the door and stepped back to allow him to enter. "What a surprise."

His uncle Harry was a frequent guest at the Cozy Cup, dropping by for a quiet meal or simply to see whether Evie had any odd jobs that needed doing. Despite Evie's best attempts to pay him for his help, Harry insisted on accepting nothing more than cups of tea and the occasional scone in exchange for repairing broken window frames, cleaning chimneys, and putting patches on the roof.

His latest project had been re-caning and re-finishing the old-fashioned Victorian chairs that Evie had found in the back of the local antique store, hidden under a tarp because the dealer thought they were fit only for kindling. She'd bought all six of them for a mere three pounds, and Harry had helped her to restore them. Now the chairs were grouped around the lace-covered tea tables, where their ornately carved backs and gracefully turned legs fit in perfectly with the rest of the shop's furnishings. From the overly-elaborate scroll work to the carved acanthus leaves on the arms, Evie loved every bit of them.

Now she saw Nigel's eyes sweep the tea room, linger briefly on the chairs, then move on to the glass case in which she kept the day's baked goods on display, all with the same dispassionate expression with which Evie imagined he would regard a crime scene.

"I didn't have time for breakfast this morning," he said. "And since I was passing by, I thought I'd stop in for a cup of tea and anything you have to eat."

Evie was tempted to point out that although Nigel Brewster might be an excellent interrogator, he was significantly less skilled at telling a convincing lie than the criminals he investigated. He sounded as stiff and wooden as a school child reciting the multiplication tables.

But she said, only, "Of course. I haven't baked anything yet this morning, but you can have a cup of tea and one of yesterday's bannocks."

Scottish bannocks were a staple of her repertoire, since they relied heavily on oats and thus allowed her to stretch her flour rations a little further.

"Thank you."

Nigel sat down stiffly on one of the newly-refinished chairs, and Evie departed for the kitchen. She didn't especially relish leaving him alone and unattended in her tea room, but making him aware of that would be a serious mistake.

At least he didn't seem to have taken the opportunity to poke or pry into anything. When Evie returned with a cup of tea and one of the bannocks on a plate, he was still sitting exactly as she'd left him, ramrod straight in his chair and drumming the tips of his fingers against the table.

"Thank you," he said again, when Evie had set the cup and plate down before him.

"You're welcome."

He made no move to pick up either the tea or the bannock, however, only gave her an unreadable look. "So you inherited this place from your grandmother?"

"That's right." Evie wasn't entirely sure where he was going with this conversation, but she had an inkling.

"I met her a few times," Nigel said. "She took sick and had to close down the business soon after I was appointed to the police station here. But she came to me once because she'd lost an amethyst ring that had been her mother's. She probably told you about it: an amethyst in a circle of pearls, with Evelyn engraved on the inner band."

Evie sighed. Sometimes it was tiresome to be proven right. "That would be surprising," she said. "Since my great-grandmother's name was Juliette. Juliette Eleanor Thurgood, married name Armstrong. It would also be extremely surprising if she ever had anything as valuable as a pearl and amethyst ring, given that she was a coal miner's daughter and married a clergyman— in 1868, if you want to be particular— who was as poor as the proverbial church mouse."

Nigel opened his mouth, but Evie went on before he could respond. "You know, if you suspect me of being an impostor and not really the granddaughter of the woman who owned this place, you could just come right out and ask me for an account of the family history. Although I'm not honestly sure which is the more insulting: that you think I'm not who I claim to be. Or that you imagine that I wouldn't have done my homework and have memorized every detail of the real Evelyn Harris's family and background in order to avoid being tripped up by exactly the sort of questions you apparently came here to ask."

She might— possibly— have succeeded in embarrassing Nigel. His expression didn't alter, but there was a slightly heightened flush of colour on his cheekbones.

He was spared having to answer, though, by the chime of the bell over the front door and the arrival of Evie's second customer of the day, a thin middle-aged housewife with a shopping basket over one arm and a weary expression.

"Hello, Mrs Campbell," Evie called to her.

Then she bent over Nigel's table, pretending to adjust the tablecloth as she spoke in an undertone. "You can go ahead and drink your tea. If I'd wanted to harm you, you can be certain that I'd find a far more untraceable method than dropping poison in a cup in my own place of business."

Chapter Six

Harry

Harry Jenkins was sipping tea at his small kitchen table, thoughts unsettled as he watched the steam curl up from his mug. His visit to Sedgwick's office lingered in his mind. The superintendent's words about "natural leadership" and the future of the constabulary had left him with a sour taste. That new lad, Barkley Robbins—son of the mayor, war-wounded from the Blitz, and all too comfortable in his role as the upcoming favourite—had made quite an impression on Sedgwick. Harry knew how men like Barkley moved through the ranks, riding their connections and letting their last names open doors. And when people like Sedgwick started noticing, men like Nigel, who'd earned every scrap of respect through hard work, rarely came out on top.

Harry couldn't shake the feeling that Sedgwick was already eyeing a replacement for his nephew.

The sharp knock on the door snapped him back to the moment. He set down his teacup, glancing around his snug, worn-in kitchen—a place he'd made his own since leaving the chaos of London. He opened the door to find Nigel standing on the stoop, shoulders slumped, an unmistakable weariness in his eyes. It seemed Harry wasn't the only one feeling the strain.

"Nigel?" Harry gave him a nod, stepping aside to let him in. The last time he'd seen Nigel, there'd been hints of trouble, but now it seemed to have settled over him like a shadow.

Nigel entered, looking older somehow, the kind of weary that ran deeper than lack of sleep. "It's about Sally Roe," he said quietly. "She called the station last night—sounded terrified. She claims someone's trying to kill her." He paused, glancing away. "Used to be lady's maid at Hawthorne Manor, but she's been in the asylum nearly a decade now."

Harry felt a twinge of recognition—a case like this was exactly what he'd expect them to hand Nigel, something tangled and impossible to solve cleanly. The kind of case that could trip a young inspector up, especially if there was someone waiting in the wings to step in if he faltered.

"Sally Roe?" Harry kept his tone neutral, though his mind was working quickly. They'd put Nigel on a case that was sure to be nothing but trouble. It would give Sedgwick all the reason he needed to shuffle his nephew out and move Barkley Robbins in. He motioned for Nigel to join him in the kitchen and poured him a fresh cup of tea, setting it down in front of him as they sat. "And what do you think?"

Nigel wrapped his hands around the mug, his expression strained. "I don't know," he admitted. "She's had... episodes before, but this time felt different. I thought maybe you could come along, get a read on her. You've handled situations like this before."

Harry leaned back, crossing his arms as he studied his nephew. Nigel's shoulders were slumped, his gaze fixed on the tea as if it held answers he couldn't find. They're setting him up, Harry thought grimly. This case was a minefield, every misstep just another excuse for Sedgwick to bring his favoured recruit into the fold.

Harry met his nephew's gaze, giving him a steady nod. "All right," he said, grabbing his coat from the hook by the door. "Let's pay Sally a visit."

As they stepped outside, Harry was expecting to see Nigel's familiar black Wolseley saloon, but he stopped short when he saw a different car parked by the gate. It was a boxy little Ford Prefect—its paint fading to grey and no doubt with a sputtering engine that Harry could practically hear just from looking at it.

"Not the Wolseley?" Harry asked, glancing at Nigel.

Nigel's jaw tightened slightly, and he gave a quick nod. "Re-assigned, they said. Needed for... other purposes."

Harry's eyes narrowed, catching the unspoken meaning. So this is how they're doing it, he thought, the frustration simmering as he climbed into the Ford beside Nigel. They weren't just shifting him onto dead-end cases; they were stripping away everything that marked him as an inspector with real standing. And that little Ford, worn and beaten as it was, was just one more reminder of how they were quietly pushing him out.

Harry settled back, jaw clenched, as they drove down the lane.

Chapter Seven

Evie

"Just an intimate little gathering," Lady Gwendolyn Hawthorne said.

The matron of Hawthorne Manor was a tall, lean woman of around fifty-five, with brassy blond hair that she wore cut in a short bob and a long-nosed, aristocratic face. For their meeting this morning, she wore an exquisitely tailored tweed coat and skirt over a pink silk blouse. Even with the recent shortages, her stockings were— of course— silk, and around her neck hung a string of pearls that probably cost more money than Evie would see in an entire year.

"A hundred people." Lady Gwendolyn tapped the tip of her gold pen against the leather-bound notebook she was holding on her lap. "Or at most a hundred and fifty, but certainly no more."

If a hundred and fifty guests was Lady Gwen's idea of an intimate gathering, Evie would love to hear her definition of a grand ball.   But then again, living in a home with no fewer than twenty-three bedrooms probably tended to alter one's perspective.

Sitting on the outskirts of the village of Crofter's Green, Hawthorne Manor was a stately mansion, built of grey stone with large windows, ivy-covered walls, and a sweeping drive-way that was lined with poplar trees.   Everything about the interior was as stately and perfectly curated as the outside.

Lady Gwendolyn had received Evie in the morning room, which was a big, high-ceilinged room in the eastern wing of the house.   The walls were painted in dark green with a white plasterwork frieze around the ceiling.   The carpets were plush orientals, and the furniture was antique walnut and mahogany, fashioned in the old English style.   Paintings that Evie assumed were for the most part old family portraits hung on the walls, although she was reasonably certain that an oil painting of a summer landscape had been done by Constable.

"Your tea cakes are really quite good," Lady Gwendolyn went on.   She had sampled one already from the tray that Evie had brought.   "So I feel quite confident that any sweets you bring will be up to standard."

It would be easy, Evie thought, to dismiss Lady Gwendolyn as one of the idle rich, the sort of woman who was born with a silver spoon in her mouth and had never done an honest day's work in her entire life.   But that wouldn't be quite fair.

Lady Gwendolyn *had* been born into a life of oriental carpets and silver spoons. The daughter of a duke, her every experience, every aspect of her education— from the books chosen by her expensive French governess to her dancing lessons to the finishing school in Paris where she had learned etiquette and deportment— everything had been designed to mould her into exactly what she was now: the lady of the manor. It wasn't entirely her fault that she seemed never to question her privileged place in the world or her worthiness to fill it.

Nor was she without human feeling. Evie knew that Lady Gwendolyn gave generously to local charities. And the moment Evie had telephoned earlier this morning to explain why she was going to be delayed, Lady Gwendolyn had insisted that Dorothy wasn't even to think of going to her husband by train. Instead, Lady Gwendolyn's own chauffeur had rolled up to the front of Evie's Cozy Cup five minutes later with orders to drive Dorothy all the way to London in the Hawthorne family Daimler.

That alone would have been enough to make Evie ignore the unconscious note of condescension in Lady Gwendolyn's words, *up to standard.*

Lady Gwendolyn consulted her notepad and seemed about to say more, but at that moment a flurry of barking erupted from the veranda that ran along the outside of the morning room's double French doors.

A frown appeared between Lady Gwendolyn's arched brows and she rose to open one of the doors and peer out.

A furry brown streak shot past her ankles and into the room, still barking furiously.   The small Pomeranian dog tore in a circle around the room—upsetting a small gimcrack table and sending an ornamental vase tumbling to the floor—then rocketed out again into the hall, where Evie heard his high-pitched yips fading away as he raced off into some other part of the manor.

"Really, Walter."   Lady Gwendolyn turned to the man who had followed the dog in through the French door and gave him a disapproving frown.   "What have I told you about letting Bonzo get away from you while on your morning walks?   And for pity's sake, shut the door behind you!   You'll let in flies."

Her husband ducked his head, chastened by his wife's rebuke. But he didn't appear to notice the second part of Lady Hawthorne's admonishment, since he made no move to shut the French door onto the terrace.   "Sorry, my dear.   There was no holding him.   He saw a squirrel and slipped his lead."

Lord Hawthorne was a tall man, some ten years older than his wife, and in appearance, he looked more like an absent-minded scholar than the lord of the manor.   He had stooped shoulders and grey hair growing thin over the crown. His face was narrow and ascetic, with a high forehead and thin lips.   His eyes, behind a pair of gold-rimmed spectacles, were a shade of pale washed-out blue, framed by colourless lashes. They blinked at the world with a mild, vaguely surprised gaze, as though he were constantly forgetting where he was and what he was doing and then being reminded of it again.

Evie had met him before and found him perfectly pleasant, even if he could never remember her name and had called her Emily, Ellen, and Edith, all in the space of a single conversation.

Now she looked at Lord Hawthorne, shocked by the change in his appearance since the last time they had met. The hands that were holding Bonzo's empty lead were trembling, and his hollow, bloodshot eyes were ringed by dark circles. His skin had an unhealthy greyish tinge, and seemed too tightly drawn over his cheekbones and temples. Dorothy's report on what the groundskeeper had said about Lord Hawthorne being afraid of his own shadow seemed to be all too accurate.

"Well, don't just stand there," Lady Gwendolyn said impatiently. "Go and catch him! You know how annoyed Cook gets when Bonzo bursts into her kitchen and gets underfoot while she's trying to prepare lunch."

"Yes, my dear." Lord Hawthorne ducked his head again and started to shamble out of the room.

"And find Diana," Lady Gwendolyn added. "Last I saw her, she was in the library. Bonzo always behaves better for her than anyone—"

"No need." A platinum-haired woman appeared in the doorway. She wore a powder blue dress with a narrow gold belt fastened around her waist. Her high-heeled shoes matched the colour of her dress, and her face was painted with so much rouge and eyebrow pencil and lipstick and powder that it was difficult to tell what she actually might look like under the layer of cosmetics. She also carried the dog Bonzo tucked firmly under one arm. "I caught the naughty boy, didn't I, Precious?" Diana Lovecraft touched Bonzo's small black nose with the tip of her finger and shook her head. "How often have I told you, you mustn't run away from Uncle Walter?"

Her voice was sugary enough to sweeten an entire batch of tea cakes, but her eyes flashed momentarily to Evie's in a blink-and-you'd-miss-it level look.

Evie returned the glance with one of her own.

However good Diana was at impersonating a charming but brainless nitwit— and she was very good— the persona that she presented to the world at large was just an act. Diana Lovecraft was in fact an agent of the SOE, or the Special Operations Executive. And Evie, so far as she knew, was the only person in Crofter's Green who knew Diana's secret.

The SOE had been formed the previous year to conduct espionage, sabotage and reconnaissance in German-occupied Europe and to aid local resistance movements. Diana was genuinely an old school friend of Lady Hawthorne, and Lady Hawthorne had no idea of Diana's real purpose in coming to the neighbourhood. But she had been sent here to investigate reports that a ring of black-market smugglers called the Iron Dukes were operating out of Crofter's Green.

Diana hadn't specifically admitted as much, but Evie suspected that the Iron Dukes must have ties to Germany and a finger in the espionage pie as well as smuggling. Otherwise, the SOE wouldn't have been concerned with tracking them down and would have left them to conventional law enforcement.

Now Evie couldn't entirely interpret the look that Diana had just given her.

She and Diana met occasionally in the normal flow of life in Crofter's Green: while shopping for groceries at Mercer's Emporium or at a meeting of the women's institute. But by common consent they never exchanged more than a few words.

Evie didn't know whether, if they had met under normal circumstances and in a time of peace, she and Diana would ever have been friends. Possibly. Or possibly they were too similar. But regardless, Diana knew secrets about Evie, too, secrets that made it safer for both of them never to give the impression that they were more than the most distant of acquaintances.

Now, though, Evie thought there was something like an unspoken request in Diana's gaze.   As though Diana wanted her to do or say something.

Before Evie could make up her mind on what that something might be, Diana turned to take the dog's collar and lead out of Lord Hawthorne's hands and buckle it firmly around Bonzo's furry neck.

"There." She set the dog down on the floor. "The naughty boy is quite ready to finish his walk with Uncle Walter.   Run along, now."

She might have been addressing the Pomeranian, but Lord Hawthorne turned at the order and shuffled back towards the French windows.   He looked dazed, still, almost as though he were sleep-walking as he pulled Bonzo with him back out onto the terrace.

Chapter Eight

Harry

G reenview Asylum stood bleak and imposing on the outskirts of Ashford, its grey stone walls looming against the overcast sky. Harry knew the place's type well enough—crumbling institutions like these dotted the country, each with their own secrets locked behind iron gates. They were a far cry from the bustling streets of London, but in Harry's experience, fear and desperation were the same everywhere.

A nurse met them at the door, leading Harry and Nigel through the quiet halls to a small exercise garden. The muted sounds of a gramophone played somewhere in the distance, and Harry's practiced eye caught the faded edges of peeling paint on the window frames, the damp in the corners. It was a place where time moved slowly, but never kindly.

Sally Roe sat hunched on a weathered bench.

She was a thin, nervous woman in her mid-fifties, her hands gripping her shawl tightly, as if holding on to it for dear life. Her pale, wide eyes darted around the garden, searching for threats only she could see.

"Sally," Harry said gently as he approached. "It's good to see you. We're here to help." He kept his tone even, his expression calm. It was a voice that had reassured hundreds of witnesses and suspects alike, and though his years of working the streets were behind him, the skill came as naturally as breathing.

Sally looked up, her voice barely above a whisper. "They're watching me." Her thin frame shook beneath her worn shawl, and Harry caught a glimpse of a fear that ran deeper than mere paranoia. He'd seen that look before, in the faces of Londoners peering from bombed-out windows, in the eyes of men trying unsuccessfully to maintain their stiff upper lips.

"Who is?" Harry asked, sitting down beside her, his tone calm.

"I don't know," she whispered, her hands shaking. "But they leave things for me."

Harry glanced at Nigel before turning back to Sally. "What kind of things?"

Sally hesitated, glancing around as though expecting someone to overhear. Then, with trembling fingers, she reached into her coat pocket and pulled out a crumpled piece of paper, handing it to Harry as though it burned her fingers.

Harry took the note, glancing at the jagged, angry words.

"Keep your mouth shut, or we'll shut it for you."

He quickly folded the note and slipped it into his coat pocket, deciding to examine it later in more detail. Right now, his priority was getting Sally to open up, despite the note-writer's threat.

"Why do they want you to keep quiet, Sally?" Harry asked gently. "What do they think you know?"

Her breath hitched, and she shook her head violently. "I can't say... I can't. They'll come for me if I do."

"You're safe here," Harry said, though he wasn't so sure himself. "No one's going to hurt you."

Sally's eyes darted around, but her lips pressed tightly together. She wasn't going to say more, not today.

Harry exchanged a glance with Nigel and stood up. "Thank you, Sally. We'll look into this, I promise."

Sally gave a slight nod, but her haunted eyes followed them as they walked away.

Outside the asylum, Harry pulled the crumpled note from his pocket and handed it to Nigel. As his nephew scanned the paper, Harry's mind was already ticking through the possibilities. "That's no delusion. That's a real threat."

He wasn't saying it just to reassure Nigel. Harry's instincts, the same ones that had kept him alive during his years as a detective, told him that Sallie's fear was rooted in something real. Someone had gone to the trouble of getting a message to her, and that meant there was more going on at Hawthorne Manor than anyone wanted to admit.

"We need to find out how this ended up in her room," Harry said. "Let's talk to the matron." He could hear the edge in his own voice—the same determination that had kept him chasing leads long after wiser men would have let them go.

The matron's office was as cold and sterile as Harry expected. Matron Foster sat behind her desk, her grey hair tightly pinned back, her severe features a perfect match for the drab surroundings.

"Mr Jenkins, Inspector Brewster," she greeted them with a curt nod. "What can I do for you?"

Harry pulled the note from his pocket and placed it on the desk in front of her. "This was found in Sallie Roe's possession. She claims it was left on her pillow."

Matron Foster's sharp eyes flicked to the note and her expression tightened. She quickly picked it up and read the harsh words before setting it back down with a sigh.

"I assure you, we take patient safety very seriously," she said, her voice clipped. "We have strict procedures in place. No one but staff has access to the patients' rooms."

"So how did this get there?" Nigel asked, crossing his arms. "Are you suggesting Sallie wrote it herself?"

The matron stiffened. "Sallie has a history of... delusions. She's paranoid, often convinced people are following her or trying to harm her. It's possible she found this note elsewhere and imagined it was left for her."

Harry frowned. "You're saying she's imagining the threat?"

"I'm saying it's not unusual for her to misinterpret things," the matron replied, her voice growing colder. "But I will, of course, investigate how this could have ended up in her possession."

Harry wasn't buying it. "Who's been paying for her care all these years?"

The matron hesitated, her expression tightening even more. "That would be Lord Hawthorne."

Harry exchanged a quick look with Nigel. "Lord Hawthorne?"

"Yes," the matron said, a slight edge creeping into her voice. "He's been quite generous. He insisted that she receive the best care when she was first admitted, and he's continued to pay for her care ever since."

"Why?" Harry pressed. "What's his connection to her?"

The matron's face grew even more guarded. "I'm afraid I don't know the details. Lord Hawthorne was a private man. But he felt responsible for her well-being."

"Responsible in what way, exactly?" Nigel asked.

The matron's lips thinned. "As I said, I don't know the specifics. My job is to ensure the well-being of our patients, and that is exactly what I do."

Harry nodded slowly, tucking the note back into his coat. "Thank you for your time, Matron. Please let us know what you find in your investigation."

Matron Foster gave a tight nod, her eyes following them as they left the office.

Once outside, Harry turned to Nigel. "Sallie's scared out of her mind. Someone wants her quiet. And Lord Hawthorne's paying for her care. We need to find the connection."

Nigel nodded, his expression grim. "We need to dig deeper into Hawthorne Manor's past. Sallie's the key to this—whatever she knows, it's dangerous."

"And Lord Hawthorne's generosity isn't as simple as it seems," Harry added. "We need to find out why he's so invested in keeping her here."

"Agreed." Nigel paused as they walked a few paces along the gravel drive, then asked, in a different tone, "Have you seen anything of Mrs. Harris lately?"

Harry felt his eyebrows inch upwards in surprise. "Evie? I stop in at the tea shop once or twice a week for a cup of tea. Help her with any odd jobs she needs a hand with. Why?"

"No reason." Nigel's tone was slightly too casual and he wasn't meeting Harry's gaze.

Harry scrutinized his face. "I hope you're not worrying that I've got any sort of romantic designs on her. For one thing, she's young enough to be my daughter, and for another, she's not been a widow for six months yet."

And apart from that, Harry's own wife Margaret had died less than three years ago. They'd been married for thirty years. Harry liked Evelyn Harris well enough, but he couldn't even imagine trying to replace what he and Margaret had shared.

"What? Good heavens no, that's not why I asked!" Nigel looked so honestly shocked by the idea that Harry believed him.

"Then why are you asking about her?"

"No reason."

"You wouldn't be trying to lie to a policeman, would you?" Harry asked.

Nigel gave him a brief smile, though Harry thought it was edged with something that verged on grimness. "Fine. It's just she strikes me as someone who's more than what she first appears to be."

"That's true of most of us," Harry said.

"I suppose."

Harry looked out across the flat stretch of the asylum's lawns. The grass hadn't been mowed recently. Greenview was probably short on help like everywhere else these days. "I've no doubt Evelyn Harris has her secrets. After all, she lived an entirely different life before settling down in Crofter's Green. But I imagine she'll share those secrets when she's ready."

Nigel didn't look entirely convinced, but he didn't argue, only put his hands in his pockets and continued down the drive.

"I had a telephone call last night from your mother," Harry said.   He hadn't intended to bring it up. He was a firm believer in letting a man wrestle with his own demons. But as long as they were discussing uncomfortable subjects, next week marked a year since Nigel's older brother had been killed in action. "She's hoping you might come out this weekend for a visit."

Harry's younger sister Julia and her husband lived in a village on the outskirts of Dover. Harry went to see them when he could.

Nigel shrugged his shoulders in a gesture Harry recognized. His nephew had done that when he was small whenever anything made him uncomfortable.

"She called me as well," Nigel said. "I told her it would depend on what cases I've got open,"

Harry let the matter drop. Nigel might not know it, but he and Evelyn Harris had at least one thing in common: they'd both talk when they were ready and not before.

Chapter Nine

Evie

With an impatient huff of breath, Lady Gwendolyn strode over to shut the door to the terrace behind her husband.

Diana went quietly to pick up the table that Bonzo had knocked over and retrieve the vase, which had fortunately fallen onto the carpet and wasn't broken. She didn't look at Evie again, but Evie had already received the message she thought Diana intended to convey.

"I hope I'm not prying, Lady Hawthorne, but is his lordship ill?" she asked. "He doesn't look very well."

Lady Gwendolyn turned from the window, a line between her brows. Evie gave it roughly even odds that the older woman would expel her from the manor for impertinence as answer the question. But maybe Lady Gwendolyn was more worried than she appeared. With a sigh, she sank back into one of the needle point chairs opposite Evie's and said, "He's not ill— not physically, that is.   It's this ridiculous business of seeing ghosts."

"Ghosts?"   Evie repeated.

"I know!" Lady Gwendolyn's words burst out as though they'd been bottled up for too long and were now determined to force their way out.   "It's preposterous— like something out of an Edgar Allen Poe story.   And yet Walter seems to believe it.   Nothing I can say will convince him that what he's really suffering must be indigestion, or his eyes playing tricks."

"I see."

Diana still wasn't looking at her, but Evie saw her give just the faintest fraction of a nod, which clearly meant, Go on.

"What exactly has Lord Hawthorne seen?" she asked.

"Oh— I don't know." Lady Gwendolyn gestured impatiently.   "He says it's a kind of strange, glowing figure.   Ghostly white, but with a greenish glow.   As I said, it's absurd!"

"Has anyone else seen these . . . apparitions?" Evie asked.

"Not a soul.   Which only goes to prove what I've been telling Walter about their being just a trick of the light or some sort of bad dream.   It's happened only at night, when all the rest of the household has already gone to bed."

"I see."   Evie wondered whether she ought to ask whether the eerily glowing figure by any chance appeared outside of his lordship's bedroom window, or whether that would be showing her own hand too much.

But Lady Gwendolyn was already continuing, gripping the edges of her leather notebook tightly in her lap. "Yes, Walter doesn't sleep well, you see. He never has, ever since we were married. The doctor even prescribed him some tablets to take on nights when he can't drop off, but he doesn't like them. So he often gets up and walks about downstairs here, where he won't disturb anyone." Her sweeping gesture included the room and the ground floor of the manor house beyond. "That's when he's seen the ghost— or whatever it really is. He says it appears to him at the foot of the stairs and stands there, beckoning to him."

Despite its long history, Hawthorne Manor seemed an entirely unlikely place for a haunting. Bright sunlight streamed in through the tall windows, illumining a room that held nearly all of the creature comforts and luxuries that Evie thought money could buy. And yet she almost shivered as she recalled the figure that had hovered outside of her bedroom window at dawn.

She also wouldn't have said that she and Lord Hawthorne had very much in common. But apparently they shared a common unknown enemy, and that thought was far more disturbing than any ghost, whether real or imagined.

Aloud, she asked, "Could it be a trick of some kind? Someone playing a prank on his lordship?"

Lady Gwendolyn looked surprised, as though the possibility had never occurred to her. "I don't know. I suppose it's possible that one of the servants—" she stopped and shook her head. "But it's too absurd! Why should any of the servants want to play such a ridiculous trick? They're very well paid here, and they know it. With the war and so many young men away fighting, we're dreadfully short staffed. And not just the men; half our maids left to join the WRENS or to train as nurses. We've only got Alfred the groundskeeper and the three maids left, plus Cook. Oh, and of course Mrs Vickers, our housekeeper. They're all having to put in more work than usual, of course, with our usual staff gone, so we've adjusted their pay accordingly. I can't imagine why any of them would jeopardize their position here to play a silly practical joke."

It had clearly never occurred to Lady Gwendolyn that she herself might pitch in and take over some of the duties left behind by the absentee servants. But Evie let that pass by. Many in Lord and Lady Hawthorne's position probably wouldn't have even offered their remaining staff higher pay.

"And Lord Hawthorne hasn't any enemies?" she asked. "Anyone bearing him a grudge who might wish to unsettle or frighten him?"

The furrow appeared between Lady Gwendolyn's brows again, deepening as she considered that. But then she dismissed the idea with an impatient shake of the head. "No, of course not," she said. "Who on earth would carry a grudge against Walter? He scarcely goes anywhere or sees anyone outside of Crofter's Green, and he's far too absent-minded to quarrel with anyone. No." Lady Gwendolyn shook her head again. "It simply must be indigestion or too much port after dinner. For myself, I think he's falling asleep without realizing it and dreaming the entire thing."

She spoke firmly— perhaps a shade too firmly, Evie thought, as though she were trying to convince herself.

Diana had sat down on the sofa and was idly flicking through the pages of a women's fashion magazine. She didn't look up or appear at first glance to be paying any attention to their conversation, so Evie assumed that she didn't have anything to add.

But all the same, Evie could tell just by the set of her shoulders that Diana was far from satisfied.

That made two of them.

Lady Gwendolyn opened up her notebook again and said, "Now. I feel quite happy about hiring you to provide the refreshments for the charity tea. Before you leave, you ought to consult with Mrs Vickers about the details of what she and Cook can provide you for the party— ah, there you are, Walter."

She broke off as Lord Hawthorne stepped back through the French doors, leading a much more compliant Bonzo on his lead.

"Walter," Lady Hawthorne said. "Give Bonzo to Diana. I want you to take Evie here to speak to Mrs Vickers."

The fresh air and sunshine didn't appear to have done Lord Hawthorne any perceptible good. He still looked grey and drawn, and he started nervously at his wife's address, his pale blue eyes blinking in confusion.

"Eh? What's that you say?"

A frown of annoyance crossed his wife's features. She spoke loudly and with very clear enunciation, the way that one might speak to a small child or someone hard of hearing. "I said give the dog back to Diana and take Evie to see Mrs Vickers. I think she said she was going to take an inventory of the bottles in the wine cellar this morning."

Lord Hawthorne blinked again and remained silent for so long that Evie expected Lady Gwendolyn to lose all patience and simply find the housekeeper for herself. But at last, he nodded as though finally taking in the request. "Certainly, my dear." He shambled over to hand Bonzo's lead to Diana.

Then he turned to Evie. "Come right this way."

Chapter Ten

Dorothy

"This way, dear." The nurse's shoes clicked on the linoleum floor as she led the way down the long hospital corridor.

Dorothy followed, almost running to keep up with the uniformed nurse, who seemed to be in as great a hurry as she was.

Everyone in St. Thomas' hospital seemed to be hurrying somewhere. The air smelled of antiseptic and floor wax, and the halls were crowded with doctors in white coats and nurses in blue, all rushing this way and that way.

The woman at the front desk had told Dorothy that they were overwhelmed with patients just now between wounded soldiers back from the fighting and civilians who'd been hurt in the bombings. She'd also said that Tom was in Ward B, which made the weight of fear on Dorothy's chest lighten just a little bit. She wouldn't have said that unless Tom was still alive.

Now the nurse who'd been assigned to take her to Tom pushed open a door on the right-hand side of the corridor and said, briskly, "Here we are, dear.   Now let's see."   She consulted a chart that hung on the wall.   "Yes, that's right.   Your husband's in cot number 14.   Fifth one in on the right."

And with that she swept away, sailing off down the hall and leaving Dorothy to peer cautiously into the ward.

The beds were arranged in two long rows, and each bed had a wounded   soldier in it.   They were all of them covered in bandages.   Some had their legs wrapped in plaster and hanging in a complicated-looking traction apparatus made from hooks and wires.   Others wore bandages around their heads, while others had bandaged arms.

One poor man whose arm was clearly gone below the elbow was groaning in his sleep.

Dorothy's heart pounded as she made her way down the ward, trying to remember the nurse's hurried instructions.   A couple of the wounded men were speaking in low voices to visitors who sat by their beds.   A fair-haired boy who looked barely older than Tommy was talking to an older couple whom Dorothy took to be his mum and dad.   But otherwise the men were all either asleep or just lying still, staring up at the ceiling with blank-looking eyes.

She didn't see Tom at first, and thought for a second or two that maybe the nurse had got it wrong.

But then she saw a head of red hair lying on one of the white hospital pillows. Bright copper red, just like Tommy's.

Dorothy's heart pounded even harder as she made her way to his bedside.

"Tom?"

It was Tom. Through the blurring of her vision, Dorothy saw that it really was him. Dreadfully thin and pale-looking, but definitely Tom.

He didn't answer her, though. His eyes were closed and he seemed so deeply asleep that for a moment Dorothy's heart pounded all over again. But he was still breathing. The blue woollen blanket drawn up over his chest rose and fell.

Dorothy's knees gave out and she sat down on the hard wooden chair by his bedside. She blinked hard. She wasn't going to break down crying. Not that anyone here would likely notice. No one was paying her any mind—

"Are you Dorothy, by any chance?" a voice behind her asked.

Dorothy started and turned to find a young woman about her own age standing next to her. The woman was tall and slim, with golden blonde hair that she wore in a coronet braid around her head. Her pale oval face was pleasant and sensible-looking rather than beautiful, with clear-cut features and intelligent-looking blue eyes. Her smile was warm and she was looking at Dorothy with a sympathetic expression. And

also— unlike everyone else Dorothy had seen in the hospital—
she was giving Dorothy her undivided attention.

That fact alone was enough to make Dorothy's eyes sting all
over again.

"That's right." She swallowed. "Did Tom tell you—"

"Oh, no." The blond woman shook her head. "No, he
hasn't been awake to speak to anyone. At least, not so far
as I've seen. But he had a packet of letters with him. I
didn't read them," she added quickly. "But I just saw the same
return address when I was putting them away in his locker
there." She gestured to a small metal lock-box that stood
under the table beside the bed. "They were all from Mrs
Dorothy Baker."

For some reason— Dorothy didn't even know why— that
made the tears that had been pressing behind her eyes suddenly
spill over.

"I'm sorry." She fumbled for a handkerchief in her handbag. "I'm Dorothy Baker. He's my husband. Tom." She
swallowed hard, trying to stop crying, but the tears kept right
on spilling out. "I got a telegram this morning saying that he
was wounded, but I don't even know what's wrong with him
or how he's been hurt—"

"I might be able to help you there, at least." The blond
woman reached for a clipboard that was attached to the foot
of Tom's bed and scanned it, her brow furrowed. "These

can be a bit tricky to read until you get the hang of them.

All the doctor's abbreviations— not to mention that their handwriting is like nothing on earth! Hmmm, yes. It says here that his right tibia— that's a bone in the lower part of his leg, or one of them— was shattered by a bullet, and then the wound went septic, forcing them to amputate below the knee—" She stopped short and looked up. "I'm sorry. One gets used to just rattling off all the medical terminology. But I shouldn't have sprung it on you like that."

"Tom's leg is . . . gone?" Dorothy faltered.

She hadn't been in a frame of mind to register it— or much of anything else— before. But now that she looked, she could see the empty space under the blankets where Tom's right foot should have been.

"I'm sorry." The blond woman seemed to hesitate, then she put a hand on Dorothy's shoulder. "I know some of the men's wives have a difficult time adjusting—"

"Oh, no, no, I don't care about that!" Dorothy shook her head fiercely. "I wouldn't care if Tom came back with both his legs and both arms gone. I'm just so thankful he's alive."

Alive and safe. This meant that no one in the government could possibly send him back out to war.

"But is he— will he be all right?" she asked. Tom's eyelids hadn't so much as flickered the entire time they'd been talking.

"He doesn't seem to hear us."

The blond woman looked down at Tom's chart again. "It says here that they're giving him morphine for the pain. That's probably why he's so soundly asleep. And that his temperature has been slightly elevated for the past two days, which has the doctors a bit worried that he still has an infection somewhere."

"An infection?" A cold hand wrapped around Dorothy's heart and squeezed.

"But he's only running a slight fever," the blond woman said. "If the infection was really bad, his temperature would be much worse. And they'll take good care of him, I promise. The doctors are all practically run off their feet around here. But they're very good."

"Are you a nurse?" Dorothy asked.

The woman's plain blue skirt and white blouse looked as though they'd originally belonged to someone both stouter and shorter than she was. The blouse was too loose, but the sleeves only just came down to the woman's wrists, and the skirt was on the short side. They definitely didn't look like a nurse's uniform, but she spoke as though she were familiar with the hospital's workings.

"Me? Oh, no. That is, I don't think so," the woman added.

"You don't think so?" Dorothy had been sneaking glances at Tom all the time that the other woman had been talking. She hadn't seen him in nearly a year, and now a part of her couldn't believe that she was really sitting beside him. She felt almost afraid that he might somehow suddenly disappear. But now she glanced at the blond woman, confused.

"I don't remember, you see." The blond woman gave her a small, crooked smile. "The technical term is neurological amnesia. Or so they tell me. My home was bombed. Or at least, that's what I think must have happened. The doctors here tell me that I was brought in via ambulance with other bombing victims, so it seems likely. But all I remember is waking up here in this hospital, without a single idea of how I'd come to be here or what my life had been before."

Dorothy stared at her. "You don't remember anything?"

"Nothing at all. Not even my own name— which I can tell you is an extremely uncomfortable state to be in." The woman smiled crookedly once again. "Although I'm more or less used to it, now. I decided to call myself Viola. Have you read any Shakespeare?"

Dorothy shook her head. She'd barely muddled her way through the assigned readers in school; Shakespeare was out of the question.

"That's all right, I don't really know whether I did, either, before," Viola said. "But I hadn't anything with me when I was brought into the hospital. No ration cards or identity papers. I was wearing only pyjamas and a dressing gown— both made in thousands and bought at Woolworth's— so you see that's no help.   But the one thing I did have was a copy of Shakespeare's *Twelfth Night*.   It was tucked into the pocket of my dressing gown.   There wasn't anything helpful like my name written onto the fly leaf.   But it looks as though the book must have been mine."

"I suppose so."   Dorothy blinked.   Viola's story was fascinating enough to almost distract her from worrying about Tom.

"I read it while I was in bed recovering," Viola said.   "As well as losing my memory, I had a broken leg, a broken collar bone, and three cracked ribs, so I couldn't get around or do very much.   I had to give people something to call me.   Being addressed as 'Miss' and 'You, there,' you gets tiresome very quickly.   And the heroine of Twelfth Night— Viola— is shipwrecked and has to build a new life and a whole new identity for herself in a foreign land.   So it seemed appropriate."

"How long ago was that?" Dorothy asked.

"It's been just over six months, now," Viola said.   "At first, the doctors thought my memory would come back.   But it hasn't.   Then they thought that if I had family, someone would come looking for me.   But no one ever has."   A hint of sadness slipped through her expression.

"And you can't remember anyone at all?" Dorothy asked.

Viola shook her head.   "Sometimes— usually when I'm just falling asleep or just waking up— I get a kind of a glimmer of

. . . someone? Some feeling of not being alone, at least. But it's always gone before I can really remember or grasp hold of anything definite. Perhaps I did have a family and they were all killed in the same bombing that struck me. The doctors tell me I haven't had any children. I had to know, you see.

I'm not sure which would be worse, having children who were alive but thought that I was dead. Or having children— living or dead—whom I couldn't even remember."

Viola shivered, something forlorn and lost shadowing her blue gaze. But then she said, "I was here at the hospital recovering for months. And then, since I'd nowhere to go afterwards— and since they're so short-staffed— the hospital director let me stay on. I can't do any work that requires a nurse's training, of course. But I can deliver mail and help the patients who can't feed themselves, that sort of thing. And I come through all the wards at least once a day with our library cart and offer books to anyone who wants something to read."

Viola nodded to a plain metal trolley that Dorothy hadn't noticed before, parked in the aisle between the rows of beds. It was stacked high with what looked like well-worn books, both hardcover and paperback.

"We don't have much of a library yet," Viola said. "Just what people have donated. But it gives people a way to pass the time when they're stuck in bed. I read Twelfth Night about six times while I was recovering. That's what gave me the idea to start collecting books. Would you like to pick one?"

Dorothy was startled. Apart from the newspapers, she hadn't read anything since she left school. "Oh, I don't think—" she began.

"Take one," Viola said. "You'll get frightfully bored sitting here and waiting for your husband to wake up enough to speak to you. Or you'll just sit here worrying, which is far worse. That's the best part about books: they make you forget your own troubles and think about someone else's for a while."

Again the flicker of something sad and lost-looking showed in her eyes. She blinked it away, though, and said briskly, "Here. Take this one." She picked up a paperback book and handed it to Dorothy. "You'll enjoy it, I promise. It's one of my favourites."

Dorothy looked down at the cover of the book, which read, '*A Study in Scarlet*, by Sir Arthur Conan Doyle.'

"Thank you," Dorothy stammered.

"You're very welcome."

Viola looked as though she were about to move on, but Dorothy stopped her with a question. "Do you know—" she stopped, swallowing. "Does it say anywhere on Tom's chart whether he knows? About his leg, I mean?"

Viola shook her head. "I'm afraid it doesn't give any details like that, no." She gave Dorothy a searching look. "You're thinking about how he's going to feel?"

"Yes." Dorothy swallowed hard again, looking down at Tom's face. He was thin and pale, but he looked so peaceful lying there. "I said I don't care— and I don't. I'm just hoping that he doesn't hate it too much."

Tom's work before the army had been cabinet making. He could do that all right with only one leg. But he'd always been so active. Swimming and diving in the ocean when they took a holiday to the seashore in the summer. Playing rugby with Tommy—

"He probably will hate it, at first," Viola said in a practical, matter-of-fact kind of tone. "They all do. You can't really blame them. But he'll find a way to manage and be all right in the end. The sort of man who saves every single one of his wife's letters and carries them with him isn't going to be brought down easily."

"Thank you," Dorothy said again.

Viola squeezed her hand. "I'm glad to have met you, Dorothy. I'd better finish my rounds, now. But I'm sure I'll see you here again."

Chapter Eleven

Evie

Lord Hawthorne led the way down a long hallway towards the rear wing of the manor. He didn't speak. Evie wasn't even sure that he recalled her presence beside him. He simply strode along, his arms crossed behind his back, his shoulders slightly hunched, and his brow furrowed in a worried frown.

A dark-haired girl in a housemaid's uniform was dusting the tops of the framed gallery of paintings that lined the walls. She stopped to curtsy at their approach, but his lordship passed her by without appearing to notice her. Striding forward, he threw open a door on the left-hand side of the hall and called out.

"Mrs Vickers? Mrs Vickers!"

The room inside was narrow, high-ceilinged, and seemed at first glance to be as long as a cricket field. As Evie followed Lord Hawthorne in, she caught the scent of aged paper mingled with a hint of wood polish and faint traces of tobacco smoke. Tall, oak-panelled walls were lined with shelves that held row upon row of leather-bound books. The embossed gold on the spines reflected the soft glow from a crystal chandelier that hung from the ceiling. Large, mullioned windows framed the room, covered in curtains of dark red velvet, while overstuffed armchairs, upholstered in deep green velvet, sat on either side of a grand fireplace adorned with an intricately carved marble mantelpiece.

In one corner, a globe sat atop an ornate stand, and a rich, Persian rug covered the floor beneath a sturdy mahogany table that was covered with what looked like stacks of parchment and a few scattered notebooks.

"I've been working on a history of the Hawthorne Family," Lord Hawthorne said with a wave at the table. "Mrs Vickers!"

A woman at the very far end of the room started at the address, nearly dropping the book she'd been holding.

"Mrs Vickers." Scowling, Lord Hawthorne strode forwards to snatch the volume out of her hands. "That is my William Caxton edition of the Canterbury Tales, printed in 1477! Have you any idea how much it's worth?"

The Hawthorne Manor housekeeper was a plump, matronly-looking woman in her middle fifties, with grey hair parted in the middle and drawn smoothly back into a bun at the nape of her neck. She wore a dark green dress with a grey knitted cardigan, and her face was broad and placid-looking, with a wide forehead and large brown eyes.

She regarded her irate employer without any appearance of being especially bothered by his anger.

"No, I can't say that I do." Her voice had the tolerant patience of a nursery governess addressing a recalcitrant child who refused to eat his spinach. "But what I do know is that it and all the rest of the books on this shelf are disgracefully dusty." She gestured with the feather-duster she carried in one hand. "It is the duty of Grace, the second housemaid, to clean the library. I shall be speaking to her about being slack in her attention to detail."

Lord Hawthorne's face darkened. So far, Evie had seen him only as a slightly eccentric but essentially harmless dodder-er. Now it occurred to her that despite his mild looks and absent-minded ways, Lord Hawthorne might be a hard man to cross.

"Grace doesn't dust those volumes because I have expressly forbidden her to touch them!" he snapped at Mrs Vickers. "You will kindly leave their care to me and to me alone!" Turning back to Evie, he said, "They are by far the most valu-able works in my collection. In addition to the Chaucer, I have a first edition of Faust and the 1760 edition of the Works of Homer as translated by Alexander Pope."

Mrs Vickers merely looked at him with tolerant patience. "Very well, Lord Hawthorne. Just as you like, of course."

"Thank you." Lord Hawthorne snorted, inspected the leather-bound volume in his hands, and replaced it on the shelf with tender care.

Then he frowned, peering at the shelf more closely. "Mrs Vickers! Have you taken any books from my shelf? I have a first edition copy of Johnson's *The History of Rasselas, Prince of Abissinia* that ought to be right here."

"Well, I certainly haven't moved it," Mrs Vickers said. "I'd only just started with the dusting."

"Then where is it?" Lord Hawthorne demanded.

"I'm afraid I really don't know, your lordship." The housekeeper still looked entirely unbothered by his angry frown. "Perhaps you took it with you upstairs? Or into your study? You often do that with books you're especially interested in, you know."

Lord Hawthorne's frown remained, but he didn't argue, only stared moodily at the shelves. "Yes, I suppose that's what must have happened." He fell silent.

"Was there something you wanted?" Mrs Vickers asked.

"Eh?" Lord Hawthorne had been frowning at the row of books on the shelf. "What's that? Oh— oh, yes. This is Evie Harris. My wife wants you to have a word with her about the food for some sort of charity do she's putting on." He jerked a hand at Evie without looking at her and went back to staring at his shelves. He finally selected another leather-bound volume and tucked it under one arm.

Evie would have wagered an entire month's worth of the Cozy Cup's profits that he'd once more forgotten her presence. But then with an abrupt jolt he swung around to face her.

"Once you've finished here, come out and see me. I'll be out in the garden with Bonzo," he said. "There's something I'd like to talk to you about."

He didn't give Evie the chance to answer, just strode from the room with the antique book still tucked under his arm.

"Don't mind his lordship," Mrs Vickers said. She directed another tolerant smile at Lord Hawthorne's retreating back.

"He's something of an odd bird. The sort who'd lose his head if it weren't fastened on, as my mother used to say. And he cares more for those old books of his than he does for any human— his family included— I sometimes think. But there. It takes all kinds, doesn't it, and you won't find a fairer employer."

Evie swiftly weighed her options. She could ask Mrs Vickers directly about the rumours of haunting, but it wouldn't necessarily be prudent for word to get around Crofter's Green that she was particularly interested in the Hawthorne Manor Ghost.

Option two was to simply draw the housekeeper into conversation and hope that she brought up the recent trouble on her own. Mrs Vickers looked to Evie like the sort of woman who enjoyed talking.

"Does his lordship have any family, apart from Lady Gwendolyn?" she asked.

"There's a grown-up daughter. Peggy." Mrs Vickers glanced around the room and lowered her voice. "But she doesn't come around here. Had some sort of a falling out with her father years ago, and as far as I know, they've not spoken since. I believe she still writes to Lady Gwendolyn now and again, but of course it's not my place to ask for any details."

"You don't know what caused the quarrel with her father?"

"No, I'm afraid I don't." Mrs Vickers didn't appear to notice anything odd about the question. Evie's estimation of her character seemed to be proving accurate, in that she seemed too happy for the chance to gossip to wonder why, if Evie were simply here to discuss ration tickets, she would want to know the Hawthorne's family difficulties. "All that happened before my time. I've only worked here about five years, now, and Peggy was gone by then. I heard all this from Cook. She's been with the family . . . oh, I believe she told me thirty years. But of course, being in the kitchen she never got the chance to hear much in the way of what was really happening the way the housemaids and the parlour maids might. And she said there wasn't even much of a ruckus. One day soon after she'd come home from finishing school, Miss Peggy was just gone, and no one's seen her since."

"How strange.   His lordship doesn't seem like the quarrelsome sort," Evie said.

"Oh no, he's not.   At least, not so long as you don't disturb his books or mess about with the bottles in his wine cellar."

Mrs Vickers gave Evie an amused smile.

"Wine cellar?"

"Oh yes.   That's his lordship's other great passion: all the bottles of old French port his ancestors stored down in the cellar.   Does he ever serve any of them?   No, he does not. He just likes knowing the old bottles are there."

"So you find this an agreeable place to work overall?" Evie asked.

"Oh yes.   Of course, it's different now than it was before the war," Mrs Vickers said.   "We've all got to make do with less and do our part to pitch in.   But even so, we're a lot more comfortable than most are these days.   I've no complaints. And now I suppose we'd better put our heads together and get to work on the menu for this charity affair of her ladyship's," she added in a brisker tone.   "She's not nearly so absent-minded as her husband, and she'll have a few words to say if I stand here talking all day instead of getting on with the job at hand."

Chapter Twelve

Evie

Evie found Lord Hawthorne sitting on one of the marble benches on the stone-tiled terrace. Beyond, green lawn and formal garden beds with fountains and statues stretched out towards a copse of trees. But even the manor wasn't entirely untouched by the war. Evie also saw portions of the lawn had been hacked out to create hastily-dug vegetable patches, just as she had in her own back garden.

Lord Hawthorne was seated with his back to her, petting Bonzo. The little dog was being quiet and docile for a change, lying with his head and front paws across his lordship's lap and apparently tolerating the attention. Although the minute Evie approached, the dog raised his head and bared his teeth at her in what looked like a warning not to try anything.

"Lord Hawthorne?"

Lord Hawthorne, too, turned to look at her, blinking in surprise. Evie had the impression that not only did he not remember that he'd asked her to come find him here, he was also not entirely certain of who she was.

But then recognition dawned in his gaze. "Ah, the woman from the tea shop! Ellen? Esther?"

"Evie," Evie said.

Lord Hawthorne appeared not to fully register that. "I've heard of you, you know."

"Only good things, I hope," Evie said lightly.

Lord Hawthorne ignored that, as well. He was rather like a creaky old organ grinder that, having begun a tune, must play doggedly on to the song's end.

"Heard that you helped solve that business a few months ago when old Colonel Smythe got himself murdered."

"That's true," Evie said cautiously. There was no point in denying it. In a place like Crofter's Green, a murder and the exposure of a criminal conspiracy had been talked about at every meal in every house in the village for at least a month.

Lord Hawthorne nodded. He stared down at the terrace tiles a moment, then said, "I suppose my wife's told you that I'm losing my mind. It's probably all over the village, too: Poor old Hawthorne's seeing ghosts. Must be on his way to being locked up in a madhouse." He stopped, exhaling a mirthless half-laugh. "Maybe I am. No one else has seen the spectre when it appears. Only me. And a couple of months ago, I'd have been to first to agree that anyone seeing ghosts was crazy myself."

He hunched his shoulders as though trying not to shiver, his gaze focused on the terrace tiles beneath their feet.

"What do you think you're seeing?" Evie asked after a moment.

"I know what I'm seeing!" Lord Hawthorne looked up and glared at her. "It's Wentworth."

His mild, scholarly face kindled with enough intensity to make Evie wonder whether his grip on reality was, in fact, beginning to slip. But that wouldn't explain her own early-morning visitor.

"Who is Wentworth?" she asked.

Lord Hawthorn scuffed at the tiles moodily with the toe of his polished shoe. "Gwendolyn's first husband."

"I didn't know that Lady Gwendolyn had been married before," Evie said.

Lord Hawthorne nodded and jerked one shoulder. "Doesn't talk about it much. Painful, you see. They weren't very happy, and Wentworth— Gerald was his Christian name— poisoned himself. Gwen took it hard. They'd been arguing, you see. Nothing anyone said could convince her that it wasn't partly her fault . . ."

Lord Hawthorne's voice trailed off, his gaze staring without focus into the middle distance as though at some scene from the past that only he could see.

"And you think the ghost you've been seeing is Gerald Wentworth?" Evie kept her tone matter-of-fact.

"Could be.   Restless spirits and all that." Lord Hawthorne again moved his shoulders as though settling an uncomfortable weight.   "And yet—" he stopped, kicking at the ground again.

"And yet?" Evie asked.

Lord Hawthorne swung around and gave her a surprisingly shrewd look.   "What if it's not Wentworth?   Eh?   What if it's someone playing a trick on me?"

"That would be a nasty trick," Evie said.

"Of course it would."   Lord Hawthorne jerked an impatient hand.   "Look here, though.   Every time, I see the same thing—a glowing figure that vanishes the second I try to get too close.   But the other night— the other night when I got to the place just at the foot of the stairs where the figure had been—I found this."

He reached into the pocket of his waistcoat and drew out a folded slip of paper, handing it over to Evie.

"What do you make of that, eh?"

Evie unfolded the paper, which was almost as thin and brittle as tissue. "It looks as though it's been torn out of an old copy of *The Book of Common Prayer*," she said.

"Exactly! And look there!" Lord Hawthorne stabbed a finger at a circle that had been drawn around one particular passage.

Evie read aloud, "The remembrance of our sins is grievous unto us, the burden of them is intolerable." She stopped and looked up at Lord Hawthorne. "Clearly someone left this for you to find."

Lord Hawthorne nodded with satisfaction. "And not a ghost, either. No ghost ripped that page out or made those marks with a pen. Must have been someone living."

"Who?" Evie asked.

"I don't know. That's what I want you to find out."

Chapter Thirteen

Alice

"What shall we do for the afternoon?" Tommy Baker asked. At eight years old, he was a healthy, sturdy-looking little boy with a mop of fiery red curls, a scattering of freckles across his nose, and inquisitive green eyes. Right now, he was peering around Alice's garden with interest.

"Well, to start, I thought we might bed out some of the lettuce plants I started in the greenhouse over the winter," Alice said. "We're past the point when we need to worry about frost overnight."

"All right." As well as being curious, Tommy was an agreeable child. As a spinster who'd passed the age of 60 some time ago, Alice didn't have much experience with children. But Tommy had been a frequent visitor to her cottage for months, now, especially since his mother had started working at Evie's Cozy Cup next door. Dorothy would bring him to the tea shop with her, and Tommy would come bouncing over to

Alice's, his red hair appearing over the top of her garden fence as he craned his neck to peer down at her and ask what she was planting in the garden beds this week.

Alice had grown to look forward to his company. But today she had gone over to the Crofter's Green school to collect him when his class was let out. She'd kept her explanation to a minimum, saying only that his father had been taken to a hospital in London and that his mother had gone up there to visit him. It helped that she honestly didn't have any more details to give, even if she had wanted to burden the child with more.

Tommy had nodded in response to the news and said very little on their walk back here to the cottage. Alice hadn't pressed him. She might not have a wealth of experience with child-rearing, but it seemed to her that there was no reason that children couldn't be afforded the same sort of consideration for their privacy that adults were.

Now she saw Tommy's downcast eyes and tight lips, but she said nothing. The boy would talk when he was ready, and until then she could offer him a distraction and a safe place to ask questions if and when he wanted to.

She led the way into the small greenhouse that leaned against the back of her cottage. She pushed open the door, letting out a waft of rich, warm, earth and peat-moss scented air. Alice breathed deeply. As long as she lived, she would never tire of the smell of healthy, growing plants.

At this time of year, the long work tables that ran down the length of the greenhouse were crammed with plants waiting to be put into the ground. Especially now, with rationing growing ever stricter and food more and more scarce, Alice wasn't going to waste a single inch of the ground she had available for planting. She already had leeks and potatoes in the ground and was planning to add turnips, beets, onions, and vegetable marrows as well as the lettuce she and Tommy were due to bed out today.

"Here's our lettuce," she said, picking up a tray of small pasteboard pots in which leafy sprouts were poking up.

Tommy nodded, but continued to look around the greenhouse. "What are those over there?" He pointed to a smaller table at the back, which was covered with pots of herbs.

"Those are the plants I'm growing for the County Herb Committee," Alice said.

Tommy's brow crinkled. "The what?"

"One of the more sensible things the government has ever done," Alice told him. "You see, a lot of medicines are manufactured in Germany. And since the Germans aren't exactly likely to sell them to British importers anymore, our country is beginning to be critically short of medicines that doctors and hospitals need."

Tommy gave her a swift look, but didn't say anything.

Alice led the way over to the small table. Tommy followed.

"So because of the shortages of medicines, the County Herb Committee is encouraging people to grow medicinal plants," Alice said. "Things like this Foxglove here." She pointed to a plant with dark green spear-shaped leaves. "Foxglove gives us digitalis, which doctors use to treat heart disease."

"And the others?" Tommy asked. "Are they all for medicines, too?"

"Oh, yes." Alice pointed to the plants in turn. "There's belladonna— that's good for muscle pain and is sometimes used for eye disease— colchicum, Hyoscyamus, stramonium, valerian . . ."

"Do you think my dad's going to be all right?" Tommy burst out.

"I don't know, dear." Alice dropped a hand on the boy's shoulder. "But I very much hope that he will be. It's surely a good sign that he's been sent back to London. They keep the really bad cases— those wounded men who wouldn't survive a long journey— over in France."

Tommy nodded, his eyes still downcast.

"I'm sure your mother will get in touch with us as soon as she's able." Alice gave his shoulder a squeeze. "Until then, I'm sure both she and your father are counting on you being brave—" she stopped abruptly.

"What's wrong?" Tommy asked.

"Nothing. That is, I'm not sure." Alice was staring at her table of County Herb Committee plants, frowning. The table was as crowded as the rest of the greenhouse, but there was a gap between the belladonna and the valerian where a pot should have been—but now wasn't. "Tommy, you haven't been in here without me, have you?"

She tried not to make her voice sound accusing, but Tommy shook his head vigorously. "Oh no, Miss Greenleaf. I'd never come in here on my own! I wouldn't want to make a mess of anything for you."

Alice forced a smile. "That's all right, dear. I'm sure you wouldn't." Unfortunately, she believed the boy completely. Which meant that someone else had been inside her greenhouse recently. Someone who had removed one of her medicinal plants.

And these plants weren't just medicinal. Most could also be poisonous if taken in the incorrect dose.

Alice cast her mind back, trying to identify which plant among the jumble of others was missing. Valerian, foxglove, stramonium—

Her frown deepened as she realised exactly what it was that was missing.

Chapter Fourteen

Dorothy

"How'd it go with your husband?" Mr Murphy asked as Dorothy climbed into the back seat of the Daimler again.

She'd been grateful beyond words to find him waiting for her outside of the hospital, just as he'd promised. She wouldn't have believed that just sitting next to Tom's bed would be so exhausting. But she felt as spent as though she'd just worked a double shift at the King's Arms and then walked a couple of miles, besides.

Now early evening shadows were lengthening across the London streets, and workers were beginning to hurry home before the blackout regulations took hold.

"All right," Dorothy said. "Although Tom's not awake. He's being kept under sedation for the time being. But he doesn't seem to be in any immediate danger."

Both a nurse and a doctor had paid visits to Tom's bedside during the time Dorothy had spent there. Very hurried visits— not that that was surprising— but the nurse had checked Tom's temperature and looked at the dressings on his leg, and the doctor had read his chart. Neither of them had spoken to Dorothy beyond a brief nod of greeting, but at least they hadn't looked worried by whatever they'd seen.

"Well, that's the main thing," Mr Murphy said. He started the ignition and put the car into gear. "Give him a few days, and he'll be sitting up and happy to see your pretty face beside him."

Would he? Dorothy didn't doubt that Tom would be glad to see her. But she kept trying to picture Tom's face when he found out that his leg was gone.

He probably will hate it, at first, Viola had said. *They all do.*

She tried to put that thought aside. Tom was alive. As Mr Murphy said, that was the main thing.

"We've just one more stop to make, if you don't mind," Mr Murphy said. "Her ladyship asked me to drop some crates off at Sotheby's."

"The auction house?" Dorothy was surprised. "Is she selling something?"

"Not sure. Mrs Vickers just said her ladyship had some crates to be taken up to Sotheby's, and I could manage it at the same time as driving you to the hospital." Mr Murphy shrugged and angled the car to join the oncoming traffic.

"Mine not to reason why, eh?" He gave her a wink and a grin in the rear-view mirror and turned onto Lambeth Palace Road.

The piercing wail of a siren cut the air.

Mr Murphy's hands tightened on the steering wheel. "Air raid warning."

Dorothy wouldn't have needed him to tell her. She'd lived through enough of the air raids herself, before she and Tommy had left London for Crofter's Green. Dozens of nights she'd spent, huddled with Tommy in the damp, earth-scented Morrison shelter that Tom had installed for them in the back garden. And yet somehow it hadn't even occurred to her that there might be an air raid today, while she was up here in town.

"What d'you think, luv?" Mr Murphy glanced at her in the rear-view mirror. He was trying to speak calmly, but Dorothy could hear the tension in his words. "Should we try to find a tube station, or make for Sotheby's? I hear they've turned their basement into a public shelter."

Dorothy's heart was hammering in her chest, but she tried to think above the fear that clogged her throat. She wasn't going to help anyone by letting her nerves get the better of her, or by picturing a bomb hitting Tom in the hospital. Or killing her before she could get back home to Tommy and Mum, for that matter.

"Sotheby's," she said after a moment.

All around them, the streets had turned from the usual London bustle to scenes of complete chaos as people raced to find the nearest bomb shelters, clutching whatever valuables they could carry. Mothers raced by, carrying babies and dragging older children by the hand. Others were hugging boxes or bags that bulged with hastily packed clothing. One older woman ran by with a ginger-coloured cat in her arms.

The cat didn't look as if it appreciated the attempt to keep it safe and was hissing and trying to scratch its owner's face.

"Sotheby's would probably be less crowded," Dorothy said. "The tube stations are always packed like a sardine tin. People practically on top of one another. There's more chance that we'll be able to find space at the auctioneers."

"Right you are."

Mr Murphy tramped a little harder on the accelerator and the car leaped forward. He was a good driver. Dorothy was grateful for all the years of practice he must have had working for the Hawthornes as he steered the Daimler skilfully from Saville Row to Maddox Street and then finally turned onto Bond Street.

The classical facade of the famous auction house loomed up ahead of them. Dorothy had sometimes come walking here when Tommy was a baby, pushing him in the pram. Not because she'd ever in a hundred years thought she might be able to afford to bid on one of the auctions or buy anything at one of the fancy shops that lined the street on either side.   She'd just enjoyed looking at all the pretty things in the windows, especially all the beautiful old vases and silver creamers and carved chairs.

And now here she was hoping to escape getting flattened by one of Hitler's bombs by hiding in Sotheby's basement.

Life was funny, if you stopped and thought about it, but Dorothy didn't have time now.

Chapter Fifteen

Dorothy

S he couldn't yet hear the roar of aeroplane engines above the continuous wailing of the siren, but she didn't doubt that they were coming.

Mr Murphy pulled the car over alongside of the road without bothering to look for a proper parking space and hopped out. He came around to open the door for her, but Dorothy had already climbed out on her own.

The auction house had large, ornate windows framed by intricate stonework and a front entrance marked by a set of grand double doors. A huge sign reading *Sotheby's* hung above the entrance.

With Mr Murphy beside her, Dorothy raced up the front steps and plunged through the doors into an elegant, marble-lined lobby, although right now the lights were all out save for a couple of electric torches held by women in air raid warden uniforms. The room was crowded with people of all ages.   Dorothy and Mr Murphy joined the group, stepping in behind a mother who had a baby in her arms and a girl a little older than Tommy beside her.

A worried-looking man in a grey suit was shepherding people along, pointing them down a long hallway that led towards the back of the building.

Dorothy stumbled with them, trying to keep her footing as the frightened people all around her pushed and shoved, ignoring the man who was trying to get them to stay in an orderly line.

The little girl up ahead of them tripped.   Her mother had her hands full with the baby, so Dorothy reached out and took the girl's hand so that she wouldn't get trampled underfoot.

"Th-thank you."

The mother gave her a distracted smile, but the baby was wailing and she was struggling to keep her own footing.   The little girl looked as though she was trying not to cry, too.

Dorothy was still trying to catch her breath and stop her own heart from pounding out of her chest, but she smiled down at her and asked, "What's your name?"

"Jane."   The girl had blond pigtails and a gap between her two front teeth.   She was wearing knee socks and a blue plaid dress with puffed sleeves and had a matching blue ribbon in her hair.   She also had on metal leg braces over the stockings, the kind that children who'd had polio wore.

"That's a nice name." Dorothy gave her another encouraging smile as they inched forward another few feet. "Have you ever been here before?"

Jane nodded. "We only live a few streets away from here, so we usually come here when the German planes come. I was going to be sent away in the country, but they couldn't find anywhere that would take me on account of my braces and needing to see the doctors so often." She nodded to the metal splints on her legs, but she didn't sound as though she were feeling sorry for herself, just stating a fact. "And then mummy decided I could just stay because the bombs weren't falling so often anymore. But I still don't like it when the planes come."

The girl's voice wobbled. "Mummy says I have to be a brave girl and not cry. It's just mummy and me and Nancy." She nodded to the baby in her mother's arms. "My father's away fighting in the war. He sends us letters, sometimes. And I can read them myself! I'm learning how to read at school," she added proudly.

"I'm sure you're a good reader. I have a little boy who's just about your age," Dorothy said.

"Can he read?" Jane asked with interest. She sounded less close to tears, now.

"Yes. But he likes arithmetic best."

"Where is he?" Jane looked around them. "Is he with you now?"

"No, he's back at home with his granny in the village where I grew up."

"Oh." Jane looked momentarily disappointed. But then she frowned, looking over Dorothy's shoulder. "He's going the wrong way."

"Who?" Dorothy turned to look.

"That man. There!" Jane pointed to a tall man who was just disappearing down a hall that led off towards their left.

 Dorothy couldn't see where the hall led; like everything else in the auction house, it was unlighted. "This is the way to the basement," Jane said. "I don't know where that way goes."

"Perhaps he works for Sotheby's," Dorothy said. "Maybe someone sent him to make sure that the valuables are locked up and safe."

Mostly Londoners were all pitching in and getting through the war together. But there were still plenty who'd help themselves to any valuables left unguarded. And nowhere—not even an upper-class place like Bond Street— was safe from being looted after a bombing raid.

"Maybe." Jane's leg braces clinked together and caught, making her stumble again.

"Here, now." Mr Murphy had been keeping silent as he walked along behind Dorothy, but at Jane's stumble, he stepped up, hoisting the little girl into his arms.

Jane frowned harder and gave him an indignant glare. "I can walk by myself, I'm not a baby!"

"Of course you're not," Mr Murphy said. "But are you sure you're not a princess?"

"A . . ." Jane looked puzzled.

"Because as soon as I saw you, I said to myself, that girl's got a royal look about her. And it wouldn't do for a princess to dirty her feet with walking, now would it?"

Jane giggled.

Craning her neck, Dorothy could see a door up ahead of them with another air warden standing beside it. At least there were no windows here, so they could have lights. Electric bulbs in the ceiling showed a steep flight of steps that people were going down, two at a time.

Dorothy was almost about to breathe a sigh of relief. Then in the distance she heard the rumble of approaching planes and the sound of the ack-ack, the anti-aircraft guns.

"Steady," Mr Murphy said. His voice was tense once more. "Let's get you down to the shelter quickly. Looks like Herr Hitler's up to his old tricks again."

Chapter Sixteen

Evie

E vie was silent a moment, considering, before she finally asked, "Do you have any suspects, Lord Hawthorne? Is there anyone who might dislike you enough to try frightening you this way?"

She asked nearly the same question of Lady Gwendolyn, but she was interested to hear what her husband would answer.

"Can't think of anyone." Lord Hawthorne patted the top of Bonzo's head. His hand trembled slightly, and the bright springtime sunlight picked out with merciless clarity the shadows around his eyes and the lines of strain bracketing the corners of his mouth. "There's one or two collectors of rare books who I've beaten out at an auction. But no one would go to all this trouble over an early edition of Milton or Keats."

"What about the torn-out page, then," Evie said. "With the circled passage? Clearly it's intended as a message. Do you have any idea which sins the author of the message wants you to remember?"

"No idea." Lord Hawthorne's answer came quickly. A shade too quickly, Evie thought.

She simply waited. Sometimes silence was a better inducement to talk than further questions would have been.

"Well, no sins that ought to be worth this amount of trouble. But . . . well." Scowling, he kicked at the ground again, then said, "I suppose you might as well see this, too."

Reaching into his pocket once again, he drew out another scrap of folded paper, almost identical to the first.

"Whoever your anonymous messenger is doesn't appear to be terribly original. I take it that's another torn page from the Book of Common Prayer?" Evie said.

"It is. And . . . well, you can see for yourself." Unfolding the paper, Lord Hawthorne pointed to the passage circled in ink, about halfway down the page.

"Whom God hath joined together let no man put asunder," Evie read.

"But we didn't break any marital bonds!" Lord Hawthorne's voice rose a trifle. "Gwen and I loved each other, just as I told you. Wentworth, her husband, realised he had lost, and killed himself. Even wrote a note encouraging Gwendolyn to remarry. So you see that can't be it."

Evie didn't answer   for a moment. She was trying— and largely failing— to imagine the dried-up, scholarly man beside her as a player in the story of passion and tragedy that he had just described.

"Someone's trying to drive me mad!" Lord Hawthorne burst out.

Trying and quite possibly succeeding, Evie thought.   His lordship looked to her like a man on the very edge of a breakdown.

"Is there anyone who might benefit from that?" Evie asked.

Lord Hawthorne hunched his shoulders.   "No one."

"I don't mean to bring up painful memories," Evie said. "But what about your daughter, Peggy?   She's estranged from you, is that right?"

"Peggy?" Lord Hawthorne gave Evie a startled glance.   Apparently, he didn't remember that he hadn't told Evie about his estranged daughter, though, because he didn't question her knowledge.   "Haven't seen Peggy in . . . it must be ten years."

"What would happen if you were to die?" Evie asked. "Would Peggy inherit the manor here?"

"Peggy's taken care of."   Lord Hawthorne continued to scowl at the ground.   Then he stood up, so abruptly that Bonzo was dumped off his lap.   The little dog scrabbled to his feet with a short bark and a resentful look at his lordship.   But

Lord Hawthorne didn't seem to notice. "Thank you. That will be all," he said with a nod.

Evie blinked, but turning on his heel, Lord Hawthorne strode off without another word.

Chapter Seventeen

Harry

H arry couldn't shake the feeling that Sally's fear was more than just paranoia. Someone—or something—was getting to her.

It had been a few days since Harry's first visit to the asylum, and things seemed to have worsened for Sally Roe. He'd received word from Nigel that she had grown more agitated, more fearful, and the asylum staff seemed at a loss for what to do. The note Sally had given him weighed heavily on his mind, though no one had been able to explain how it had found its way onto her pillow.

When Harry arrived at the asylum, Matron Foster greeted him with her usual mix of professional courtesy and stern formality, though there was something new in her eyes—perhaps annoyance, or even suspicion.

"Mr Jenkins," she said, her voice clipped but polite. "I wasn't expecting you."

"I thought it best to follow up with Sally Roe," Harry replied evenly. "I'd like to speak with her again."

The matron's lips pressed into a thin line. "She's not been well these past few days. More... agitated." She paused, her eyes narrowing slightly. "I don't know how much use another conversation will be."

"I'll take that chance," Harry said, his tone leaving little room for argument.

The matron hesitated but then gave a stiff nod. She turned and led him through the now-familiar winding corridors of the asylum. The air inside felt heavier today, as though the walls themselves were closing in. Finally, they arrived at a small, dimly lit patient's room.

There, Sally sat by the window, her hands clutched tightly around the edge of her shawl. She looked smaller than the last time Harry had seen her—her shoulders hunched, her face pale. Her wide eyes darted nervously to the door as Harry stepped in.

"Sally," Harry said softly, taking a seat across from her. "How are you feeling?"

She didn't look at him directly, her gaze flicking to the window and then back to her lap. "They're still watching me," she whispered, her voice so low that Harry had to lean in to hear her.

"Who's watching you?" Harry asked gently.

Sally's trembling fingers gripped her shawl even tighter. Her eyes darted toward the window again. "The ghost."

Harry felt his brow furrow. "A ghost?"

Sally nodded quickly, her breath quickening as though just speaking the word had frightened her even more. "I saw it," she whispered, her voice shaking. "A figure... outside my window. Pale, like smoke. It was watching me."

Harry hesitated. He'd expected fear from Sally, but this? This was something different. Still, her mind had been fragile for years, and he knew well enough not to take everything she said at face value.

"Sally," he said gently, "are you sure you didn't just have a dream?"

Sally's head jerked up, her eyes wide and wild. "No," she said fiercely, shaking her head. "No, it was real. I saw it. It's always watching. It wants something... it wants me to stay quiet."

Harry's heart began to beat a little faster. "Quiet about what?" he asked, leaning in slightly.

But before Sally could answer, the door creaked open, and Matron Foster stepped into the room. Her eyes immediately locked onto Sally, and the flicker of annoyance Harry had seen earlier was sharper this time.

"Mr Jenkins," she said, her voice cool and businesslike. "I'm afraid this conversation is upsetting her. Sally needs her rest."

Sally's panicked eyes flicked between the matron and Harry, her voice dropping to a desperate whisper. "Don't let them get me."

Harry stood slowly, offering Sally a reassuring nod. "I'll make sure you're safe, Sally. I promise."

The matron stepped aside as Harry walked toward the door, but he could feel her eyes watching him closely—calculating, perhaps even suspicious. As soon as they were out in the hallway, the matron shut the door behind them with a click, her expression tight with disapproval.

"Sally's condition is delicate," the matron said sharply, folding her arms. "I would appreciate it if you didn't agitate her further with these... questions."

Harry's tone hardened. "Delicate or not, someone left a threatening note in her room, and now she's claiming to have seen a ghost. If she's in danger, I need to find out who's behind it."

The matron's eyes narrowed, but she remained silent, her lips pressed tightly together.

Harry studied her for a moment longer, a gnawing suspicion forming at the back of his mind. Something about the matron's demeanour had been off since he arrived—too guarded, too quick to shut down the conversation. She was hiding something, of that he was certain.

"I trust you'll look into the matter of the note," Harry said, his voice even but firm.

"Of course," the matron replied, her tone clipped. "I take my duties very seriously, Mr Jenkins."

Harry nodded, though the doubt lingered. As he stepped out of the asylum into the brisk spring air, his thoughts raced.

Sally's talk of a ghost—whether it was a figment of her imagination or something else—had rattled him more than he cared to admit. There were too many unanswered questions, too many secrets hidden within the asylum walls.

And then there was Lord Hawthorne. Whatever his connection to Sally Roe, Harry was sure he wasn't paying for her care out of the goodness of his heart.

Chapter Eighteen

Dorothy

D orothy had forgotten how much she hated air raids. Somehow between leaving London and settling in Crofter's Green, she'd managed to block out the memory of the boom of the anti-aircraft bombs, and the dull and yet deafening thud of the bombs as they struck the ground.

The basement of Sotheby's was large, with electric lights and sturdy concrete walls. It was cold, but at least it was dry, without the clammy feel of most cellars. Dorothy supposed they'd have to find a way to keep out the damp, if they usually stored valuable antiques down here.

Still, the walls shook every time a bomb hit. The lights flickered, and plaster shook down from the ceiling.

Dorothy sat with her back braced against one of the walls, her eyes squeezed shut as she waited for the echos of the latest bomb to die away. She'd never get back home tonight, not now; they'd likely be stuck here until morning.

Unless one of those bombs struck and brought the building above them down on their heads. Then they'd be trapped until the rescue workers could dig them out. If they survived at all.

Dorothy shut her eyes even more tightly. *Please, please let me get back home. Please don't let one of the bombs hit St. Thomas' hospital and kill Tom.*

Alice Greenleaf would look after Tommy for tonight, and no doubt Mum, too. They'd be all right. Dorothy just had to stay alive for tonight, and then tomorrow she'd be back home with all of them in Crofter's Green. Maybe she could even stop by the hospital again and see Tom, if he was awake.

Only when the ringing in Dorothy's ears stopped did she realise that Jane, who was huddled beside her, was crying.

Jane's mother had her arm around her daughter, trying to comfort her. But she was also trying to rock baby Nancy, who was still wailing, and she looked as though she wanted to break down herself.

"Here," Dorothy said, holding out a hand to Jane. "Don't cry." If Tommy were ever frightened sometime when she couldn't be there to help, she hoped some kind stranger would take care of him.

She wracked her brains, trying to think of some sort of amusement or at least a distraction before she remembered the book that Viola had given her back in the hospital ward.

Dorothy had stuffed it into her handbag and almost forgotten about it while she was sitting by Tom's bedside, but it was still there. She pulled the volume out and showed it to Jane. "You told me you like to read, didn't you? What if we try reading this together? I'll read out loud and you can help me with any hard words, what do you say?"

Jane looked at the book, still sniffling, but finally nodded. "All right."

Dorothy let out a breath, opened the book and read out loud, raising her voice a bit so as to be heard over the other noises within the shelter. "Chapter 1. Mr Sherlock Holmes."

The story was better than anything Dorothy had expected. She knew the name Sherlock Holmes. She'd given Tommy money a few months ago to see a film with some of his mates called, The Hound of the Baskervilles. She remembered him coming home excited to tell her all about some monstrous dog with glowing eyes. But she'd never read any of the stories.

Now, though, reading out loud, Dorothy found herself swept right along with Dr. Watson, meeting Sherlock Holmes in the hospital laboratory, trying to discover just what his mysterious flat mate did for a living.

She might not be much of a reader, but ever since Tommy was small, she'd told him make-believe stories every night, using different voices for different characters and funny accents that always made Tommy laugh. She did the same now, trying to make the story as lively for Jane as she could.   Every now and again she stopped and pretended not to know how to read a word, too, so that Jane could have the fun of reading it for her.

By the time they got to the part of the story where Holmes and Watson were summoned to an abandoned house on Brixton Road, Dorothy was so interested that she could almost block out the sounds of the bombs.   She worried for a minute or two that a story about murder might be too much for a little girl.   But then again, any child who'd lived through the Blitz in London had probably seen worse than anything Sherlock Holmes ever did.   And Jane was flipping the pages for her eagerly and waiting, breathless, for Dorothy to read some more.

Not just Jane.

Dorothy had just read about the word, "Rache" written in red on the wall when she looked up to realise that almost the entire roomful of people had stopped talking and murmuring and had turned towards her to listen.   Even baby Nancy had finally quieted down and fallen asleep with her head on her mother's shoulder.

Dorothy could feel a hot blush come up into her cheeks. She wasn't really clever, even if she was only pretending to need Jane's help with the words. And make-believe stories for

Tommy were one thing, but she wasn't any kind of a proper performer, either.

But then an old man in a chequered cloth cap who was sitting near the corner called out, "Go on, ducks, read some more!"

He was echoed by a chorus of others. "Yes, go on!" and, "Keep reading, it's getting interesting!"

Mr Murphy grinned and gave her an encouraging nod. Almost everyone in the cellar was smiling at her. All except for one thin, grey-haired woman with a squashed-looking black felt hat and a pair of gold pince-nez on her nose. She was sitting against the opposite wall and was staring at Dorothy as if her nose had just turned blue.

She could try doing voices for two separate Scotland Yard inspectors and making them sound different from each other.

Dorothy looked back down at the book. Outside, more bombs fell with thuds that made the electric lights flicker again.

Dorothy swallowed hard so that her voice wouldn't shake, and kept on reading. "You may mark my words, when this case comes to be cleared up, you will find that a woman named Rachel had something to do with it."

Chapter Nineteen

Harry

The call came just before dawn, rousing Harry Jenkins from a restless sleep. The moment he heard Nigel's voice on the other end of the line, he knew something was terribly wrong.

"Uncle Harry," Nigel had said, his voice tight. "We've got a body. Lord Hawthorne—at the manor."

Harry was out of bed and pulling on his clothes the moment the call had ended, his mind already racing through the possibilities. This was Crofter's Green, after all, not London. Things like this weren't supposed to happen here.

The pre-dawn mist clung to the air as Harry and Nigel arrived at Hawthorne Manor in Nigel's little Ford. The grand estate loomed in the faint early morning light, its stone facade dark and forbidding, framed against the fading night sky. Harry had always found something imposing about the old place, even on his first day in the village when he'd passed it on a morning walk into the hills outside town. Now, though, he could almost imagine that the house was holding its breath, bracing for the inevitable.

As they crunched across the gravel drive, Harry's eyes caught sight of Mrs Vickers, the housekeeper, standing at the entrance, wringing a dishcloth. Her face was pale, her usual calm replaced by wide-eyed shock. Harry could see she was struggling to keep her composure, and he'd seen that look enough times to recognise it—the look of someone who'd seen something they wished they could forget.

"Inspector," she whispered, her voice trembling. "It's... it's Lord Hawthorne. He's—"

"We know, Mrs Vickers," Nigel said gently, placing a hand on her arm. Harry noted the gesture—his nephew had a good way with people.

Harry gave her a small, reassuring nod as they stepped inside, trying to project the steadiness that had always served him well. He'd learned that in moments like these, a little calm could go a long way. But as he moved through the grand foyer, the air felt heavy with the kind of stillness that only comes after something terrible has happened. The echo of their footsteps seemed unnaturally loud against the polished floors, as if the house itself was listening.

"Where is he?" Harry asked quietly, keeping his voice low out of respect for the dead—and perhaps for the housekeeper's frayed nerves.

"Down the main staircase," she said, her voice shaky. "He... he must have fallen."

Harry caught the way her eyes flitted away as she spoke, as if she couldn't quite believe her own words. He'd seen that, too—people trying to convince themselves that what they'd found couldn't be as bad as it seemed.

He exchanged a glance with Nigel, noting the tightness in his nephew's jaw. Harry could tell the lad was holding back his thoughts—likely trying to keep Mrs Vickers calm. But Harry had the same suspicion itching at the back of his mind. He followed her toward the grand staircase, each step feeling heavier than the last.

When they rounded the corner and the staircase came into view, Harry's breath caught in his throat.

Lord Hawthorne lay crumpled at the base of the staircase, his body twisted at an unnatural angle, as though he'd been thrown from a great height. His nightgown was stained with dirt from the carpet, his face pale and still. But it wasn't just the sight of the body that made Harry's skin crawl.

It was the faint, glowing material scattered around his head.

A strange, almost phosphorescent dust clung to the edges of the carpet, faintly illuminating the area around the body.

Harry's eyes traced the glowing trail up the side of the stairs, where the same substance speckled the steps. It was as though someone—or something—had left a trail leading from the top of the staircase down to where Lord Hawthorne had met his end.

Harry knelt beside the body, taking in the details with a methodical eye. It was a habit that never left him, even here in the countryside. He noted the unnatural twist of the man's neck, the position of his arms. "This wasn't just a fall," he muttered, more to himself than to Nigel. "His neck's snapped—clean."

The old instincts, the ones that had served him for decades in London, came rushing back, sharpening his focus. It was clear that Lord Hawthorne's death hadn't been an accident. The question was whether he'd been pushed—or whether the cause of death had been something far stranger.

"What do you make of the glowing material?" he asked, leaning closer to inspect the strange substance. It was fine, almost like powder, and seemed to catch the faintest light as it glimmered on the edges of the carpet. His mind flipped through the catalog of substances he'd encountered over the years—none of them quite matched this.

Nigel, crouching nearby, frowned. "Never seen anything like it. Could be some kind of chemical... but it's not natural."

Harry's thoughts turned to Sally Roe, and the fear in her eyes when she spoke of the ghost she'd seen outside her window. The note warning her to keep her mouth shut. And now this—glowing material at the scene of Lord Hawthorne's death. Could the two be connected? Had Sally somehow known that something was going to happen?

He didn't believe in ghosts. Not really. But after what he'd seen, he couldn't dismiss the notion entirely. A rational explanation might be buried somewhere beneath the surface, but until he found it, he'd have to keep an open mind.

"What do we know about Lord Hawthorne's movements last night?" Harry asked, keeping his tone steady as he glanced at Mrs Vickers. The matronly housekeeper still hovered nearby, her hands clasped tightly in front of her.

"He went to bed early, as usual," she said, her voice low. "I didn't hear anything in the night—no noise, no shouting. Just... I found him like this when I came down early this morning."

"Did anyone else see him before he went to bed? Any visitors?" Harry pressed, focusing on her expression, the way her hands tightened around the dishcloth.

Mrs Vickers shook her head. "No, sir. He's been keeping to himself lately. Ever since..." She trailed off, biting her lip.

"Ever since what?" Harry prompted, watching her closely. He knew that look—someone balancing on the edge of telling a secret.

She hesitated, her eyes flicking between Harry and Nigel. "Well... ever since he started seeing things."

Harry held her gaze, waiting for her to continue. "Seeing things?"

She nodded, her voice dropping to a whisper. "He said he'd been seeing a figure. Pale, glowing—like a ghost. He wouldn't speak of it much, but it's been haunting him for weeks now. At first, I thought it was just his nerves. But after this..."

Harry's blood ran cold. Lord Hawthorne had seen the same thing Sally Roe had described. A glowing figure. A ghost.

But ghosts didn't leave trails of glowing powder, did they?

"Show me his bedroom," Harry said abruptly. "But turn out the lights first."

Chapter Twenty

Alice

"Do you think my mum will telephone soon?" Tommy asked.

Alice looked up from the pan of eggs she'd been scrambling. Since Dorothy hadn't returned the night before, she had spent the night in the small flat Tommy shared with his mother and grandmother. Joan, Dorothy's mother, was nearly an invalid, crippled by rheumatism. She was still asleep now, possibly thanks to the valerian tincture that Alice had given her the night before, so Alice was making Tommy his breakfast before school.

Now, looking into his eager, anxious face, she wished that she had it in her to lie. It wasn't difficult to guess why Dorothy would have failed to return to Crofter's Green last night. Air raids in London might not be a nightly occurrence anymore, as they had been for nearly 8 months. But Hitler's Luftwaffe still flew over to drop their payloads of bombs with horrible regularity.

It really wasn't fair that Tommy should have to worry about his mother and father both.   But then, if there was one thing that Alice had discovered in her more than sixty years, it was that life was very seldom fair.

"I'm sure she'll be in touch just as soon as she's able," she told Tommy.   "Now.   What about some—"

Eggs, she was about to say.   But her words were interrupted by the sharp trill of the telephone.

"Mum!"   Tommy raced to snatch up the receiver.   But his face— which had instantly brightened at the sound of the phone— fell again when he heard whoever was on the other end of the line.   "What?   Oh.   Oh yes, she's right here."

He held the receiver out to Alice.

Alice reached out to take it from him, puzzled as to who in the world would be contacting her here.   "Hello?"

"Alice?"   A man's deep baritone came through the receiver.

"Harry Jenkins here.   I was wondering whether we could enlist your expertise on some trouble that's cropped up at Hawthorne Manor."

"Trouble?" Alice repeated.   Her pulse had already quickened at the sound of Harry's voice, which called up immediate memories of a close encounter she'd had with a murderer a few months before.

She could think of no entirely harmless reasons why the retired Scotland Yard Inspector would have taken the trouble to track her down at Dorothy Baker's flat and   telephone her at 7 o'clock in the morning.

So she wasn't entirely surprised when Harry's voice went on, "I'm sorry to have to tell you, but Lord Hawthorne is dead.   Tripped, fell down the stairs, and broke his neck last night."

"Lord Hawthorne?   Dead?"   Alice might have been bracing herself for some dire announcement, but she was still shocked by the news.   Back in her youth, Lord Walter Hawthorne had been the county's most eligible bachelor and had set the hearts of all of Alice's friends fluttering, even though there was no chance whatever that a man of his station would ever marry a village girl.

"I'm afraid so."   Harry's voice changed, and he went on as though choosing his words with care, "I'm here at the manor with Nigel, now.   We were wondering whether you might be able to come up and have a look at something?"

"What—" Alice realised belatedly that Harry's voice was extremely carrying, and that Tommy was watching her, wide-eyed, clearly hanging on every word of this conversation.

"What sort of something?" she asked.

"Just something odd that we've found here on the staircase.   There's an odd sort of glowing residue."

"Did you just say, glowing?" Alice's heart jumped hard, and she momentarily forgot all about Tommy listening in.

"That's right," Harry said.   "We could send it to one of the laboratories in London, of course, but that would take time, and they're overworked as it is.   So we were wondering whether you might be able to help identify it, what with your background in chemistry and such."

Alice gripped the telephone receiver more tightly.   Physically, she might still be in Dorothy and Joan's tiny but immaculately clean flat.   But in her mind's eye, she was back in her own greenhouse, looking down at the County Herb Committee plants and noticing that one pot— one very puzzling pot— was missing.

"Yes," she said out loud.   "Yes, I think there's every chance that I might be able to tell you exactly what this glowing residue might be."

Chapter Twenty-One

Dorothy

Dorothy stepped through the Sotheby's main entrance and back out onto the street, blinking at the dazzle of morning light. She hadn't finished *A Study in Scarlet* the night before, but she'd read until well past midnight, when the lights in the cellar had been put out so that everyone could try to get some sleep.

The all-clear had been sounded about that same time, so some of those who'd taken shelter had decided to leave and go back to their own homes for the rest of the night. Since Dorothy and Mr Murphy had hours of driving to get home— and since the London Streets were bound to be in a horrible state right after a bombing raid— they'd decided to stay.

Dorothy had wadded up her cardigan to use for a pillow and managed to get a few hours of sleep on the hard cellar floor.

Now the streets as far as her eyes could see were covered with a haze of dust and smoke, and the air was filled with the acrid scent of burning. The wail of fire engine and ambulance sirens echoed up and down the street, and a bomb must have hit not too far off, because further up Bond Street Dorothy could see a huge crater in the road and a building that was now just matchsticks and broken bricks.

She shut her eyes. She was grateful to be alive, but at the same time it felt wrong to be thankful for the bombs having fallen somewhere else. Others hadn't been as lucky as they'd been.

"Look at that," Mr Murphy said, beside her. He didn't seem to be feeling any guilty qualms; his voice was cheery as he pointed to the Daimler, still parked across the street. "The car's even still here. I was afraid some bright lad might've nicked it during all the hullaballoo."

He and Dorothy were among the last to leave the auction house. The others who'd remained in the cellar for the night had all thanked Dorothy very nicely for her reading before they'd gone on their separate ways. The old man in the chequered cap had actually had tears in his eyes as he'd squeezed both of her hands, and Jane's mother— whose name turned out to be Maud— had hugged Dorothy and made her promise to come and visit if she was in London again.

Mr Murphy unlocked the boot of the car and hefted a wooden crate up onto his shoulder. "May as well run this inside, since her ladyship wanted it— " he stopped, his usually cheerful face etched in a frown.

"Is something wrong?" Dorothy asked.

"That man up there." Mr Murphy nodded to the figure of a man who was just turning the corner onto Maddox Street. "I'd have sworn it was Alfred."

Dorothy's brows went up in surprise. "You mean Alf Travers, the groundskeeper?"

She peered down the street, too. But they were too far away, and the man was already gone, vanished along with the rush of other pedestrians out this morning. She hadn't had a good enough look to even think there was anything familiar about him.

"I must have been mistaken." Mr Murphy shook his head. "What'd Alfred be doing in Bond Street? There's not even a racetrack anywhere for him to bet on."

He settled the wooden crate more firmly on his shoulder. The crate clinked, as though it was filled with glass bottles. Dorothy saw three more in the boot of the car.

"Do you want some help?" she offered.

"Nah, thanks all the same." Mr Murphy gave her a cheery wink. "Old and feeble and maybe half-blind I may be, but I can manage this lot. You sit yourself down in the car."

"If you don't mind," Dorothy said. She'd spotted one of London's bright red public telephone boxes up the street a little ways. "I want to try telephoning to my mother. She's bound to have been worried, since I didn't make it home last night."

She might even be able to speak to Tommy, too. The hour was early enough that he probably hadn't yet left for school.

"Of course, of course." Mr Murphy waved her off. "I may be a little while, depending on whether the Sotheby's bloke I'm supposed to give these to has turned up for work yet. I've got his name." He patted the pocket of his uniform, one-handed.

"But who knows whether he's here. Tell you what, why don't you go back to St. Thomas's and see if you can get in to see that husband of yours again?"

Dorothy's heart jumped. She might really get to see Tom a second time.

"You don't mind?" she asked.

"Not a bit. I'm sure it'd put your mind at ease to know he got through last night's business all right," Mr Murphy said.

"Besides, maybe he'll be awake this morning. You run along and I'll pick you up there in an hour or so."

He turned to carry the crate towards Sotheby's main doors.

Dorothy rummaged through her handbag for coins. She was third in line to use the telephone; others besides her were anxious to let their friends and families know that they were all right and had survived the bombing raid. But finally she was able to shut herself inside the little glassed-in booth, and after the usual clicks and buzzes, she heard her mother's voice say, "Hello?" at the other end of the line.

"Hello, Mum."

"Dorothy!" The relief in her mother's voice was plain, even through the phone line. "You're all right?"

"Fine. There was a bombing raid last night, that's all," Dorothy said. "But we were able to get to a shelter."

"And Tom?" her mother asked.

"He's—" Dorothy hesitated. This wasn't the kind of news she wanted to give over the telephone. "He's going to be all right," she said. "What about you and Tommy? Did Alice stay with you two last night?"

Alice had offered when Dorothy asked her to pick Tommy up from school.

"Ye-es."

Dorothy frowned. It might be only the fault of the connection, but there seemed to be an odd note in her mother's voice. She couldn't imagine why, though. Alice Greenleaf was her mother's oldest friend. They surely hadn't quarrelled?

"She stayed until early this morning," Mum went on. "Then the police— well, then she had to leave—"

"The police?" Dorothy cut in. She'd have said that the only thing less likely than Alice and Mum quarreling was Alice getting hauled off by the police.

"Well, no, not the police, really."   Mum's voice was hurried, now.   Dorothy recognized the tone; it was the one her mother used when she was hoping you wouldn't ask her any awkward questions.   "It was that nice Harry Jenkins, you know.   The one who retired to Crofter's Green a few months ago?"

"I know who Harry Jenkins is," Dorothy said.   "Mum, what's been going on?"

"It's all right, Mummy!" Tommy's voice came over the line, only slightly muffled.   Dorothy pictured him leaning over his grandmother's shoulder to shout into the receiver.   "It's just that Granny's trying not to tell you about the murder."

Chapter Twenty-Two

Dorothy

Dorothy was being followed.

It took her a while to notice. Most of her attention was taken up with trying to take in the news from Crofter's Green. Her mum had been quick to hush Tommy and explain that no one had been murdered. Lord Hawthorne had tripped going down the stairs the night before and been found dead in the front hall early this morning. Yes, the police had been called in, but that happened any time there was a sudden death.

Even still, Dorothy was struggling to absorb the shock of Lord Hawthorne's passing.

After ending the telephone call with her mother, she had found a taxi cab that could drive her from Bond Street to St. Thomas', although thanks to whole sections of streets being closed off after last night's bombing, the cab had wound up letting her off a few streets away from the hospital on Royal Street. Dorothy hadn't minded. As tired as she was, she still was glad for the chance to walk and stretch her legs and work the kinks out of her back after the hours of being cramped up in the cellar. And walking gave her time to think, too.

For as long as she could remember, Lord Hawthorne had been head of the Hawthorne family and a permanent institution up at the manor. Like the Bank of England or the Tower of London, he was one of those unchanging constants you might not think much about every day, but you knew were there. And now he was . . . gone. Fallen down the stairs and had his neck broken. Just like that, his whole life snuffed out in a blink.

Dorothy was so taken up with wondering whether Lady Gwendolyn would stay up at the manor or find somewhere else to live that she didn't really properly notice the woman in the black hat until the third or fourth time she'd seen her.

The air was thick with the scent of damp brick and the occasional waft of smoke, but people were still out and about, hurrying along the pavement, some clutching ration books as they tried to get to the shops before food supplies were completely sold out. Street vendors were calling over the noise of the crowds, offering everything from newspapers to flowers, trams rattled past, ambulances wailed, and bulldozers rumbled through piles of debris. London was battered but determined to carry on, as all the war time posters that plastered the building walls were telling people to do.

When uneasiness prickled across Dorothy's skin, she thought at first that she was just tired. Or worried about Tom. Or remembering the bombing from last night. Really, there was a whole laundry list of reasons why she might be feeling on-edge. But then she happened to glance behind her and saw a slightly squashed-looking black felt hat, trimmed with a ring of purple silk flowers. And she realised abruptly that she'd been seeing that same squashed felt hat ever since leaving Sotheby's. The thin, grey-haired woman wearing the hat had climbed into a taxi cab that had pulled up just behind Dorothy's own. And then Dorothy had noticed her— but without consciously paying much attention— at least two more times among the crowd of other people standing on a corner with her and waiting to cross a street.

Now she was fully paying attention, and she realised that her acquaintance with Mrs Squashed Hat went back further than Bond Street. The same woman had been down in the Sotheby's basement with everyone else last night. She was the one who'd been staring so hard at Dorothy while Dorothy had been reading the story about Sherlock Holmes to Jane and everyone else in the shelter.

Dorothy's thoughts raced, skipping back and forth. On the one hand, maybe this was just a coincidence. It wasn't impossible to think that maybe Mrs Squashed Hat was also going to visit someone who was a patient at St. Thomas'.

Just like the nurse had told Dorothy yesterday, the hospital wards were filled with people who'd been hurt in the bombing raids.   On the other hand, though, maybe the woman really was following her.

Just a couple of months ago, Dorothy had seen more than she would have liked of some of the criminal gangs that were operating out of London these days.

She was only about a few streets away from the hospital now.   Dorothy quickened her pace, fighting the urge to look behind her as she hurried along the crowded street.   She reached the main entrance to St. Thomas' and almost ran up the front steps.   Only then did she let herself glance back over her shoulder.   The woman with the black felt hat was nowhere in sight.

Dorothy released a long breath.   She'd just been letting her imagination run away with her, after all.

Even better, the hospital didn't look as though it had taken any damage in the bombing raid last night.

She entered the lobby and once again gave her name to the nurse on duty at the front desk, who was just as busy and harried-looking as she'd been yesterday.   Today she seemed to be answering the telephone while also making notes on a sheet of paper in front of her and handing a man in an orderly's uniform some sort of form to fill out.   She only nodded distractedly when Dorothy said that she remembered Tom's ward and didn't need anyone to show her.

Dorothy made her way along the scrubbed and sanitised hallways, but she hadn't quite reached Tom's ward when she rounded a corner and almost bumped into Viola.   Viola was dressed in more clothes that didn't fit her quite right: this time, a plaid woollen dress and a cardigan that were both much too large.   She was pushing her wheeled cart of books, and her eyes widened in surprise at the sight of Dorothy.

"Mrs Baker!   But how did you get here so quickly?"

"Quickly?   How do you mean?"

"They only just telephoned—" Viola stopped speaking as though she'd just realised she might have said too much.

But it was too late.   "Telephoned?   Why?   Has something happened to Tom?"   Dorothy only just managed to get the words out.   Her lungs had squeezed into a tight, frozen knot.   She couldn't breathe.

She could barely hear anything over the hard pounding of her own heart in her ears.   But she saw Viola give a quick shake of her head, and that at least reassured her enough that she was able to take a quick gulp of air and catch the last part of the other woman's reply.

"—Just that his fever has gone up a bit overnight."

Chapter
Twenty-Three

Alice

A lice looked down at the smear of pale greenish residue that marked her fingers. "Its scientific name is Panellus stipticus," she said. She was standing at the foot of the main staircase at Hawthorne Manor, speaking to Harry and his nephew Nigel Brewster, who was also the local police inspector.

At least half of her attention was taken up with trying not to picture Lord Hawthorne sprawled out dead on the floor under her feet. His body had already been photographed by one of Nigel's constables and taken away, but that didn't stop Alice from picturing the grisly scene over and over again in her mind's eye.

She and the two men were currently alone at what sensational newspapers would probably call the scene of the crime.

If it was in fact a crime, and not a simple case of a man tripping and falling down the stairs.

Harry and Nigel hadn't outright told her, but Alice was observant enough to read the grimness in the two men's expressions and conclude that things were certainly trending towards murder rather than accident.

Lady Gwendolyn was upstairs in her room, lying down after the shock, while the servants were gathered downstairs in the servants' hall, waiting to be interviewed by the police. The manor had never in Alice's memory been a lively place, but now it had a hushed, oppressive feeling of silence, almost like a tomb.

"Panellus . . ." Nigel frowned. He was a tall, lean young man. Well, perhaps not so young, in that he was probably approaching the age of forty if he hadn't reached it already. But everyone whose age was less than a half-century was beginning to look young to Alice these days. He had red-brown hair and an angular face that typically revealed very little.

Alice imagined that criminals might make the mistake of thinking that his lack of expression and rather stolid, humourless appearance meant a lack of intelligence, as well. But about that, they would be quite wrong. She had seen firsthand that Nigel Brewster was by no means a stupid man. Nor did she think that he was entirely without humour, although she hadn't yet worked out whether he was simply very formal or perhaps merely shy.

But since the answer mattered rather less than the fact that he was currently waiting patiently for her to explain herself further, Alice pulled herself back from her reflections.

"Stipticus," she repeated. "It's a type of the bioluminescent fungi commonly referred to as foxfire— though that name includes several varieties of fungi and other mushrooms. This particular species is also called the bitter oyster. The mushrooms start out as tiny white knobs, which eventually develop into fan- or kidney-shaped orange-yellow to brownish caps. They attach to decaying wood by short stubby stalks, and are most commonly found on oak, birch, alder, beech, hazel, chestnut, and ash trees. The fungus typically feeds on dead wood, but it will also grow opportunistically on a live tree if the conditions and climate are right. It is a saprobic species, and as such causes white rot, meaning in other words a form of wood decay in which the wood assumes a bleached appearance and where lignin as well as cellulose and hemicellulose is broken down by enzymes secreted by the fungus."

"I see."

Nigel blinked, possibly to stop his eyes from glazing over at her explanation. Alice reminded herself that not everyone was as fascinated by the science of fungi as she was.

"And you were growing some of these . . . bitter oyster mushrooms in your greenhouse?" Nigel asked.

"Studies have shown them to be effective in stopping bleeding, and they also make for a highly potent purgative," Alice said. "So yes, I was growing them for the County Herb Commission. Or rather, I was until I discovered that my pot of the fungi had gone missing."

"When was that?" Harry had been silent, turning his head this way and that as though observing every detail of the manor's main hall, but now he turned to Alice.

"I discovered the theft yesterday afternoon," Alice told him. "As to when the pot of panellus stipticus was actually taken?" she shook her head. "I'm afraid I can't say with any very high degree of accuracy. I know I watered the plants around it three days ago. And I think that the panellus was there then. But I wouldn't be able to swear to it absolutely. I have a good many plants on that table, and I was in a hurry to get out and dig another bed for potatoes. I might not have noticed that the pot was missing."

"You would have noticed," Harry said with certainty. "I'm all for honesty and accuracy in witness statements. But I've a better opinion of your powers of observation than to think you'd have overlooked a thing like that."

"We'll say that the theft most likely occurred within the past three days, then," Nigel said. He made a note on the pad he carried. "Now, this stuff that seems to have been smeared about the stairs. Could someone just have crushed up some of these mushrooms and spread them around?"

"Oh, no." Alice looked down at her smudged thumb and forefinger once again. "No, the bioluminescence is only visible when the mushrooms are in the wild, attached to the wood on which they feed. No, in order to use them to create this sort of an effect, a rather complicated chemical process must be carried out on the harvested mushrooms. Briefly put, the compounds within the mushroom which emit light must be treated with salt of ammonia in the presence of iron, hydrogen peroxide, and a cationic surfactant. Then a chemiluminescent reaction occurs which causes the resulting substance to emit light."

Nigel blinked again, but to his credit seemed to have been paying attention. "I see." He glanced at his uncle. "So it seems we're looking for someone with a background in chemistry. Or at the very least a layman with a high degree of technical knowledge."

"Ought to narrow the field quite a bit," Harry agreed. He rubbed his jaw. "Can't think of anyone like that in the village, though."

"Except for me?" Alice asked dryly.

Harry gave her a grin and a wink. "There aren't many safe bets in life these days. But I'd be willing to stake my policeman's pension on you not being a homicidal maniac. If you ever got the urge to murder someone, you'd have better sense than to use a method that would point straight back to you, for one thing."

"Well, thank you. I think." Alice drew out a handkerchief and used it to wipe her fingers. "But I'm not entirely clear. How is this phosphorescent material related to Lord Hawthorne's death?"

Harry and his nephew exchanged glances. Then Harry said, "This is all conjecture, mind you. But I suppose you've heard the rumours about Lord Hawthorne recently seeing ghosts?"

"Certainly," Alice said. "I imagine every man, woman, and child in Crofter's Green has heard those rumours by now, and paid far more attention to them than the latest reports on the BBC about the war."

Harry nodded. "Well. What it looks like to us is that whoever was staging these ghostly apparitions somehow lured Hawthorne out of bed and to the staircase last night with a show of glowing lights. Then he was either tripped or given a good hard shove."

"It's possible, isn't it, that someone was just playing a nasty prank on Lord Hawthorne, and that his death really was an accident?" Alice asked. "That is, whoever was responsible might only have wished to frighten him, and might not have foreseen that he would fall down the stairs and be killed."

"It's possible," Harry allowed.

"But you don't think it's likely," Alice said.

"Nasty, suspicious minds we policemen have got," Harry said. "Prone to assuming the worst of everyone."

"To be fair, the worst is so very often true," Alice said.

Harry chuckled, then glanced at his nephew. This time, Alice thought there was a silent question in the older man's look. Nigel gave a barely perceptible nod before saying, "Well, I'd better be taking official statements from the servants. The longer I let it go, the more time they'll have to talk among themselves and 'remember' all sorts of exciting occurrences last night."

"Is that how it goes in a murder investigation?" Alice asked curiously. She had left Crofter's Green only to attend university in her youth, and had otherwise spent her entire life here in the same small village. She didn't regret it, but she was interested to hear what Nigel and his uncle would say. This was an eye-opening look into the inner workings of a world entirely different from her own sphere.

"Generally speaking." Nigel's solemn expression lightened briefly in a small smile. "The housemaid will start the day by saying that she slept straight through the night without hearing a sound. But then the more she thinks it over, she'll decide that maybe she was woken up by a sort of moaning sound. And by the time she's told that story to all her closest friends, the possible moan will have been transformed into a blood-curdling scream and she'll also swear that she looked out her window and saw a madman carrying a ten inch knife dripping blood."

"So people are liars by nature?" Alice asked.

"Put it that most people want to be important and to be a part of any excitement that's going around," Nigel said. "Wish me luck." With a nod, he strode off in the direction of the green baize door that led to the kitchen and the servants' wing.

Alice was expecting Harry to say that, having identified the probable source of the greenish glowing substance, she was now free to go.

But instead he said, "If you've got time for it, could we have a quick word?"

Chapter Twenty-Four

Dorothy

D orothy's heart was hammering as she made her way down the ward's central aisle to Tom's bedside. Viola clearly had been trying not to frighten her, but even a glance was enough to show her that Tom's fever was more than just a little worse since the day before.

Tom's cheeks were flushed bright red, and he was tossing and turning his head on the pillow.

"Tom?" Dorothy said softly. She put her hand on his forehead and found his skin dry and burning hot.

Tom's eyes fluttered open, but his gaze seemed to look at her and through her all at the same time without any trace of recognition.

"Mum?" His voice was hoarse and cracked-sounding. "Mum, is that you?" He struggled as though he was trying to get up.

Dorothy swallowed down the lump in her throat and put a hand on his shoulder.

"Just rest now, Tom. You'll feel better soon."

"Dorothy?" Just for a second, Tom looked at her as though he actually knew who she was. Then his gaze went bleary and he twisted his head restlessly on the pillow, his face contorting in a grimace. "Why does my leg hurt so much? Where am I?"

Dorothy blinked her eyes hard. She could cry later. Right now, Tom needed her to be strong. And calm.

"You're in St. Thomas' hospital, Tom. You were hurt in the fighting. Do you remember?"

But Tom's eyes had flickered closed. "Hurts," he mumbled. "Should never have got onto that bicycle."

A nurse in a starched white cap and apron bustled up before Dorothy could answer.

"I'm sorry, but I'll have to ask you to leave for a short while. The doctors have ordered that this man be given a cold bath to help bring his temperature down and then have strict quiet with no visitors."

"But . . . but I'm his wife," Dorothy stammered.

The nurse was middle-aged and grim-looking with a square, determined jaw and a pursed-up mouth that looked as though she disapproved of the entire world. But Dorothy thought that even she looked sympathetic for a second or two.

Then she shook her head. "I'm sorry, but hospital rules are hospital rules. When a patient's fever spikes like this, it's of the utmost importance that they remain absolutely quiet. Even family members can cause too much excitement and agitation. You can come back tonight or tomorrow."

Dorothy stared at her stupidly. "But I don't live here in London. I've got to go home."

This time, the nurse's look seemed to convey that Dorothy's living arrangements weren't anyone's problem but her own. Although actually, Dorothy wasn't even sure that the older woman heard her. She was busily erecting a folding screen around Tom's bed. Two more nurses came up to join her, one pushing a wheeled cart with a basin of ice water on the top.

A hand touched Dorothy's arm. "Come with me."

Dorothy hadn't heard her approach, but Viola was beside her. "We can go and have a cup of tea in the hospital canteen."

Dorothy nodded, following behind Viola as she led the way out of the ward. She couldn't think what else to do. Maybe it was the shock and the worry and the near-sleepless night— as well as having had practically nothing to eat for the past two days— but she felt almost as though she'd been wrapped up in layers of thick, muffling cotton wool, unable to do anything but stumble along mutely behind Viola along hospital hallways and down a flight of stairs.

They ended up in a large, sanitised room that Dorothy took to be the hospital canteen.

"Sit here; I'll fetch the tea and something to eat," Viola told her.

Dorothy sat down at one of the scarred wooden tables. She was aware of other people in the room— men in pyjamas and bathrobes who must be patients, people with bandaged heads and arms in slings who were probably casualties from the latest bombing raid— but she couldn't bring herself to look at them directly or meet anyone's gaze.

When someone dropped into the chair opposite her own, she thought for an instant that it must be Viola. But Viola hadn't been wearing a drab brown overcoat—

With a jolt of shock that penetrated even the muffling layers of cotton wool, Dorothy's head jerked up and she looked into the lined face of the woman who had followed her from Sotheby's, the same thin, grey-haired woman with the squashed black felt hat who had stared at her during the bombing raid the night before.

"Who are you?" Dorothy gasped.

Seen up close, the woman looked to be no more than thirty or maybe thirty-five, far too young for her grey hair and drab, dowdy clothes. In fact, Dorothy realised that the grey hair had to be a wig. It was too stiff and unnatural-looking to be real, and she could see tiny wisps of dark hair that had to be the woman's natural colour escaping at the nape of her neck.

Even with the wig and the old woman's disguise, Dorothy could see she was beautiful, with large dark eyes and an olive cast to her tanned skin. When she spoke it was with an Italian accent. One of Dorothy's neighbours when she and Tom had lived in London had been Italian.

"Who I am is not important," she said. "But you should listen to what I have to tell you."

"Why?" Dorothy asked. "What do you mean?"

"Are you Lady Gwendolyn Hawthorne?" the woman asked.

In spite of everything that had happened and the crushing weight of fear on her chest, Dorothy almost laughed out loud.

"Me? Lady Gwendolyn? That's a good one."

The other woman frowned. "You arrived at Sotheby's in her car and with her chauffeur driving."

"How do you know that?" Dorothy asked.

The woman made a quick, impatient gesture. "The same way I know a great many things." She cast a quick look around the canteen as though checking to make sure that they weren't being spied on, then leaned forward, lowering her voice. "You must at least know Lady Gwendolyn, so I will give you a message for her. Quickly. I have not much time before someone notices that I am gone."

Chapter Twenty-Five

Dorothy

"**G**one?" Dorothy asked.

Gone from where? And why should the Italian woman care about anyone noticing? A part of Dorothy wondered whether she was touched in the head. But somehow, she knew deep down that wasn't it. The woman's eyes were frightened, but completely sane, and she spoke with a desperate kind of earnestness.

"Please. Don't interrupt. A man called Rosco brought me to this country with sweet words and empty promises. One of which was that he would marry me."

Anger simmered beneath the woman's expression— not the hot kind of rage, Dorothy thought, but the sort that cold fury that had lasted so long it had turned hard like ice.

"He lied," the Italian woman went on. "It amuses him that I have no family here, no friends, no choice but to stay with him or starve on the streets. He does not even know that I can speak any English. But I have learned. My one tiny weapon against him is that I am not as stupid and ignorant and helpless as he thinks that I am. Not anymore. I have listened and learned little by little to speak the language here. I have played the innocent fool enough that Rosco even allows me to go out on my own sometimes. Shopping, that is what I tell him. Oh, he used to send one of his men to follow me. But they always returned to him to report that I did nothing but go into dress shops or a jewellery shop, and never did I say a word to the ladies who worked there, but only pointed to what I wanted.

"Now he believes that I am quite content to remain with him and receive a new dress, a new bracelet as a reward— like a child being bribed with sweets. He does not even bother to send anyone to follow me when I go out anymore. But I— I have begun to follow him and his men. Once he even passed by me in the street when I was dressed this way"— she made a gesture that included her wig and clothes— "and he did not recognize me. He would never believe that I would be clever enough to disguise myself or work out what he is up to."

Again, Dorothy heard the cold, steel-hard fury beneath the woman's tone. She shook her head, though, frowning, "I'm sorry, but I don't understand why you're telling me all this—"

"I am explaining it!" the woman interrupted. "Rosco leads a gang here in London called the Iron Dukes."

Dorothy jerked back, drawing in a sharp breath. The Italian woman nodded. "I can see you know that name. That makes this simpler, then. The Iron Dukes have been stealing valuables— antiques, old bottles of wine, books and the like— from a place called Hawthorne Manor. They steal them and then bring them up here to London to sell at auction houses."

A cold, sick feeling bloomed in the pit of Dorothy's stomach. "Stealing? Do you mean that Mr Murphy is stealing from his lordship and her ladyship?"

Mr Murphy had been so nice to her. But maybe he'd had reasons of his own for wanting to come up to London. Maybe it hadn't been Lord Hawthorne at all who'd sent him to Sotheby's with cases of wine to put up for auction.

The Italian woman shrugged. "I don't know who is doing the actual stealing." Clearly she wasn't at all concerned about Dorothy's feelings in the matter. "All I know is that the goods are brought up here to that big auction house where we were last night, the one where all the rich people go to buy and sell."

"Sotheby's."

"Yes. Rosco has two or three men who work there— or who pretend to work there— doing the unloading and the packing in the store rooms. Really, of course, they are stealing whatever they can."

"So it's not just Lord and Lady Hawthorne that they're robbing?"

"Oh, no." The Italian woman shook her head. "I over-heard one of them say something about Lady Hawthorne of Hawthorne Manor. But I am sure there are others."

"What were they saying about her ladyship?" Dorothy asked.

"That I do not know." The other woman looked regretful. "Sometimes even still Rosco and his men speak too fast for me to quite understand. I thought that they said something about, *when she's dead*, but I cannot be certain."

"When she's dead?" The cold numbness in Dorothy inten-sified. "Are you sure they didn't say, When he's dead? Could they have been talking about Lord Hawthorne instead of Lady Hawthorne?"

The Italian woman tilted her head, considering. "Perhaps," she said at last. "Yes, perhaps I was mistaken. As I say, I do not always understand what Rosco and his men are saying, and I must be very, very careful always never to let them think that I am listening."

Dorothy opened her mouth, about to mention Lord Hawthorne's death, but then changed her mind. She was pretty sure that the woman sitting opposite her was telling the truth. But pretty sure didn't really count for very much when there was a potential murder involved, and after all she didn't even know the Italian woman's name.

So she asked instead, "Why are you telling me all of this? Just to get back at this man Rosco?"

"That, of course." The woman nodded.

"Why not just leave him, though?" Dorothy asked. "If he's stopped watching you closely, why not just take some of the jewellery and clothes he's bought for you and disappear?"

"First, because it is not so simple as that. I doubt very much that there is anywhere I could hide where Rosco would not find me." The Italian woman shivered and looked, for the first time since sitting down at Dorothy's table, afraid. "But also, I do not wish only to get away from Rosco. He must be stopped— destroyed." Her hands clenched on the edge of the table.

Dorothy opened her mouth, but before she could get a word out, the Italian woman went on, her words coming in a low, furious rush. "Just because I have lived in England now for many years does not mean that I do not love my country. And now— now Rosco is dealing with that . . . that *stronzo* Mussolini who is setting fire to Italy and watching it burn to the ground."

"The Iron Dukes are working with Mussolini?" Dorothy was trying to imagine what interest the Italian dictator could have in a London street gang.

"In a manner of speaking." The other woman made another quick, angry gesture. "Mussolini and Hitler are in one another's pockets. And Rosco . . . Rosco is happy to take the money German agents pay him to spy or carry out their dirty work for them. He cares nothing for who wins this war, so long as it makes him richer."

"German Agents?" Dorothy repeated. "There are German agents here in London?"

The Italian woman gave her a pitying look. "There are German agents everywhere." She glanced around them once again. "I must go. You have family here at the hospital?"

"My husband," Dorothy faltered.

The other woman nodded. "Very well, then. You must tell Lady Hawthorne what I have told you so that she may be warned and so that the police may capture Rosco and his men. If I have anything more to tell you, I will contact you again here."

With that, she stood up and swept out of the canteen, to leave Dorothy staring after her.

It might have been ten minutes or it might only have been one before Viola set a tray with two cups of tea and a plate of biscuits down on the table.

"Here we are," she said. "I'm sorry that took so long. They'd just run out of tea and had to brew a fresh batch. Not that you'll probably be able to tell, it's usually so weak it might as well be dishwater."

Dorothy raised a cup to her lip and took a sip. It wasn't particularly strong tea, but at least it was warm.

"Thank you."

"Of course." Viola smiled at her. "I know how worried you must be about your husband. But the doctors here really will take the best possible care of him. And I've seen many men worse off than him pull through. They have new medicines nowadays to treat infections. Sulfa drugs like Prontosil that are doing wonders with infected wounds."

"Thank you," Dorothy said again. She took another swallow of tea, then said, "Do you think I could just look in on Tom again before I have to leave?"

"The nurses may not like it, but we'll find a way to smuggle you in," Viola promised her.

Dorothy nodded. She needed to see Tom just once more. Whether he was aware enough to know it was her or not, she had to kiss his cheek and tell him to keep fighting for her and for Tommy.

Then . . . then she needed to get home to Crofter's Green so that she could tell someone everything that the strange Italian woman had just told her.

Chapter Twenty-Six

Evie

"Carrot biscuits?" Mrs Benton's three double chins quivered in indignation. Her thin lips pursed with an expression of distaste. "You really have nothing at all else to offer?"

Evie squelched the urge to say that a missed meal was hardly likely to cause someone of Mrs Benton's ample proportions to starve. A stout, matronly lady, she wore a black straw hat pinned firmly atop her thinning grey hair, and a flowered dress with buttons that looked as though they might at any moment give up the struggle and pop like so many miniature champagne corks.

"I'm sorry, Mrs Benton," Evie said instead. "War time rationing, you know."

Mrs Benton snorted, but raised the offending carrot biscuit doubtfully to her lips and took a small bite.

Evie waited. She loved opening the shop up and serving her customers— even those like Mrs Benton, who made a positive hobby out of finding things to complain about.

"Why— why these are quite excellent!" Mrs Benton's eyes rounded in surprise. "I would never have thought that carrot biscuits could be so appealing."

"Thank you."

This week, Evie had been experimenting with some of the recipes suggested in the government-published pamphlets on wartime cooking. The majority of the recipes tended to sound more like propaganda pieces, touting the virtues of potatoes and carrots. Both those crops were cheap and easy to grow. Evie had her doubts about potato pastry for a pie crust, but the carrot biscuits— spiced with ginger and cinnamon and studded with raisins— had turned out surprisingly well.

If Mrs Benton had been impressed, then Evie could definitely mark that recipe down in her 'successes' column.

She refilled Mrs Benton's teacup and made a mental note that she would have to top up the milk jug after Mrs Benton left. With Dorothy away in London, Evie was left alone to do the work that they usually divided between them all on her own. Not that she begrudged Dorothy the time away. All that mattered was finding out whether her husband was all right—

Evie's thought snapped off as the door to the tea room opened and Diana Lovecraft swept in, accompanied by the usual cloud of her favourite scent. Women's fashions these days tended to be practical and mostly utilitarian in style: narrow skirts, plain blouses with straight sleeves. New clothes required coupons to purchase— the same as butter and sugar and flour— so no one had extra fabric to spare for fripperies.

Diana's clothing choices didn't just ignore those current trends, they thumbed their noses in the direction of everything utilitarian or practical. Today she was wearing a poppy-red dress with a black belt, the fabric swirling around her calves. Patent leather shoes encased her silk-stocking clad feet, and a hat with a ring of scarlet silk flowers perched at a jaunty angle atop her peroxide blonde curls.

In a way, it was an effective type of camouflage, Evie thought. Diana's outward appearance drew so much atten-tion that very few people thought to wonder much about the actual woman inside the flamboyant clothes. Diana also car-ried Bonzo the Pomeranian under one arm. The little dog was looking, if possible, even less thrilled about the arrangement than usual, and bared his teeth at Mrs Benton as Diana passed by her table.

None of that mattered at the moment, however. Diana was here, at Evie's tea shop, which violated all their unspoken rules about having as little contact with one another as possible.

Something must have happened.

"May I help you?" Evie offered Diana a pleasant smile.

"Oh— thank you. Yes." Diana's smile was also fixed firmly in place, but her usual sugary-sweet tone was less sweet and fluting than usual. Something really had happened. "I was just wondering whether you might have any of those lovely little dog biscuits you made for Bonzo the other week? I called at Mercer's, but they're out of anything for my precious boy to eat."

"Of course," Evie said. "As it happens, I've just mixed up a fresh batch. If you'd like to come through into the kitchen with me, I'll just wrap them up for you."

Chapter Twenty-Seven

Evie

S ince Evie had never sold— or made— a dog biscuit in her life, she would be in an awkward position if Mrs Benton expressed any curiosity on the subject or asked how the biscuits were made. Fortunately, though, Mrs Gertie Spenlow— another of Crofter's Green's habitual complainers— entered the shop at that moment and dropped into the chair opposite Mrs Benton's.

Comparing their grievances against the world in general would keep them both occupied for a quarter of an hour, at least.

"I'll be with you in a moment, Mrs Spenlow," Evie said. "I'm just going to see to Mrs Lovecraft's order and put a fresh kettle on for tea."

She led the way into the kitchen with Diana following closely on her heels.

As the swinging door closed behind them, Diana gave the kitchen a swiftly appraising glance.

"You've certainly done wonders with the place since the last time I was here."

Evie filled a kettle at the tap and set it over one of the cooking range's burners. "Thank you."

As much as she loved the outer tea room, the kitchen was by far her favourite room in the house, with its white porcelain sink and old-fashioned black cooking range. She hadn't done anything to update the space, just restored it to the way it had always looked in her grandmother's time.

The linoleum on the floor was slightly faded with age, but still showed the lovely pink and green floral pattern that her grandmother had chosen years ago. A big pinewood Welsh dresser in the corner held a hobnail glass lamp and some of the nicest pieces of Gran's china: blue Wedgwood cups and Willow Ware teapots, and a cake stand patterned with gilded lilies of the valley.

The second tray of the carrot biscuits that Evie had baked this morning sat cooling atop the work-smoothed farmhouse table in the centre of the kitchen.

Diana eyed them hungrily.

"Help yourself," Evie told her.

"Thank you." Diana shifted Bonzo in her arms so that she could take one of the biscuits and bite off half in a single mouthful. "I came out without any breakfast. I'm starving."

Bonzo gave a short, peremptory yip, and Diana broke a second biscuit in half and gave him one of the pieces.

"Trying to find things to feed him these days makes for excellent cover." As before when Diana dropped her assumed identity, her voice was brisk and tinged with a slightly sardonic lilt. "I can talk my way into the butcher's, the fishmongers, even the bakers to ask whether they have anything that might suit him. But in reality the little blighter's tastes are quite indiscriminate; he'll eat practically anything."

Bonzo gulped down the second half of the biscuit and then started scratching at the fur around his neck with his back paw.

"What's happened?" Evie asked.

"Lord Hawthorne was found dead first thing this morning at the foot of the grand staircase."

Evie stared at her. "Dead?"

"Yes, I know. It's difficult to take in, isn't it?"

Wartime accustomed one to the idea of sudden death. Especially living in London during her days of working as an air raid warden, Evie had made peace with the idea that one of the countless German bombs that fell on the city might end her life, and that someone she spoke to in the evening might easily not live to see the sunrise.

But she still had a moment of disbelief at hearing Diana's news. She'd seen Lord Hawthorne only the day before. He'd asked her to investigate the strange business of the ghostly sightings and the apparent messages from the Beyond.

That thought snapped Evie out of her shock and back into the present.

"I suppose it must have been murder?" Diana wouldn't be here otherwise.

"I haven't asked what the police think— for obvious reasons," Diana said. "But I'm fairly confident that your retired policeman friend Mr Jenkins and his nephew the police inspector don't think that it was a simple accident that caused poor old Walter to shuffle off this mortal coil."

A note of regret slipped into Diana's voice and she shook her head. "I can't say that I ever liked him particularly. I always thought Gwen could have done better in the way of a husband. But I'm sorry he's gone."

Evie sorted rapidly through the crowd of questions she wanted to ask. She and Diana couldn't be gone too long or else Mrs Spenlow and Mrs Benton would start to wonder just how long it took to wrap up a batch of dog biscuits.

"Do you have a theory about the haunting?"

Diana grimaced. "No. It's quite embarrassing, isn't it? Here's a crime that's being committed practically under my nose, and not only do I not know who is responsible, I don't even have a clear idea of the motive. Did Walter ask you to look into the matter when he spoke to you yesterday?"

"He did. He seemed torn between the idea that the ghost was in fact the spirit of Lady Gwendolyn's first husband and the alternate theory that it was a human playing a cruel prank. He asked me to find out who that human might be. Or rather, that's what he wanted at first. But he ended our interview quite abruptly when I asked him about his daughter."

"Ah, Peggy."

"Have you ever met her?" Evie asked.

"No, I haven't. At least, not since she was a tiny tot," Diana said. "Gwendolyn and I haven't seen very much of each other since leaving school. She was a few years ahead of me, and after she'd graduated, we went our separate ways."

"Until you needed a convincing cover to stay in Crofter's Green for the sake of investigating black market racketeering in the area."

Diana made a wry face. "Put like that, it sounds as though I'm treating Gwen rather shabbily, but you're quite right. If not for the war and the SOE, I don't suppose Gwen and I would ever have done more than exchange Christmas cards once a year. But to answer your question about Peggy, I'm not sure what caused the quarrel she had with her parents. With her father, rather. She still writes to Gwen, I know, and they even meet to go shopping or take in a show in London occasionally."

"She just never comes to Hawthorne Manor."

"No."

"Do you think she'll come home now that Lord Hawthorne is gone?"

"I don't know. Gwen sent her a telegram straight away this morning to tell her the news of Walter's death. I suppose we'll find out whether or not that entices Peggy to return to the old ancestral home."

"Lord Hawthorne said that she would be taken care of when he was gone. Does that mean that she inherits the estate now?"

"You're thinking of motive?" Diana shook her head. "I'm afraid I don't know the answer to that. My guess would be, though, that the estate goes to Gwen, with perhaps a trust set up for Peggy? But I suppose we'll find out for certain when Walter's will is read. Bonzo, stop that," she added, as the little dog scratched at his collar again.

"If Lord Hawthorne really was murdered, his death must be tied somehow to the haunting," Evie said. "You can't think of a motive for someone to want to torment him that way?"

"I honestly can't. So often in the case of sudden death, one thinks immediately of the husband or wife. But I can't see Gwen flitting about the estate with a sheet over her head for the sake of frightening Walter. I've lived in the house for the better part of six months, now, and unless she's a far better actress than I give her credit for, her feelings about him range from mild affection to slightly less mild irritation. I suppose she might have a financial motive for wanting him gone, if she does in fact inherit Hawthorne Manor. But she already has entirely free range over the place. Walter lets her do anything she likes in the way of improvements or decorating or hosting parties— like this charity affair she's hiring you to cater. And he's never stingy about money. She can buy anything she likes— or could, before the days of rationing. Why would she kill just to gain what she effectively already has?"

"I don't suppose there's another man?" Evie asked.

"Not unless she's carrying on a passionate affair with Alfred the groundskeeper, who has all the appeal of Bonzo here and a personality to match."

Diana rumpled the little dog's ears. Then she bit her lip. "It's not really funny. Poor Walter is dead, and I honestly have no idea why or who's responsible."

On the stove, the tea kettle was beginning to sputter and emit the little puffs of steam that meant it would start to whistle soon. Another minute or two and Evie would have to get back to her customers in the tea room.

"Are you going to tell the police about who you really are?" she asked.

"Not unless I have to." Diana's wry smile flashed briefly out again. "If, say, they take it into their heads to arrest me for murder, then I'll obviously have to come clean. Or if it turns out that Walter's death is somehow related to the Iron Dukes."

"Do you think it was?"

"That's the question, isn't it," Diana said. "We already know that the Iron Dukes gang specializes not only in black market goods but also in looting antiques and other valuables. Of which Hawthorne Manor certainly has a good many."

Evie tilted her head, struck by that thought. "So whoever is responsible for the ghostly appearances might have been trying to provide a distraction so that the manor could be robbed?"

"Well, yes. Although it's a little hard to see how exactly that works," Diana said. "Most sneak thieves want less attention, not more. Obviously whoever's doing the haunting either lives on the manor's grounds or can get in any time he or she wants. Why advertise that fact by creating a stir that the entire village hears about? And why only appear to Lord Hawthorne?"

"You're right, it doesn't make sense, does it," Evie agreed. "We're missing something."

Diana glanced down at the dog in her arms. "Bonzo, what on earth are you doing?" The little animal was still scratching at the fur around his collar with one hind leg.

"Maybe he has a rash or something," Evie said. "You could take him to Alice; she might be able to give him a cream or a salve for it. She has herbs to treat practically any human ailment."

"I may do that." Diana frowned at Bonzo's collar. "It's hard to tell what he's got under all of that fur." She sighed. "Walter adored Bonzo, you know. One of his redeeming qualities: how much he enjoyed taking Bonzo out around the grounds for walks. I suppose I can be glad of that, now."

The tea kettle let out a shrill whistle, and Evie crossed to take it off the burner.

"What about you?" Diana asked. "Are you planning to tell Harry Jenkins and his nephew about your activities over in France?"

Evie opened her mouth, considering whether she ought to tell Diana about the haunting figure that had appeared outside her window yesterday morning. But in the end, she closed her mouth again without saying anything. Diana was SOE and as such more than capable of defending herself. But even still, Evie had done enough in France to have Nazi enemies whom she wouldn't wish on the other woman. Until she knew how and why she and Lord Hawthorne appeared to have one of those enemies in common, she would keep the story to herself.

"You said it yourself," she told Diana lightly. "Only if I'm arrested for murder."

Chapter Twenty-Eight

Alice

"Certainly," Alice said. She waited to hear what Harry would say.

He didn't seem to be in any hurry, but frowned as though choosing his words with care.

"You were very helpful during the blackout murder affair over the winter," he finally said.

"You flatter me."

"No flattery about it. But there was also a fair bit of danger to you."

Alice thought briefly of the gun with which an extremely unpleasant individual had threatened to shoot her. She could, if she concentrated, still feel the cold bite of the gun's metal barrel pressed against her temple.

But she dismissed the memories with a brisk shrug of her shoulders. "Those were dangers I was quite willing to face. Also, I survived." She fixed Harry with a level look. "If this is your way of warning me that becoming involved in another murder investigation is likely to entail more risk, then consider me warned and get on with asking me to do whatever task it is that you clearly have in mind."

Harry exhaled a half laugh. "No beating around the bush with you, is there? Very well. It's like this: most people, when confronted with the police, will clam up and say very little. It's one of the ways that you can sometimes peg a criminal, as it happens: they've got the idea that an innocent person will talk freely, and so they smile and talk too much trying to show just how innocent they are. Nine times out of ten, they end by giving themselves away with all sorts of unnecessary detail. But they're wrong. Even if someone's not guilty of any crime, most people have a secret or two that they'd prefer not to have dragged into the light, and talking to the police makes them nervous."

"Yes, I can understand that," Alice said.

"Now, of course Nigel's got to take official statements from Lady Gwendolyn and all the household servants, that goes without saying," Harry went on. "But I've a feeling someone already well acquainted with the family might be able to get a lot more out of all of them about what's been going on up at the manor house lately."

Alice arched an eyebrow. "Someone like me, I assume you mean?"

"That's it in a nutshell," Harry agreed. "If you're willing. I mentioned a bit ago that Lady Gwendolyn's lying down in her room. If you were to go up there as an old friend and offer her a bit of sympathy and a listening ear?"

"Certainly. Do you want me to steer my expressions of sympathy in any particular direction?" Alice asked.

"Well, for one, I'd be happy to hear more about this haunting business," Harry said. "I'd like her ladyship's thoughts on what was at the bottom of it. And then if you can find out anything about any enemies his lordship might have had—anyone with a quarrel or a grudge against him, that sort of thing?"

Alice nodded. "Yes, I imagine that can be easily arranged—"

A shrill scream rent the air. A woman's voice.

Alice's first thought was of Lady Gwendolyn, but the scream hadn't come from any of the upstairs bedrooms.

Alice had observed before that for all his age and silver hair, Harry Jenkins was capable of swift and decisive movement in the case of an emergency. Almost before she had time to process the shock of what was happening, he had swung around and was running towards the wing of the manor that housed the library and the billiard room.

Alice followed after him, arriving at the door of the library just a moment or two later.

She drew in a sharp breath as she looked past Harry into the large, oak-panelled room.

A woman's body lay sprawled out on the oriental carpet in front of one of the bookcases. Alice thought for an instant that she was dead, but then the woman gave a feeble moan and tried to sit up. Alice recognized Mrs Vickers, the housekeeper.

Harry moved to crouch down beside her. "Easy, now. Just take a moment, everything's all right."

Alice didn't know Mrs Vickers especially well, since her housekeeper's duties, for the most part, kept her up at the manor. But they had served on one or two wartime committees together for rolling bandages and knitting for the troops.

Now the housekeeper's greying hair was coming loose of its usually tidy bun, her breath was coming in short, hard bursts, and her eyes were wide and glassy with what looked like shock. "The man— the man—" she gasped.

She raised a shaking hand and pointed to one of the library's tall, mullioned windows, which Alice saw was ajar.

"Stay with her," Harry directed.

Alice moved to kneel next to Mrs Vickers and put a steadying arm around her shoulders. "It's all right, dear, you're quite safe."

She wasn't even sure that the other woman heard her. The housekeeper merely continued to stare unblinkingly straight ahead.

The window was set very low to the ground, with a cushioned wooden seat designed for reading just below the sash. Really, Alice reflected, if someone had crafted a window specifically to function as an easy escape route, they could scarcely have done a better job.

Harry certainly had very little trouble climbing up onto the cushioned seat and then down onto the lawn outside.

He disappeared briefly from view, but was back in what must have been less than a minute, shaking his head. "No one." He swung himself back in through the window the way he'd left. "I'll have Nigel send his constables out to comb the grounds for an intruder, but ten to one whoever it was is long gone by this time." He came back to offer Mrs Vickers a hand. "Now. Can you tell us what happened?"

Chapter Twenty-Nine

Alice

"Thank you." Mrs Vickers took the hand Harry offered and got shakily to her feet, although she continued to lean heavily on Alice for support.

"Maybe we ought to sit down?" Alice steered her towards one of the dark brown leather sofas that sat at right angles to the library's massive hearth.

"Thank you." Mrs Vickers dropped down heavily onto the seat next to Alice's and looked up at Harry. "It all happened so fast, I don't know how much help I can give you."

"That's all right." Harry's voice was warm and reassuring. He was very good at coping with nervous witnesses, Alice had noticed. "Just take your time and start at the beginning."

"Very well." Mrs Vickers smoothed out the wrinkles in the apron she wore over her starched black dress and took an unsteady breath. "I know you asked that we stay in the servants' hall until we could be interviewed, but I was missing my bunch of keys— the ones I keep to the wine cellar and the other household locks. I thought perhaps that I might have left them in here yesterday, when I came to do the dusting. So I just ran up here to have a look."

The housekeeper stopped and swallowed, raising a shaky hand to push the loosened hair away from her face. "I went over to those shelves near the window, since that's where I was dusting, for the most part." She gestured. "But I'd scarcely begun to search when someone struck me down from behind."

"Struck you down?" Harry repeated.

"He gave me a hard shove and I fell onto my knees. I screamed, I remember that. Then he hit the back of my head." Mrs Vickers put her hand up to cradle the back of her skull.

"You said, He," Harry said. "And you mentioned a moment ago that your attacker was a man. What did he look like? Did you recognise him?"

"I . . . well, I can't really say." Mrs Vickers shook her head regretfully. "I did see it was definitely a man. He was wearing trousers and a corduroy jacket— both of them very dirty." She made a face. "But apart from that, I really had only the barest glimpse of him as he climbed out the window."

"That's better than nothing," Harry told her encouragingly. "Could you tell how old he was? The colour of his hair? Was he tall, or short? Thin, or fat? Anything you can remember would be helpful."

"Well." Mrs Vickers frowned and then screwed up her face as if making an effort to remember. "I don't know, I really can't say. I don't think he was especially tall, and he certainly wasn't fat. But apart from that . . . "

"Very good," Harry said. "Anything else?"

"I couldn't say, I really couldn't." Mrs Vickers opened her eyes and spread her hands helplessly.

In Harry's place, Alice would have been tempted to ask whether there was anything that Mrs Vickers could say. She had always thought of the Hawthorne Manor housekeeper as a pleasant, efficiently no-nonsense sort of woman, the type who dotted her I's, crossed her T's, and was eminently sensible.

But then, many ordinarily sensible people lost their heads when they'd had a bad shock.

"Very good," Harry said again. He nodded as though Mrs Vickers had in fact told him something helpful. "Now. Another question: do you think that he was already in the library when you came in?"

"Oh, yes."

Alice had been counting on another version of, 'I couldn't say,' and was so startled that she almost did a double take. But Mrs Vickers nodded at once in response to the question.

"Oh, yes, I'm sure he must have been. I didn't see anyone outside in the hall. And I shut the door behind me when I came in and didn't hear it open again. So he must have been here already, hiding somewhere. I didn't spot him right away. Perhaps behind this sofa, even!" Mrs Vickers eyes widened and she shivered a little at the realisation.

"Yes, I suppose that seems likely," Harry agreed. "What do you suppose he was doing here?"

Mrs Vickers looked a little surprised by the question. "I .. . well, I really couldn't say. I suppose he must be a thief. His lordship has some very valuable old books among his collection— or so he always told me. Poor soul." The housekeeper shook her head, her eyes filling with a rush of sudden tears.

It was the first evidence of grief that she'd so far shown over her employer's death, and Alice thought that it seemed to take even Mrs Vickers by surprise. She dashed the tears impatiently aside with the back of her hand and said, "Whoever broke in here must have come to steal some of them."

"Yes, I suppose so." Harry's voice was still reassuring in its warmth, though Alice had the impression that he didn't necessarily agree. "But to go back to these missing keys of yours. Is it usual for you to lose track of them?"

"No, of course not!" Mrs Vickers drew herself up, looking momentarily affronted. "No, indeed. I would be a very poor housekeeper if I made a habit of losing the valuables entrusted to me. No, I cannot recall that I have ever let my ring of keys out of my sight. But I couldn't find them this morning. Ordinarily, I keep them in a box beside my bed, but of course we were all awakened when poor Lord Hawthorne was found at the foot of the stairs." Her voice trembled briefly, then steadied. "So I never even thought of taking them out and putting them in my apron pocket as I usually would; we all just rushed out to see what had happened. Then, when I went back to my room, the keys weren't in their box. And so I thought perhaps I'd accidentally left them in here yesterday."

"Do you remember putting them away in your room last night?" Harry asked.

"I . . . well . . ."

"You couldn't say?" Alice asked. She hadn't really intended to speak, but the words slipped out entirely on their own.

Harry gave her a look that if Alice was interpreting his expression correctly was partly amused and partly censorious. But Mrs Vickers nodded quite unsuspectingly. "No, I couldn't say, not for certain. I've tried and I've tried, but I can't recall definitely putting the keys away last night. I always do, you see— take the keys and put them in their place as I'm getting into bed at night, that is. I've done it so often that I don't even think about it anymore or particularly notice myself doing it, if you know what I mean."

"Just habit." Harry nodded. "That's understandable. But if, say, these keys of yours had been stolen, what would the thief be able to unlock?"

"Why . . . why everything!" Mrs Vickers looked aghast at the thought. "All the doors and windows in the manor. The wine cellar. Everything!"

"Did Lord Hawthorne have a safe where he kept valuables, papers, jewellery?" Harry asked.

"He did. In his study. And of course, I didn't keep the keys to that," Mrs Vickers said. "Lord Hawthorne did. But do you really think that my keys have been stolen?" She still looked shaken by the idea.

"We'll have a look around, of course," Harry said. "It's possible that they've just been mislaid. But given that there was an intruder in here just minutes ago, I think we have to entertain very seriously the idea that your keys are now in the hands of that same man who knocked you down."

Mrs Vickers shivered again, rubbing her hands up and down her arms.

"We'll find him," Harry said. "Never fear. The police may be slow and steady, but we get our man in the end."

The housekeeper looked only partially reassured. She swallowed. "Mr Jenkins, we all thought that his lordship's death was a dreadful accident. We all knew that he'd been unwell lately— plagued by all sorts of nervous fancies. But if some stranger broke in and stole my keys— then came in here to rob the library of the rare books—"

"Best not to think about it," Harry told her. His voice was kind, but firm. "If you're feeling better, you might go down to the kitchen and see about having a cup of tea."

"Thank you." Mrs Vickers stood up shakily and nodded. "That sounds like an excellent idea."

Alice watched the housekeeper make her way out of the library, shutting the door behind her. Then she said, "I apologise. I clearly ought to leave the questioning of witnesses—no matter how irritating—to trained professionals like yourself."

"Ah, well. She wasn't the most aggravating witness I've had to question in my day. Not anywhere close." Harry rubbed his nose with the back of his thumb as his gaze ranged over the room. "You should have seen the time I had to investigate a murder that had happened in a theatre near Covent Garden. The ventriloquist wouldn't say a word to me straight. Had to have his wooden dummy sit on his lap and speak for him the whole time."

"Really?"

"A policeman soon learns how often real life is even stranger than anything in fiction." He smiled briefly, but his tone was abstracted, Alice thought, and his brow was furrowed as he continued to look all around the library.

"Something's troubling you," she said.

Harry didn't speak, but neither did he deny it.

"Are you wondering why a sneak thief—if that's what the intruder was—would have chosen to break in now, in broad daylight, and with the police crawling all over the estate to boot?" Alice asked.

Harry gave her a swift, appreciative look. "We'll make a police woman of you yet. And yes, that's exactly what I was wondering— well, that among other things. Doesn't entirely make sense, does it? Anyone on the police force will also tell you that the criminal mastermind is only a character you find in detective stories. Most real-life criminals are about as brainy as a bag of rocks— if that. But even the most lack-witted thief knows enough to wait to rob a place until dark, when everyone in the house is asleep. Never mind not committing a crime while the police are actually on the premises."

"It makes one wonder what exactly he was after— and why it was so urgent that he was forced to break in now, despite the risks."

Alice, too, let her gaze travel over the library. Everything looked neat and well-ordered, the leather-bound books on their shelves arranged in tidy rows, the fireplace swept, the hearthrug lying neatly in place.

"I don't see any signs that he was picking through his lord-ship's collection of rare books, at any rate," she said. "But then a book is hardly the sort of thing that he would urgently need to steal. So he must have broken in here for another reason entirely."

Harry nodded. "If it'd been his lordship's study, I'd have believed he wanted something out of the safe. His lordship's will, maybe, with an eye to destroying it before it could be read? But a lot of rare first edition books? That's the sort of thing you wait until after nightfall to pilfer."

"Maybe he thought that the safe was in here?" Alice suggested. "Instead of in the study? Or maybe—" she stopped.

"Yes?" Harry gave her an inquiring glance.

"I was just thinking that maybe the intruder didn't break in at all. What if the man who attacked Mrs Vickers was in fact the same person responsible for his lordship's murder? What if— having pushed Lord Hawthorne down the stairs— he simply hid. A thorough search of the manor wasn't conducted, was it?"

Harry shook his head slowly. "Not a thorough one, no. Not one that would have accounted for all the places in a house this size where someone could hide. My nephew's too short staffed for that, with the war on, and we were taken up with examining the body and the spot where he was found."

"Exactly," Alice said. "Hawthorne Manor is huge. The intruder could have been hiding all this time in a cloakroom or behind a screen or in an unused bedroom. Making his way to Mrs Vickers' room and stealing her keys, then searching for whatever it was he was after, whether it was in here or somewhere else. Perhaps he just happened to be in here when Mrs Vickers startled him."

Alice didn't in general consider herself a nervous woman, but a cold, nasty feeling dripped its way down her spine at the thought that a murderer had been prowling through these rooms and had perhaps narrowly avoided being seen by the police or any of the servants. Then she thought of something.

"Oh, but wait. That doesn't entirely make sense, either, does it? If the intruder knew enough to steal Mrs Vickers' keys, that means the person would have to be someone familiar with the estate, wouldn't it? Someone who knew enough to be aware of exactly where those keys were kept. That sort of person would know exactly where Lord Hawthorne's safe was located. And he would also know that none of Mrs Vickers' keys would be able to open it."

Harry gave her another approving nod. "I knew you'd the makings of a fine detective. That's an excellent point you make. Unless Mrs Vickers did misplace her keys after all, then whoever took them must have found them in the box by her bedside table. She says she didn't get a good look at her attacker, but if she had, I wonder whether she would have recognized him."

"Our field of suspects certainly seems to be narrowing," Alice said. "Someone familiar with the routines and habits of the manor house staff, who also has a fairly esoteric foundation of knowledge in chemistry and botany?" She shook her head. "I just can't think of anyone at all who would fit that bill."

"It's a conundrum, isn't it," Harry agreed.

Alice waited, but he didn't seem inclined to elaborate.

She asked, "Perhaps this would be a good time for me to go upstairs and have that word with Lady Gwendolyn, as you suggested?"

Harry nodded. "While you're there, you might see whether her ladyship knows anything about a woman named Sally Roe."

"Sally Roe?"

"She's a patient at the local asylum. Suffered a complete mental breakdown years ago. Lord Hawthorne's been paying for her care there ever since."

"Lord Hawthorne was paying to keep a woman at Green-view Sanitorium?" Alice was aware that she seemed to be repeating everything that Harry said, but she would never have expected such a thing of his lordship.

"He was," Harry said. "And I'd very much like to know why."

Harry gave the library one final, swift glance, then said, "And now, I believe I ought to go and find Nigel, so that we can make a search of the grounds. See whether this sneak thief and possible murderer of ours left any more trace of his activities outside than he did in here."

Chapter Thirty

Alice

Alice tapped lightly on the door of Lady Gwendolyn's bedroom and waited. She was fully prepared to find that Lady Gwen was asleep or simply unwilling to receive any visitors, but after a moment, a faint, "Come in," filtered through the door.

Alice entered to find the room in near total darkness, the curtains drawn and the lights all extinguished. Squinting through the shadows, she made out the figure of Lady Gwendolyn, lying on a velvet chaise longue near the window.

"Is that you, Alice?" Lady Gwendolyn, too, appeared to peer though the darkness.

"Yes." Alice managed to avoid tripping over any of the other furniture and found a chair beside the chaise. "I wanted to come and tell you how very sorry I am for your loss."

"Thank you."

The dim light was such that Alice couldn't easily make out Lady Gwendolyn's expression, but she seemed to lie motionless a moment, staring up at the ceiling.

Then she sat up with a quick, impatient movement, "Oh, for goodness sakes, let's pull open the curtains and switch some lights on. I don't even know why I have them all off, except that it seems the sort of thing one ought to do."

"It's natural when one is hurt to want to run away and hide in the dark," Alice said. She pulled the window curtains open, though, letting in a bright shaft of summer sunlight.

Lady Gwendolyn put up a hand to shield her eyes. She wore a teal blue silk dressing gown belted over a pair of pale ivory-coloured satin pyjamas. A pair of matching teal blue slippers lay on the floor beside her, but her feet were bare.

"Hurt?" She repeated Alice's word in a musing tone, as though testing it out for the first time. "Yes. Yes, I suppose Walter's death does hurt. I always knew from the time that we married that I was likely to be left a widow. He was so much older than I was. But it's a shock all the same, for him to die like this."

Lady Gwendolyn's voice had a flat, toneless quality. Her expression, too, was slack, her eyes dull as though dusted with charcoal.

"I hope the police didn't bother you too much," she said.

"The police?" Lady Gwendolyn gave an indifferent shrug. "Oh, no. They were very pleasant, very polite. Although they couldn't give me a definite answer on when I can have Walter's body back for the funeral, which is rather inconvenient."

Alice knew from personal experience that in times of shock it was natural for the human brain to take refuge in seemingly trivial details. And Lady Gwendolyn had always been a driving force behind the planning of village events. Even still, the disconcerting slackness in her voice was striking.

If Lady Gwendolyn had come into Alice's herbal shop in the high street, Alice would likely have prescribed a tincture of valerian to help soften the shock. But if Alice was any judge, Lady Gwendolyn had recently dosed herself with something in the way of a sedative with an effect stronger than any valerian tincture had to offer.

"I suppose there are formalities that have to be observed in any case of sudden death," Alice said.

"Yes. But I wanted to be able to tell Peggy," Lady Gwendolyn said. "She'll want to make plans."

Alice hesitated. She had lived in Crofter's Green before the time that Peggy had so famously decamped from her home never to return. Local gossip had run predictably rampant as to the cause of her departure, but no one had ever been able to find out the cause of the rift between the Hawthornes and their only child. All the same, even ten years later, Alice—along with all the rest of the village—knew that one simply didn't bring up the subject of the Hawthorne's estranged daughter with either Lord Hawthorne or Lady Gwendolyn. It just wasn't done.

But now her ladyship's flat, distant gaze and detached manner made it seem unlikely that she would take offence to anything that Alice said.

"Does Peggy know about her father's death?" she asked.

"I sent her a telegram first thing this morning, so I suppose she must," Lady Gwendolyn said.

She leaned back, her eyes half-closed.

"Do you think that Peggy will come back for her father's funeral?" Alice asked. "I'm sure everyone in the village will be glad to see her again."

"Oh yes, I think she will. Now that Walter is gone. That makes all the difference, doesn't it?"

"Does it?"

"Oh yes."

Alice waited, but Lady Gwendolyn didn't say anything else, only continued to lean back on the chaise with dull, distant eyes, as though she were about to drift off into a waking doze.

"Do you know a woman named Sally Roe?" Alice asked.

She wasn't sure how long she had before Lady Gwendolyn fell into a sedative-induced sleep, after which Alice would have lost the opportunity to ask any further questions. She hoped whatever dose Lady Gwendolyn had taken had dulled her senses enough to accept the abruptness of the question.

"Sally?" A faint frown puckered her brows, then smoothed out. "Oh— oh, yes. She was a maid here at the manor when Walter and I were first married. Although not for very long. She suffered some sort of nervous collapse shortly after and had to be sent to live in a sanitorium." Lady Gwendolyn stifled a yawn with one hand. "Walter has been paying for her care at Greenview— you know the big, gloomy-looking place, just outside of Ashford."

"Really? Why would he do that?" Alice asked.

"Not for the reason you're probably thinking." Lady Gwendolyn's head lifted and the faintest spark of amusement shone through the glassy-eyed dullness of her expression. "I know in books the lord of the manor is always guilty of seducing the innocent maidservant. But I can promise you that there was nothing of that kind between Walter and Sally. Walter didn't have an ounce of the seducer's spirit in him, for one thing. And for another, even if he had been inclined to stray, Sally was the last woman he would have chosen. She irritated him to no end. She was always a nervy, fidgety sort of girl. Forever dropping things. She once spilled a cup of hot tea all over one of Walter's rare manuscripts. I thought Walter would burst a blood vessel."

Her lips curved in a faint, reminiscent smile.

"And yet he's been paying for her care at Greenview all these years?" Alice asked.

"Oh, well, he felt obligated, you see." Lady Gwendolyn waved a vague hand, then yawned again. "She had no family at all. No one to look after her when she went all to pieces. She'd have been a danger to herself if we'd simply let her go off into the world. I told Walter that he was quite right to make sure that she was safe and well cared for." Lady Gwendolyn's eyes drifted shut, then she frowned again. "I must remember to speak to the Greenview people, now that Walter is gone," she said. "I don't know what sort of provisions Walter may have made for Sally in his will."

"That's a kind thought," Alice said.

"Well, as I said, Sally is quite alone in the world. Someone needs to care for her." She sighed, leaning her head back against the pillows on the chaise, her breathing beginning to deepen and slow. Alice thought that she had fallen asleep, but then her eyes— even more unfocused and glassy, now— flickered open. "Why do you want to know about Sally?"

"I heard her name mentioned recently, that's all," Alice said. She picked up a soft pink knitted blanket from the bed and draped it over Lady Gwendolyn. "Rest well, my dear."

Chapter Thirty-One

Evie

The manor house curtains were all drawn, as befitted a place of mourning, and a black ribbon had been tied over the knocker on the front door. The sobriety of the scene was marred, though, by a lone figure whom Evie recognized as Alfred Travers, the groundskeeper who had first told Dorothy the rumours of Lord Hawthorne's ghost.

Alfred was chopping sullenly at the soil in one of the vegetable garden beds that had been added to the front lawns. Lady Gwendolyn was keen on setting an example for the rest of the village with her victory garden, but it didn't look to Evie as though her groundskeeper approved of the initiative. With every lackluster swing of his shovel, he was muttering a curse under his breath.

He looked up as Evie approached and stopped working to tip his grimy-looking cap at her.

"G'day, missus."

"Good day." Servants— even outdoor servants— generally knew far more about the inner workings of a household than their employers. And this particular servant looked as though he would welcome any excuse to avoid working for a few minutes. Instead of making her way up to the front door, Evie paused to give Alfred a friendly smile. "The garden beds are coming along nicely. Are you planting potatoes?"

"And cabbage and onions." Alfred prodded a clod of earth with the toe of a boot. "It's a lot of work, I can tell you, for a man my age to do alone. And my health's not what it was. Had my appendix out last year, I did, and the doctor said I was to take it easy after. No heavy lifting, now, Alf, he said. Them's was his exact words to me. No heavy lifting and no strenuous labour—"

He stopped short as a taxi cab came speeding up the gravel drive and stopped at the front step. A man and a woman emerged from the rear passenger's seat, and instead of finishing his sentence, Alfred gave a low whistle. "Well, well. The prodigal's returned."

"What's that?" Evie asked.

"Prodigal. Daughter, not son." Alfred jerked his chin in the direction of the couple who'd just arrived. "That's Miss Peggy. I suppose the chap with her must be her husband. We'd heard she'd got married living up in London."

Evie shaded her eyes to study the pair. The woman Alfred had recognized as Peggy hadn't bothered to put on mourning. In fact, she almost rivaled Diana Lovecraft for eye-catching fashion choices. She had dark brown hair styled in tight curls and wore a trim cherry-red skirt and matching jacket over a crisp white blouse. Her feet were encased in black patent leather high-heeled shoes, and she carried a black handbag with a gold chain.

She also seemed to be less concerned about being welcomed with a fatted calf— or for that matter mourning her dead father— than with arguing with her companion.

Evie could already hear their raised voices, even as they disentangled themselves from the back seat of the cab and stepped onto the drive.

"For goodness sakes, Charles." Peggy's high-pitched complaint carried all the way over to where Evie was standing. "Stop being such a skinflint and just pay the man his fare."

The man with her— Charles— was blond-haired, and strikingly handsome with chiseled features and a square jaw. Like most young men these days, he was in military uniform and wore the dark blue coat and trousers that marked him as an officer in the royal navy. He also walked with a cane, which likely meant that he had already been invalided home on medical leave when the news came about his father- in-law.

He scowled in response to his wife's chiding and looked as though he were about to argue. But then he glanced their way, and seemed to realise that he and Peggy had an audience. His gaze connected briefly with Evie's before moving on to Alfred.

"Me fare, Mister?" came the driver's whining voice, along with a rap on the cab window.

A dull red flush crept into Charles's cheeks and he swung around, pulling out his wallet and thrusting a note in through the taxi driver's window.

The driver tipped his hat and sped off, headed back down the drive the way he'd come.

Charles walked, stiff-backed, up the front steps of the manor house and Peggy followed, teetering on her high heels. Before either of them could ring or knock, though, the door was opened by a spare, ascetic-looking man whom Evie recognized as Mr Crowley, the local solicitor.

"I saw you coming up the drive and thought I would welcome you, Miss Peggy." He extended a hand. "If I may say so, it is good to see you again after so many years, much as I regret the circumstances. It goes without saying that I am very sorry for your loss."

"Oh."

Standing off to the side of the front entrance, Evie could only see Peggy's face in profile, but she looked completely taken aback by the expression of sympathy, as though she had no idea how to respond.

It was Charles who broke the awkward silence, reaching out to shake the hand that Mr Crowley had offered. "Thanks very much. I am Charles Brentwood. As I'm sure you can imagine, it's been a great shock to my wife. She is anxious to see her mother."

"Of course, of course," Mr Crowley stepped back to allow them entrance. "You're just in time for the reading of the will."

The three of them vanished inside the house and the door swung shut.

Evie turned back to Alfred, wondering whether there was anything to be gained by resuming her questioning. But Alfred was already picking up his tools, his movements hurried.

"Well, I'd best be getting on, missus." He tipped his hat at her before pulling it down over his forehead. "Got some yew hedges that aren't going to trim themselves."

He shouldered his hoe, dropped his spade into a burlap sack, and strode off, disappearing around the side of the house.

Chapter Thirty-Two

Harry

Outside in the garden, Harry and Nigel heard the snip-snip sound of metal shears trimming a tall yew hedge.

"That's Alfred Travers," Nigel said. "The gardener."

Travers worked the hedgerow trimmers with calm, controlled hands that were as gnarled and scarred as the branches he pruned. Not a big man, but steady, self-contained. The kind who stayed quiet.

At least he seemed that way from a distance.

The man turned as they neared, tipping his head up, eyes narrowing beneath the brim of his flat wool cap.

Harry could feel the groundskeeper's gaze sweep over them. The man's coat was rough mud-streaked wool and his boots looked as if they'd tramped through every square inch of the Hawthorne estate land. Nothing polished, nothing flashy, but everything about him seemed as solid and deeply rooted as the trees around them.

Nigel cleared his throat, stepping forward with his badge in hand. "Mr Travers, we'd like to ask you a few questions about Lord Hawthorne's death."

Travers's expression didn't change, though Harry noticed the slightest flicker in his eyes—a tension there, quickly buried. He nodded, glancing briefly at the badge. "I already told the patrolman."

Nigel nodded, his voice firm. "We'd like to hear it from you."

Harry leaned in a little, his gaze sharp. "We want to know who could have entered the house."

Alfred hesitated, the faintest trace of reluctance there. "It's locked up every night," he said finally. "So I don't know how anyone other than—"

"You stay in the manor house at night?" Harry interjected.

Alfred shook his head. "No, I have a little cottage on the grounds of the estate."

Nigel asked, "You have a key, though, don't you?"

Alfred's jaw tightened. "What are you getting at?"

"Just who could have been inside the house last night, as Detective Jenkins told you."

"Well, I don't know. I was asleep in my bed after a long day's work out here."

Harry let his gaze drift over the garden, taking in the neatly arranged beds bursting with colour and growth. Late spring had set the garden into full bloom: clusters of tulips and irises swayed gently in the breeze, their vibrant petals a sharp contrast against the deep green of well-tended shrubs. The pathways wound between flowering borders, where peonies and early roses had already begun to open, filling the air with a faint, sweet fragrance. A newly turned plot at the garden's edge awaited the next planting.

"Lot of work for you, isn't it?" Harry asked, his eyes still scanning the garden's well-kept sprawl.

Alfred gave a short nod. "I get by. They don't complain."

"You do it all by yourself?"

"Sometimes I get help," Alfred replied, his voice guarded.

"Staff from the house?"

"Sometimes." He hesitated, then added, "Not lately though. No money to pay more regular help. But itinerant hands fill in now and then. Temporary."

Harry didn't miss the careful wording. "Recently?"

For a split second, something flickered in Alfred's eyes. "Well," he began, clearing his throat, "there was Willis. But I haven't seen him in a while."

"When did you last see him?"

Alfred scratched his chin, thinking. "Maybe two or three days ... "

"Before today?"

He gave a backhand gesture at the open flower bed. "I could have used him today. Had to dig out that bed for the primroses myself."

"Can you describe this Willis?"

"Thin, wore work gloves all the time. Front teeth stuck out like a rat's. Ugly chap on account of those teeth."

"Age? Hair colour ? Nationality?"

Alfred's gaze flicked downward. "About thirty, blond hair. Could have been anything, really, but I'd have said German if you asked my first impression."

"Where does he live?" Nigel asked, his voice low and serious.

Alfred shrugged. "Didn't say."

"No?"

"He just showed up one day a couple months ago. Middle of March, I think. Offered to work cheap. I needed the help." Alfred paused, studying Harry's face as if weighing how much more he should say. "He had a bicycle. Rode out here from someplace. I didn't ask questions."

"You couldn't hire more staff?" Nigel added.

"The house isn't as posh as it used to be," Alfred replied, his tone carrying a trace of resentment.

Harry raised an eyebrow. "Does this Willis live in town?"

Alfred shrugged again. "Didn't care, really. He does his work, a couple of hours a day. I pay him by the hour."

"How much?"

"A shilling."

"Not much," Harry observed.

Alfred's lips thinned. "Better than nothing. Got the impression he was hard up."

"What gave you that impression?"

"Same clothes every day. Pretty shabby, not mended. And his boots... old army boots, broken down."

Harry considered that, filing it away. "Why wasn't he in the army?"

Alfred gave a short chuckle. "Asked him that myself. Said he had stomach trouble."

"What does he eat?"

"Brought his own little packet, a brown bag. Sandwich of some sort." Alfred gave a dismissive gesture.

Harry raised an eyebrow. "Meat?"

"Didn't look that close. You think he did it? 'Cause he didn't show up the past two days?"

"Could be any number of explanations," Harry said. "But it might be good to talk to him."

Alfred gave a short nod, though his expression remained guarded. "If he comes back, I'll let you know."

Harry exchanged a glance with Nigel.

"Fine," Nigel said. "Here's my card with the number you can call."

They were about to move on. Then Harry said, "Oh, one more thing. Bonzo."

Alfred grimaced with distaste. "What about Bonzo?"

"Did this Willis ever come into contact with the dog?"

"Come to think of it, he did. Little blighter used to come around when Willis was eatin' his sandwich."

"Regularly?"

"Just about. Dogs'll eat anything any time. At least that one will. Spoiled rotten."

Chapter Thirty-Three

Evie

"So the Iron Dukes are in the pay of the Germans?" Evie was trying to keep her voice steady, her expression calm. But Dorothy's look of concern said that she wasn't entirely succeeding.

"According to the woman who spoke to me at St. Thomas's they are, anyway," Dorothy said. "I'm not sure whether or not to believe her."

They were together in the kitchen, working on spreading a marmalade glaze over the tops of some bath buns. The kitchen smelled of fresh baking and the blend of chamomile tea that Alice had made for the shop last week. With tea rations growing ever scantier— even for places like Evie's with a government restaurant license— Evie was experimenting with every herbal blend that Alice could suggest in order to augment their supplies.

The outer room was empty for now, but a tea time rush of customers would probably start trickling into the Cozy Cup sometime in the next half an hour. The longer daylight hours of the approaching summer meant that people went out to do their marketing later in the day and then fancied a cup of tea and a bun or a biscuit after.

Dorothy had stopped at home to change her clothes after arriving back from London, and wore a neat cotton dress in a blue floral pattern under her apron. But Evie could still see the stamp of fatigue in the shadows under the blond-haired woman's eyes.

"You know, you really don't have to stay and work this afternoon—" she began.

Dorothy interrupted with a firm shake of her head. "I don't want to leave you to manage alone for a second day in a row. Besides, Tommy's already next door right now having an early supper with Alice and Mum. Alice wheeled her over for a visit in her invalid's push chair at lunch time. So I can just bring her and Tommy both home after my shift here's over. And anyway—" she stopped, biting her lip. "To be honest, I'd rather keep busy with work. I don't want to just have to sit around and think about how Tom's doing and what could be happening up in London just now."

Evie could certainly understand that. "All right, then. Go on, what were you saying?"

"I was just wondering whether we can trust that the Italian lady was telling me the truth."

"Oh, I think we can," Evie said. "The Iron Dukes are exactly the sort of men whom any German agents in London would recruit— mercenary, self-serving . . . willing to do anything for the right price."

And connected to Crofter's Green.

Evie still didn't know or understand how Lord Hawthorne's death fit into the pattern that was forming. But the odds that her own ghostly visitor was, in fact, directly connected to the work she'd done over in France and the enemies she'd made there had just shot up into the stratosphere.

Hence the reason she was having a hard time focusing on spreading her share of the marmalade and kept wanting to start at any unexpected sounds.

"I wish we had a way of contacting this Rosco's lady friend," she said.

"I know." Dorothy bit her lip as she set the last of her buns on the flowered china serving platter. "I wish I'd tried harder to get her name or some other bit of information about her."

"No, no. I didn't mean to criticize. You did everything right," Evie assured her quickly. "If you'd pressed her any harder, she might have taken fright and run away. As it is, we at least can hope that she really will try to contact you at St. Thomas's again. Are you going back there?"

Dorothy took a clean rag and started to wipe stray crumbs and drops of marmalade from the kitchen table. "Yes. First thing tomorrow morning. I'll stay tonight with Mum and Tommy, and then Mr Murphy is going to drive me back up to London. Lady Gwendolyn insisted, apparently. It's very kind of her. Unless—"

"Unless Mr Murphy really is stealing from the estate and also lying about Lady Gwendolyn giving him permission to take you?" Evie finished.

"Well, yes." Dorothy rinsed the rag out under the sink and looked unhappy. "There's another possibility, too, isn't there? Lady Gwendolyn could be in on the robbery scheme, too. In which case, maybe Lord Hawthorne's death really was murder, and his wife had something to do with it. I don't like to think that, when they've both been so nice about helping me get up to see Tom, but—"

Evie looked at her, surprised, though she really shouldn't have been. Dorothy was cleverer than she usually gave herself credit for. "I hadn't thought of that," she said. "But you're right. It's a possibility we have to at least take into account."

She and Diana had dismissed the idea that Lady Gwendolyn might have a motive for wishing her husband's death. But if the Iron Dukes were involved, that altered the picture a good deal. Most people had a secret or two that they wouldn't want to become widely known, and by Lord Hawthorne's own admission the circumstances surrounding the death of Lady Hawthorne's first husband had been fraught with intrigue.

She took down the big copper tea kettle and filled it with water from the tap, then crossed to set it on the stove, thinking all the while.

If the Iron Dukes leader, the man who went by the name of Rosco, had learned some secret about Lady Gwendolyn, some sort of leverage that he could have used to blackmail Lady Gwendolyn into allowing him to strip the manor of its valuables—

"If I stay with you long enough to handle the first rush of customers, do you think you can cope on your own for a bit after?" she asked Dorothy.

"Of course I can," Dorothy said. "But why?"

"Because I think I'd like to pay another visit to Hawthorne Manor."

Chapter Thirty-Four

Harry

The drawing room of Hawthorne Manor had the kind of hush Harry associated with tense stakeouts—no one spoke above a murmur, and, as people took seats and adjusted chairs, every creak of the old wooden floorboards seemed extra loud in the surrounding silence.

Harry positioned himself in a small straight-backed chair near a corner, where he could see the faces of everyone present. He wanted to catch every shift in expression, every flicker of reaction as the solicitor read the will. His nephew Nigel sat beside him, looking as out of place as Harry felt among the velvet drapes and mahogany furniture. But the two of them were here for a reason.

Mr Crowley, the family solicitor, was also seated on a small chair, with legal papers spread out on a heavy mahogany table before him. Grey and gaunt, he cleared his throat and adjusted his spectacles. He cast a quick glance in Harry and Nigel's direction before addressing the room.

"Lady Gwendolyn has graciously allowed Inspector Brewster and Mr Jenkins to attend this reading," he announced. "She believes their presence may help ensure that all matters proceed smoothly." His tone made it clear that he considered their presence an intrusion, but he was too professional to say so outright

Lady Gwendolyn, seated near the hearth, offered the briefest nod of acknowledgment, though her eyes remained fixed on the solicitor. Across from her, Peggy Hawthorne lounged as if she were at a casual afternoon tea rather than at the reading of her father's will. Her husband, Charles, hovered near the sideboard, looking as though he'd rather be anywhere else.

Crowley shifted his focus back to his papers, adjusting them neatly before beginning the formalities. "I, Lord Walter Hawthorne, being of sound mind and body, do hereby declare this to be my last will and testament, revoking all previous wills and codicils," he intoned, each word clipped and precise. He tapped the table beneath him, as if it somehow lent an extra weight to his words. "It is my wish that my estate be divided and administered as follows, and that the executors of this will should carry out its terms with the utmost care and respect for my intentions."

Harry kept his eyes on the family as Crowley read through the legal verbiage. He had heard similar speeches before—careful, practiced words meant to conceal as much as they revealed. But it was the reactions of the family members that interested him.

Lady Gwendolyn, considering that her future was about to be revealed, appeared quite composed. Peggy's expression barely wavered, a small, amused smile playing on her lips. Charles, on the other hand, seemed to grow more impatient with every clause.

Crowley finally reached the part everyone was waiting for. He smoothed the pages in front of him and looked up briefly, as if savouring the moment before delivering the key details. "To my beloved wife, Lady Gwendolyn Hawthorne, I bequeath the entirety of my estate, including Hawthorne Manor and all its associated properties, to be managed at her discretion ..."

Crowley paused for a sip of water.

A murmur rippled through the small gathering. Harry kept his gaze trained on Peggy, noting the slight shift in her posture, the way her smile grew a touch wider. Charles couldn't hide his displeasure, his mouth pulling tight as if he'd just bitten into something sour. Lady Gwendolyn, by contrast, maintained a mask of composure, though Harry detected a flicker of satisfaction in her eyes, quickly concealed.

Then Crowley continued, his tone taking on a still more formal note. "There are, however, two specific conditions attached to this bequest."

He adjusted his glasses and read from the document. "First, a trust is to be established for the continued care of Miss Sally Roe at Greenview Asylum, with all expenses paid for as long as her condition requires."

Lady Gwendolyn inclined her head slightly, her expression giving little away, while Peggy's smile remained, unmoved. Charles shot a quick, frustrated glance at his wife, his knuckles turning white as he gripped the sideboard.

Crowley shifted in his chair, glancing down at the remaining pages. "And second," he continued, "Miss Margaret Hawthorne is to be permitted to reside at Hawthorne Manor, without charge, for as long as she wishes, should she choose to do so."

Crowley folded the pages of the will. "And this, ladies and gentlemen, concludes the reading."

Peggy let out a light chuckle, crossing her arms as she leaned back in her chair. "The old boy wanted Mum and me to reconcile, did he?" She tilted her head toward Lady Gwendolyn.

Lady Gwendolyn's composure faltered just a touch, her voice taking on a sharper edge. "And will you stay, Peggy?"

Peggy's response was smooth, but there was an edge beneath the casual tone. "For now."

Harry noted how Charles's lips thinned further, his annoyance barely contained.

Then, before anyone could speak again, the drawing room door swung open. Diana Lovecraft swept in, making a dramatic entrance. She held Bonzo, the fluffy tan Pomeranian, tucked firmly under one arm, the little dog wriggling as if trying to escape her grip. Diana's usual air of careless charm was in place, but Harry noted the tension behind her painted smile and the sharp glint in her eyes.

"Gwen, I do apologise for my late arrival," Diana announced, her tone sweet as treacle, though her eyes were sharp as steel. "And for not being here earlier."

Lady Gwendolyn rose with the air of a queen granting an audience. "We're all quite finished here," she said. "Let's talk quietly somewhere else." She moved to the door.

Diana followed, shifting Bonzo to her other arm, frowning down at the dog as he pawed irritably at his neck. "Oh, you poor thing," she cooed. "Mummy must take you to the nice veterinary chap as soon as ever we can."

Harry turned to Nigel. "We need to leave, right now."

Chapter Thirty-Five

Harry

They headed for Nigel's old Ford, battered but kept scrupulously clean. Nigel slipped into the driver's seat. Harry went around to the passenger side, the recent events at Hawthorne Manor still turning over in his mind.

Nigel adjusted his hat and glanced over. "Where to?"

"The veterinarian," Harry replied, his gaze lingering on the manor's dark silhouette in the rearview mirror. The imposing old house loomed, holding its secrets close, shadows pooling in every corner.

"For Diana's dog?" Nigel asked, pulling the car into gear.

Harry nodded. "We need to speak with the vet before Diana arrives. I've got a theory."

The Ford lurched forward as they left the gravel drive, the narrow lane twisting out ahead of them. Fields stretched out on either side, framed by lines of gnarled trees, their branches just beginning to bud. Harry kept his gaze ahead, but his mind was on Bonzo, Diana's Pomeranian—the small dog who, he now thought, might have played a role in Lord Hawthorne's strange death.

"You think she's a suspect?" Nigel asked, guiding the car around a bend in the road.

Harry leaned back, considering. "She had access to Bonzo. And the dog... Bonzo would have known Lord Hawthorne's room, and Lord Hawthorne might have followed Bonzo without a second thought."

He watched Nigel's profile, noting the tightening of his nephew's jaw as he thought it through. "You're suggesting someone could've used Bonzo to lead Lord Hawthorne out of his room?

"In the dark, yes," Harry replied. "Imagine: Bonzo's collar, or a scarf, treated with something that glowed faintly in the dark—just enough to give the impression of a ghostly presence."

Nigel's brow furrowed, understanding dawning. "And Lord Hawthorne, believing he was seeing a spectre, followed the dog straight to the stairs..."

"The killer would only need to guide Bonzo to the top step and stand aside."

"And when his Lordship came along ... a push."

They drove on in silence, the car jolting over the rutted road as the sky grew darker. A single crow took flight from a tree overhead, its harsh caw slicing through the air.

"The autopsy?" Harry asked, almost a murmur.

"Broken neck. Hawthorne's health was poor—any fall could have been fatal," Nigel replied, his gaze fixed on the winding road.

Harry nodded, his face unreadable as he absorbed the theory. "Lady G inherits. A tidy motive."

"But this feels like more than money," Harry said, voice thoughtful. "There's revenge in it—someone who knew Hawthorne well enough to exploit his superstitions, his beliefs." He glanced at Nigel, weighing his next words. "It's either Lady G... or someone who held a grudge."

They reached the narrow river bridge, the countryside stretching out in its perfect spring green and gold. Soon, Nigel turned onto a long lane that led up to a small, ivy-covered stone farmhouse. Parked out front was a battered Morris, its paint weathered and wheels coated in mud.

Nigel pulled the police Ford up beside it. Harry stepped out and pressed his hand to the bonnet of the Morris, feeling the residual warmth.

They approached the farmhouse door, its handle tarnished by years of weather and use. A small wooden sign was tacked to the right-side frame: L. Torrington, MRCVS. Farm Practice and Small Animals. After a few knocks, the door opened, revealing Torrington in a threadbare white coat, a steaming mug of tea in hand.

He looked to be fifty or so, with grey hair and a grey beard, both thinning. His weathered face spoke of long days outdoors.

His cautious expression registered the police badges with a flicker of surprise.

"Can it wait?" Torrington asked, glancing from Harry to Nigel. "I've only just arrived."

"It won't take long," Harry replied. They followed him inside, past a pair of muddy boots in the vestibule, and into a small waiting room lined with wooden benches and chairs. Dust motes floated in the slivers of light coming through the windows.

"I don't recall seeing you here before," Torrington said, his gaze assessing as he sized them up.

"Have you treated Diana Lovecraft's Pomeranian?" Harry asked.

"Bonzo," Torrington answered with a nod. "She brings him in now and again."

"She's likely to bring him in again soon. Some irritation on his neck," Harry said, keeping his tone neutral. "We'd appreciate it if you could save a sample of hair or skin if you find anything unusual."

Torrington's brows knit together as he set his mug down. "Police business?"

Harry nodded. "We suspect an irritant may have been applied to Bonzo. Possibly something to make him agitated or drowsy."

Torrington's gaze sharpened. "Lord Hawthorne's accident. You think it wasn't an accident?"

"It's possible," Harry said. "If Bonzo comes in, we'd appreciate—anything you find, really. We're considering the possibility of something topical, a sedative perhaps. Something that would change the dog's behaviour."

The vet was silent, weighing his words. "Could be something mild to keep him from barking, I suppose. Though it's a roundabout way of quieting a dog. Meat's the usual choice."

Harry shrugged. "We'd like to cover all angles. We're only asking for a sample if there's anything notable."

The vet gave a slow nod. "If she brings Bonzo in, I'll take what specimen I can and hold it for you. Are you planning to stay here?"

"No, we'll be gone," Harry said. "And please don't tell her we were here. We don't want to alarm her. For now, we're working with the theory that someone else tampered with the dog."

Torrington took that in with a thoughtful nod. "I'll help you however I can. Can't say for certain if she'll bring him in today, but if she does, I'll save a sample."

Harry handed him Nigel's card. "If she comes in."

Back in the Ford, Harry squeezed into the passenger seat, craning around to watch the vet's house as they pulled back down the lane. Nigel drove in silence, his gaze set forward, waiting. Harry glanced at him, knowing the question on his mind.

"We need reinforcements," Harry said finally.

Nigel's eyes shifted in understanding. He gave a single nod. "The tea shop," he replied, turning the wheel with purpose.

Chapter Thirty-Six

Blake

B lake stared at the photograph he'd taken down from the table by his bed. His room in Mrs Hodgekins' boarding house was bare of any other pictures or decorations, which was the way he preferred it. His walls were bare, his bookshelf held nothing but mathematics textbooks, and his desk was clear of anything save the stack of school assignments he was currently correcting for his class of third form students.

When he'd first moved in, his landlady had set vases on the mantle and paintings of the seaside on the walls and little china ornaments on the bookshelf, so many little points of distraction that they made Blake uneasy every time he set foot in the space.

He'd asked Mrs Hodgekins if she would mind him packing away all of the decorative bits into a box, and she'd agreed readily enough—although the look she'd given him had said she thought he was more than a bit strange.

Blake was extremely used to that look. He'd long ago re-signed himself to the fact that his mind simply didn't work the same way that other people's did. Generally speaking, most people either laughed, sneered, or got offended when Blake spoke to them. Sometimes all three.

Except for Katherine. Blake looked down again at the silver-framed photograph in his hands. It showed a slim, blond-haired young woman with a sensitive, intelligent face. Just a snapshot, rather than a formal pose, which Blake was glad for. This was the only picture he had of her, the one she'd given him when his unit shipped out to France at the beginning of the war. All of her other photographs— all her possessions— had been blown to smithereens when the bomb fell on her building, obliterating everyone and everything inside.

In the photo Blake held, Katherine was holding a tennis racquet and smiling at the camera in a way that seemed to invite anyone looking at the photograph to share in the joke.

Blake could remember her smiling just that way at him. Katherine had used to tease him for not understanding the point of greeting someone with a, *How do you do?* when no one actually cared about the real answer.

But she'd never made him feel like an oddity. Out of all the people in the world, Katherine was the only one Blake had ever met who'd wanted to understand why he thought about things in the way he did. Why he could stare at a complex mathematical problem and feel calmed by the neat arrangement of the numbers. Why when walking down the street he automatically tried to calculate the probability of a taxi cab passing by before an ambulance.

And now she was gone.

Probably.

No, definitely.

Blake hashed out this silent argument with himself at least twice a day, and since it had been two hundred and thirty-eight days since the bombing raid in which Katherine's flat had been flattened, that meant that he had gone through this internal conversation a bare minimum of four hundred and seventy-six times.

And yet he still kept failing to convince himself that it was unreasonable to hope that Katherine might still be alive, simply because her body had never been recovered.

He didn't expect any different outcome from the inner argument today. The illogical, hopeful part of his mind would trot out stories of people who'd gone missing and been found years later, suffering from loss of memory. The rational part of him would point out the extremely low probability of that being the case with Katherine. And at the end of the day, he still wouldn't have managed to persuade himself to stop clinging to a tiny, unrealistic and entirely illogical spark of hope.

Today, though, he was spared having to listen to his own mind going through the tired old arguments for and against.

A knock on his door startled him and nearly made him drop the photograph of Katherine, but he set it carefully back in its appointed place before calling, "Come in, Mrs Hodgekins."

No one but Mrs Hodgekins ever came to his door, so it seemed a safe assumption that the knocker was his landlady. To his surprise, though, it was the burly, grey-haired form of Harry Jenkins who stood revealed when the door swung open.

"Good evening, Captain Collins." Harry wore a lightweight overcoat over his tweed suit and carried an umbrella against the spring rain shower that had begun to spatter against the windowpane.

"Hello." Blake spoke cautiously. Unexpected visitors almost always left him not knowing quite what to say. But he also felt a stirring of interest.

Harry Jenkins was a former inspector from Scotland Yard, and his presence was a helpful reminder that Blake wasn't quite as alone as he had been since the raid in which Katherine was presumed to have been killed. Ever since the affair of the blackout murder, he even had what he might tentatively refer to as a handful of friends.

"I was wondering whether you might be available for a meeting at the tea shop this evening," Harry Jenkins said. "I'm sure you've heard about the business up at the manor?"

"Of course. Lord Hawthorne's death." The students in school had talked of little else today and had been more than usually distracted during lessons. "Do you mean that there are suspicious circumstances surrounding the accident?"

Harry's lips stretched in a grimace. "There are suspicious circumstances abounding, one might say. Not just regarding his lordship's death. That's why I was hoping you might be willing to sit in on a meeting to talk it all over. Evie, Dorothy, and Alice have all already agreed to come."

"Certainly." Blake felt the spark of interest quickening. "But I'm not quite sure what I can do, unless there's a code to be broken—"

That had been his part in the investigation a few months before.

"No codes as yet," Harry said. "But you notice patterns. You take a scattered array of seemingly random puzzle pieces and fit them into a single image that makes sense. That's what I'm hoping you'll be able to do now."

Chapter Thirty-Seven

Harry

"All right," Harry said, glancing around the room. "What do we have?"

They were in Evie's kitchen. The scent of her freshly baked scones filled the air, mingling with the steam rising from mugs of Earl Grey tea. Five scones were mostly crumbs now, resting on five dessert plates—one for each of Evie's guests.

Harry sat at the head of the table, with his nephew Nigel on his left and Evie herself on his right. Beside Evie was Alice, who listened intently, and across from her, Blake, the young schoolteacher, sat quietly observing. At the far end, Dorothy—just back from London and her visit to her husband—completed their circle. She'd told them Tom was doing as well as could be expected, but she seemed thoughtful, as if she'd brought secrets back with her.

They all began speaking at once, voices layering over each other until Harry held up a hand. "One at a time. There's a lot to sift through, and we need to focus on Lord Hawthorne's murder. Let's keep it organized. Nigel, suppose you share what the police know."

Nigel nodded. "Lord Hawthorne died from a fall, apparently, and his neck was broken. Now, that could have been the result of the fall..."

"Or," Harry interjected, "someone could've broken it before—or even afterward, for that matter."

"Then there's the matter of that strange, glowing substance," Alice said, her voice thoughtful. "Found on the staircase and in his room... and on Bonzo, the little dog."

Nigel nodded. "The veterinarian left a message for me at the station." He gave a wry grimace. "Diana brought Bonzo in. He had an irritation on his neck, but he'd recently been shampooed. So the vet couldn't find anything to analyze. Bonzo's now wearing some topical soothing cream and is doing much better." He paused, holding up a finger. "However, there were traces of harsh alkali on Bonzo's collar—some irritant that could have been applied deliberately."

Alice said, "Ammonia salts are alkaline."

Blake was looking puzzled, as was Dorothy.

Alice said, "Just so we're all working with the same information. Ammonia salts are part of a chemical process that turns a certain type of mushroom into a greenish glowing paste. And someone stole a pot of those mushrooms from me."

Harry raised a brow. "And that occurred not too long ago, I think you said?"

"This week or possibly last week."

"And when did Lord Hawthorne tell you he had begun to feel haunted?"

"He really didn't say how long it had been going on. But he told me about it last week."

"Did he say anything about greenish luminescence?"

She shook her head.

"So someone could have haunted Lord Hawthorne without the stolen mushrooms."

"Or with them," Alice said. "Or with other mushrooms of the same variety, from another source."

"Nigel, do you have anything on the stolen mushrooms?"

Nigel shook his head. "I did check, but no one has reported any mushrooms missing. Not that anyone would."

"All right, let's get back to the night of the murder," Harry said. "And Bonzo, since he was involved. How likely is it that someone could have planned this, using Bonzo as a lure?"

Evie took a deep breath. "Lord Hawthorne loved that dog. Bonzo was always curling up on his lap. He took Bonzo for walks in the garden."

"So who knew that?" Harry asked.

"Everyone in the house, most likely," Nigel said.

"Including Diana Lovecraft, Bonzo's owner?"

"The housekeeper says Diana kept her door open at night so Bonzo could roam freely."

Evie had to choose her words carefully. "Diana may come across as a bit... frivolous," she said, forcing a casual tone, "but she's hardly violent. Anyone in the house that night could have used Bonzo."

"Anyone with a key could have entered the house," said Nigel.

"You're thinking of Alfred's hired help," Harry said. "Better explain."

"Alfred's the groundskeeper. Gave us a story about a stranger. Man named Willis. Worked in the garden on and off the past few months. Last Alfred saw him was two days before the murder."

Dorothy spoke up, her voice hesitant. "I saw Alfred in London near Sotheby's. Mr Murphy was with me."

"Sotheby's? Mr Murphy?"

"Sorry. Mr Murphy is the chauffeur at the manor. He pointed Alf out to me, and I just saw him for a moment as he turned a corner. I can't be sure, but it could have been him."

"What were you doing at Sotheby's?"

"Mr Murphy was taking me to the hospital, dropping off some crates on his way. Lady Gwendolyn told him to take them to Sotheby's. But ..."

"But what?"

"There was an air raid, and I saw a woman at Sotheby's. In the shelter—" She broke off. "I'm making a mess of this, aren't I?"

"Not to worry. You're doing fine." Harry's tone was calm and understanding and it seemed to give Dorothy comfort.

She started again. "I saw a woman that night during the air raid, and then she followed me, and the next day when I was in the hospital visiting Tom, she came right up to me. With a story. And she was in disguise. A young woman, dressed up and with a grey wig to look older."

"You want to tell us about it?"

"She said she saw me getting out of the Daimler and thought I was Lady Gwendolyn. But anyway, she said that there's a ring of thieves at Hawthorne Manor and that they bring stolen goods to Sotheby's to be stored and fenced. She said her husband, a man named Rosco, is part of the gang, working for the Iron Dukes, and also the Germans. She says there are German agents everywhere."

"A story indeed," Harry said. "Nigel?"

"We haven't had any reports of things missing from the manor, if that's what you're getting at."

"There were six crates in the Daimler," Dorothy said. "I saw them. But I haven't any idea what was inside them."

"I'll check on that," Nigel said.

"Dorothy, did the woman give you a way to contact her?" Harry asked.

"She said she'd let me know. At the hospital."

"But no name?"

Dorothy shook her head.

"So. We need to find her, and this Rosco."

"We can look in at Sotheby's," Nigel said.

"Also, we'll need to take stock of Hawthorne Manor's valuables," Evie said. "See if anything's missing."

"And find this Willis, if anyone has seen him." Harry said. "He might have been doing more than just gardening."

Chapter Thirty-Eight

Blake

"It sounds to me"— Harry looked around the table— "as though we ought to divide and conquer, so to speak. Seems we have any number of unanswered questions and an equal number of directions in which this investigation can go." His gaze swept the table again and landed on Blake with a questioning look.

Blake cleared his throat and looked down at the paper in front of him on which he'd jotted down a few notes. He didn't feel as though he had anything to say except the obvious, but then maybe the various threads of the case weren't quite as obvious to the others in the room as they appeared to him.

He stared hard at the paper. "As I see it, our first unanswered question is the haunting of Lord Hawthorne, which may or may not be connected to the second mystery: that of his fall down the stairs."

Evie was sitting in the chair to Blake's left, and now opened her mouth as though about to say something. Blake waited a moment to let her speak. He sometimes had trouble reading other people's cues on when they'd like to put in a word.

Maybe this was one of those cases where he was mistaken, though, because she only shook her head and remained silent.

Nigel, Harry's nephew, gave her a swift look that might have been either suspicion or curiosity. Blake had noticed when they sat down that he'd chosen a place directly across from Evie, almost as though he wanted to be able to watch her.

Blake looked back down at his notepaper before he could get distracted. "Third, we have the death thirty-three years ago of Lady Gwendolyn's first husband. Lord Hawthorne's own private theory was that his ghostly visitors were in some way connected to the death of Gerald Wentworth. And that is certainly a possibility that needs to be investigated. Gerald Wentworth is dead, but did he have any friends or family who might blame Lord Hawthorne for the death and wish to enact revenge?"

"That'd be a very long game," Harry said from the head of the table. "To come after Lord Hawthorne thirty-three years later. But point taken. We need to find out who would have known enough about Gerald Wentworth's suicide to leave those messages for Lord Hawthorne— and why someone would have wanted to."

Blake nodded. "Fourth, Sally Roe, the woman who'd worked as a maid up at Hawthorne Manor until her breakdown, and now claims to be receiving threatening messages at the Greenview asylum."

"Yes, Sally Roe." Alice glanced at Harry. "I never got the chance to tell you the results of my conversation with Lady Gwendolyn about her. According to Lady Gwendolyn— and I'm reasonably certain she was speaking the truth— there was nothing romantic or improper between Sally and her employer. She knows no other motive apart from simple goodwill that would account for Lord Hawthorne's paying for her care at Greenview all these years."

Evie's lip's quirked in a brief, crooked smile. "Do you think you could say that in an even more sceptical tone of voice?"

Alice's expression lightened momentarily as well. "I could certainly try, but I believe the point has been made."

"Right. Why was Lord Hawthorne willing to pay for Sally Roe's care— even to the point of making sure that she was mentioned in his will?" Harry asked. "That's certainly a point that needs looking into. As well as the question of these threatening letters. The matron up at Greenview thinks Sally's making it all up to get attention, but I'm not so sure."

"Next we have the possible theft of valuables from Hawthorne Manor," Blake went on. "According to what Mr Murphy the chauffeur told Dorothy, Lord Hawthorne himself authorized the sale of the valuables he took up to Sotheby's. But we have reason to doubt whether that is true."

"It could be difficult to prove one way or the other, though," Alice said in a musing tone. "Which— if he was lying— would give Mr Murphy a motive for Lord Hawthorne's death."

Dorothy looked distressed, Blake thought, but she spoke up. "It makes the most sense for me to try to find out more about the Italian woman, doesn't it? Assuming she really does come to find me at the hospital, of course. But if she does"— she took a breath— "it would probably be helpful if I followed her. I might be able to find out where she lives. If she's telling the truth about this man Rosco, I might even be able to find out where the Iron Dukes have their base of operations."

Harry straightened up at that, looking at Dorothy intently. "Are you sure about wanting to do that?" His voice was gentler than usual.

"Yes." Dorothy swallowed as though she were nervous, but she sounded firm. "My husband risked his life— and lost his leg— fighting Hitler's army. I guess I can follow a woman through London to do the same. If it's true that the Iron Dukes are working for the Germans, then they need to be stopped."

Harry was silent for a long moment, then finally he nodded. "All right. Nigel and I"— he glanced at his nephew— "ought to go up to London and pay a visit to Sotheby's. We might as well give you a lift. Then if the Italian woman puts in an appearance— and if you think you can do it carefully and as safely as possible— you can go ahead and follow her."

Dorothy nodded. "I will. I won't go alone. I've a friend— well, not exactly a friend. A woman I met who works at the hospital. But she's someone I can trust. I'll ask her to come with me."

Harry nodded again. "Right. Now where does that leave us with the rest of our lines of inquiry?

Alice spoke. "I can pay another call on Lady Gwendolyn under the guise of bringing her an herbal tincture to help her cope with the shock, then speak to her on the subject of the valuables that her husband supposedly was sending up to Sotheby's."

"While you're there, see what you can find out about the daughter, Peggy and her husband, as well," Harry said. "That's something we haven't addressed yet: what role— if any— the pair of them play in all of this."

"You said that Peggy didn't get anything at all in Lord Hawthorne's will?" Evie asked.

"Nothing except the right to live at Hawthorne Manor," Harry said.

"That's odd. When I spoke to him, Lord Hawthorne assured me that Peggy would be taken care of after he was gone.

Although I suppose that could have been what he meant, that she'd always have a place to live at the family home."

"Possible. But we also don't know what the original quarrel was between Peggy and her father," Harry said. "I'd like to know what made her leave all those years ago and why she seems so ready to come back now."

To Blake, the idea of trying to work those sorts of questions into casual conversation sounded worse than a trip to the dentist. But Alice nodded, her expression entirely calm. "I'll certainly try to uncover anything that I can."

"And I can go and pay a visit to Sally Roe," Evie said. "Try to learn why someone would suddenly want to threaten her."

Nigel had remained entirely silent while everyone else had been speaking, but now he said, abruptly, "I'll come with you."

Harry gave him a startled look, and so did Dorothy. Blake was surprised, too. He might have suspected Nigel of wanting to spend more time with Evie. But Nigel didn't look particularly happy about the idea. His expression was . . . Blake couldn't entirely decide what sort of look that Nigel was giving Evie. The closest he could come was grim, or maybe just determined.

Evie met his stony gaze with a level look and smiled, although Blake didn't think she was especially happy, either. "Of course. I'll be delighted to have your company."

Harry looked from one of them to the other, his brow furrowed. Then he grunted, "Right. Might be just as well to have your visit be a two-person job. I've been thinking it could be helpful to get in through the back door of Greenview, so to speak. Talk to Sally without the matron being aware of our visit."

Evie gave him an interested glance. "You don't trust the matron?"

Harry pursed his lips. "Put it that I think it would be best for Sally if no one at Greenview knew that we were taking her fears seriously. Or that we were interested in talking to her more. If someone's warning her to keep quiet, we don't want them thinking she's about to go blabbing to the police."

Evie nodded slowly. "No, I can see that. All right. We'll try for a covert entrance into Greenview." Her glance fell again on Nigel and her eyes crinkled as though she were amused. "We can discuss possibilities for disguises later."

Nigel looked as though he'd have liked to grimace, but just continued to stare at her with the same stony look.

Blake spoke, hoping to dispel the strange feeling of tension at the table. "I can look into the death of Lady Gwendolyn's first husband. Not talk to people, I don't mean. But I could try to dig up any old newspaper clippings about the story, that sort of thing."

"There are bound to be police files, too," Nigel said, turning away from Evie and looking less grim. "I'll see if I can have them delivered to you, if you're willing to look through them."

"I'm willing, of course." Blake frowned. "But is that going to cause any problems for you?"

"Sharing a police report with a civilian, you mean?" Nigel barked a humourless laugh. "As short staffed as we are, I doubt anyone will even notice. But if they do, I'll take full responsibility."

Harry gave his nephew a swift glance and looked as though he wanted to say something. But in the end, all he said was, "I think that's everything covered, then. What say we all carry out our assignments and report back here two evenings from now?"

Chapter Thirty-Nine

Harry

"We're looking for Rosco," Harry said.

The shipping clerk glanced up, a slender man with a lined face and the kind of restrained manner Harry associated with old family butlers. He wore a crisp navy waistcoat, his name tag polished to a gleam that matched his wary eyes. Here at Sotheby's, Harry thought, silence and discretion ruled the day. There was no unnecessary chatter, no movement beyond the minimum needed to keep things in order.

The man became cooperative, after Harry and Nigel showed their police identification cards.

"Rosco," the clerk repeated, lips pressing into a thin line. "Yes... Rosco Leonato. He works in the shipping area, but he isn't here at the moment."

Harry exchanged a look with Nigel, who stood near the door, scanning the room. This all felt familiar—the subtle tension, the way people went quiet when you came looking. He could almost imagine he was back on the London force, trailing smugglers through the shipping docks and dark alleys, where men like Rosco made their way just out of reach of the law. Not every crate in a shipping room was aboveboard. Some hid more secrets than the artifacts packed inside.

The clerk adjusted his cufflinks, eyeing Harry with that polite, measured stare. "Perhaps I could be of assistance?"

"We'll see," Harry said, keeping his tone neutral. "We were told Rosco's been using the shipping room for some temporary storage. Any crates from Hawthorne Manor here, by chance?"

The clerk's gaze flickered, his fingers tightening around the edge of the desk. "I wouldn't be privy to such details," he replied carefully.

Behind him, rows of shelving stretched from floor to ceiling, lined with brown paper-wrapped bundles tied with thick twine, and wooden crates. They sat on metal racks, each one bearing a neatly printed tag: *Paris, New York, Cairo.* A lot of places they could come from—or disappear to, Harry thought, eyes narrowing.

A young woman carrying a parcel brushed past them. Wearing a navy-blue dress with a crisp grey apron over it, she paused just long enough to turn her gaze toward a small door off to the left—a quick flick of her eyes before she carried on, disappearing around a corner.

Harry caught the gesture and followed her glance. "Mind if we have a look around?" he asked, though he was already moving toward the door she'd indicated, hoping it might lead to a storage area for crates like the ones he sought.

The clerk's face tightened. "I'm not sure that would be appropriate—"

"It'll be quick," Nigel said, stepping in beside Harry, his tone just firm enough to shut down any further protests.

Without another word to Nigel or the clerk, Harry pushed the door open and stepped through. The air shifted immediately, cooler and carrying the faint scent of old wood and ink—a quieter part of the building, out of view from the main shipping area.

The room beyond was smaller, lined with shelves that reached from floor to ceiling, each one crowded with crates stacked three or four high. This was a more hidden storage space, a place where items in transit were kept under closer guard, perhaps to be rerouted discreetly to a buyer or held back from official listings. Here, the crates were less conspicuous, labeled only by stencilled numbers or vague identifiers like "Estate."

Harry scanned the rows, looking for any that bore signs of being from Hawthorne Manor. He ran his fingers lightly over the stencilled letters on one crate. *Tudor Collection*. The lid was loose, and he lifted it, revealing tarnished silver goblets wrapped in thick burlap. Were goblets missing from Hawthorne Manor, he wondered? He would have to check on that.

Then, on a lower shelf, he spotted a crate marked "HM." No full name, no elaborate markings, just two simple letters.

He crouched down, fingers tracing over the faint letters—enough to catch his attention, even if it didn't prove anything yet. The lid was nailed down, firm and tight.

The door creaked, and Nigel leaned in. "Anything?"

Harry straightened, giving one last look at the crate. "Possibly. But nothing we can confirm here."

As they returned to the main shipping room, the senior clerk cleared his throat, standing ready by the desk. "If you're looking for further information about Mr Leonato, our employment office should have his current address," he offered in a tight voice, his discomfort evident.

Harry nodded, filing the suggestion away as they returned to the main room. He caught sight of the woman with the apron again, her face still as unreadable as when she'd guided them with that slight flick of her gaze. Harry tipped his head in her direction, a silent acknowledgment of the help she hadn't needed to voice.

Once they were back in the corridor, Nigel fell into step beside him. "Seems they're glad to see the back of Rosco."

Harry grunted in agreement. "Sotheby's clerks don't like trouble. They'll guard their reputations as fiercely as they'll guard the valuables. But Rosco... he's not a Sotheby's type. He's the kind who keeps his head low, his pockets full, and his friends few. Never thought I'd be trailing after his sort again."

As they walked, Harry's mind wandered back to the London streets he'd patrolled, the shipping docks, and the countless men who came and went, ghosts who left no trace but their bootprints and unpaid debts.

At the employment office, a thin man in round spectacles looked up from his desk, squinting at them from behind a wall of paperwork. After a quick exchange, Harry and Nigel secured Rosco's address, written in neat script on a slip of paper.

Harry folded the paper, slipping it into his coat pocket. "Now, let's see if Rosco's home."

Chapter Forty

Harry

They climbed into Nigel's little Ford, the car rattling slightly as it started up. The small, aging vehicle wasn't exactly cut out for London's winding streets, but Nigel had learned to navigate the city with a deftness that surprised Harry. The Ford chugged along, weaving through the narrow lanes, the engine occasionally protesting as they passed street after street of dense, gritty buildings—each one more worn than the next.

Harry glanced out the window, watching the streets change as they moved closer to the area where Rosco would likely live. The edges softened from neat rows of terraced homes to a patchwork of narrower, older streets, each one hemmed in by tall, mismatched buildings. *Not the kind of place you'd expect a Sotheby's employee to call home,* he thought.

"Too bad we can't search those crates," Nigel said as he manoeuvred around a slow-moving lorry. "The ones marked

'HM' were the best lead we've got, but there's no chance of getting a warrant without a proper identification on them."

Harry nodded. "Especially not from a London judge. Without evidence that those goods are stolen property, they'll turn us away faster than we can ask." He shifted in his seat, frowning as they took a right turn onto a street so narrow the buildings seemed to lean in, conspiring. "And even if Lady Gwendolyn did send them to be sold, that information's locked up behind Sotheby's confidentiality rules."

He paused. "Maybe Evie will learn something from Lady Gwendolyn."

"Maybe." Nigel stared straight ahead through the windscreen.

"It was good of you to offer to go with her to see Sally Roe at Greenview," Harry said. Although he thought privately that it had been nothing of the kind.

Nigel didn't answer at once. Finally he spoke, as though choosing his words with care. "Would it surprise you to hear that someone telephoned the police station a few weeks ago? An anonymous caller— a man— claiming to have information about Evelyn Harris."

Harry's eyebrows went up. "What sort of information would that be?"

"Claimed that she'd worked as a German agent in the past and might still be spying for the Germans now," Nigel said, still focused on steering the car through the narrow, cobbled lane.

Harry digested that. "I'd say if that's the case I'd be not so much surprised as curious as to what our anonymous caller had to gain by making such a claim. But meanwhile—"

"Meanwhile, we're here," Nigel finished for him.

They had arrived in front of a modest row house that looked like it had weathered a few too many seasons without fresh paint. The brick facade was soot-stained, chipped in places, with narrow windows staring down at them like dark, cautious eyes. Nigel parked along the curb, cut the engine, and they climbed out, standing in front of the house as they took in the place Rosco called home.

Harry stepped up to the door and knocked. After a moment, they heard shuffling from inside, followed by the faint aroma of something simmering—garlic, onions, maybe a hint of rosemary. The door opened a crack, revealing a woman with Italian features and dark hair streaked through with silver, pulled back in a loose knot. She wore an apron dusted with flour, and her eyes, though softened with age, were sharp and appraising.

"Yes?" she asked. There was an edge to her expression, a guardedness Harry understood immediately. With the country at war with Italy, a woman like Mrs Leonato had every reason to keep her head down. He imagined what she must go through every day, trying to hold on to her sense of place and dignity while feeling like a stranger in her own home.

"Mrs Leonato?" Harry asked.

She tilted her head. "Yes, but call me Emilia." She opened the door wider, letting them see into a small, tidy sitting room crowded with cooking ingredients—bundles of herbs drying by the window, jars of spices lining the mantel, and a worn but polished kitchen table set for two.

"Is Rosco home?" Nigel asked.

She shook her head. "No, he's at work," she replied, stirring a pot simmering on the small stove nearby. The rich aroma filled the air, and Harry couldn't help but be reminded of his own kitchen back in Crofter's Green.

"You're his wife?" Nigel asked, glancing around, his gaze pausing on a photograph on the wall—a scar-faced young man smiling proudly, with his arm around a smiling woman, who looked just as Italian as Emilia though younger.

"No," she said, a faint smile touching her lips as she followed Nigel's gaze to the photograph. "That's my Rosco, but I'm his mother. His wife left him several months ago."

Something the woman who'd called herself Rosco's wife had neglected to mention to Dorothy, Harry thought. He wondered if the woman would ever show herself to Dorothy again, and, if she did, what else about that woman's story wouldn't add up.

But Rosco's mother here didn't seem at all disturbed about the news she'd just given Harry. He sensed no tension in her voice, just a weary acceptance.

"Did she, now? And Rosco moved back in with you?"

Emilia nodded, adding a pinch of something into her pot, stirring slowly. "He needed a place to stay. The work he does—it isn't always steady, and the hours are strange. Sometimes he's home, sometimes he's gone. Not the easiest man to live with."

Harry exchanged a look with Nigel. He could feel there was more she wasn't saying, some part of the story she kept back, either out of loyalty or discretion. He decided to play it slow, giving her a little time to get comfortable.

"Well, if it's all right with you, we'll come back later. Or if you hear from him, tell him Harry Jenkins and Inspector Brewster would like to speak with him."

Emilia's gaze sharpened, curiosity flickering in her eyes. "Is he in some kind of trouble?"

"Just a few questions," Harry replied calmly. "Nothing to worry about."

She nodded, but Harry could tell she was already processing it, turning it over in her mind. He couldn't help but admire her composure. She wasn't rattled easily, not even by two men asking after her son in the middle of a weekday afternoon.

"Thank you, Emilia," he said, tipping his hat slightly. "We'll be in touch."

As they stepped out onto the street and climbed back into the small Ford, Nigel cast a glance back at the house. "So who is that woman who followed Dorothy from Sotheby's to the hospital? Could she really be Rosco's wife?"

"If she'd left him, you mean?" Harry adjusted his hat and looked thoughtfully at the quiet row house. "Hard to see how he could have been watching her every move."

Chapter Forty-One

Evie

The last golden pink rays of sunset were staining the horizon and deep purple shadows were beginning to gather as Evie looked across the lawns to the towering outlines of Greenview asylum. By arrangement, she and Nigel were meeting in a small copse of trees behind the Greenview Sanitorium. Nigel had spent the earlier half of the day with his uncle in London, and so had only just arrived. But Evie had been here for two hours already, making a thorough reconnaissance of the place.

Anything like real security— except for childishly simple locks on the windows and doors and a nurse sitting behind the desk in the front hall— seemed to be practically nonexistent, but old habits died hard.

Nigel was staring down at the small heap of supplies that Evie had brought with her from home.

"Those are our disguises?"

Shortly after moving to Crofter's Green, Evie had adopted a stray ginger tabby cat. Or rather, the cat had decided that it would come and go from her cottage as it pleased and any arguments that Evie made would be futile. The tabby chased mice and fully expected to be compensated in food for the effort, but it had established quite firmly that Evie was by no means allowed to think of it as a pet. Only once had she attempted to lift the cat up into her lap. The tabby had stared at her with a mixture of outrage and disbelief, as though unable to comprehend how Evie could have dared to commit such an act of effrontery.

Nigel was looking at her with an almost identical expression now, although fortunately for Evie, she had found the cat's round, golden-eyed stare to be far more intimidating.

"Almost no one pays attention to maintenance workers," she told him calmly. "In my experience, you can go almost anywhere if you're carrying a ladder." She pointed to the small wooden collapsible step ladder that she had brought along.

She was already dressed for the role, in a pair of men's corduroy trousers, an oversized fisherman's knitted jumper, and heavy workman's boots. She'd knotted a grubby bandanna around her neck and tucked her hair up under a flat-brimmed hat.

The disguise wouldn't pass muster if anyone looked at her closely, but that was just the point: if the disguise worked as intended, no one would stop for a closer look.

"I brought a coat for you," she told Nigel. She pointed to a folded-up tweed jacket that had definitely seen better days. The cuffs were threadbare and moths had nibbled holes in the collar. "You'd better scuff up your shoes a bit and dirty your trousers, but otherwise you'll pass. You can carry the bucket and mop."

She pointed to the articles in question. They'd been easy, she'd just packed up the ones she kept back at the Cozy Cup for mopping the tea room floor after a busy day of customers eating and spilling crumbs and tea all over.

She watched Nigel struggle with it for a moment. Then at last he said, "Fine."

She had to give him credit, once he'd made up his mind, he didn't argue, only bent without a word to scoop up handfuls of dirt and rub them across the shiny tops of his shoes and the knees of his trousers. He shrugged into the tweed coat.

"Will that do?"

Evie raised an eyebrow. "What, no comments on why I know so much about getting into places where I have no business to be?"

She didn't know why she said it. Given that he was already suspicious of her, it was idiotic to bring the question up herself. But there was something about Nigel Brewster that seemed to bring out the worst in her.

He glanced at her as he picked up the mop and bucket, his expression unreadable. "My uncle thinks that you have secrets that you'll share when you're ready."

For that to happen, the world would have to be a far safer place than it was right now. "Your uncle is a wise man," she said. "Now we'd better go. There's a terrace at the back of Greenview where they bring patients out to sit in the sun. But no one ever seems to go around to this side of the place, although there's a door there. Can you see it?"

She pointed through the screen of trees to the door that was just visible on the building's grey stone side.

"It's locked," Evie said. "But that shouldn't pose much difficulty. You hang back here until I've got it open. I'll raise my hand like this"— she held up her right hand in demonstration— "when it's safe for you to come and join me."

It was Nigel's turn to raise an eyebrow. "You can pick a lock?"

Evie swung the step ladder up onto her shoulder. "Unless you want to be the one to risk getting arrested for breaking and entering, you'd better hope so."

Chapter Forty-Two

Alice

"Is my dad going to die?" Tommy asked.

Alice, as before, was tempted to offer him a comforting platitude. She dismissed that thought at once, but she thought fleetingly that no child should have to ask that question or look the way that Tommy was currently looking now. But at this moment thousands of boys and girls all over Great Britain — and no doubt over in Germany, as well— were plagued by that identical worry.

"I very much hope not," she said aloud.

She and Tommy were walking up the long sweep of gravel drive that led to Hawthorne Manor, which this afternoon seemed to huddle sullenly against the darkening sky. Even the last rays of the fading sunset looked ominous, as though the sky was bleeding.

Dorothy had left for London with Nigel and Harry first thing this morning, after which Tommy had suddenly developed an acute stomach ache that he'd insisted made it absolutely impossible for him to go to school.

Alice hadn't pressed the issue. If she were in Tommy's shoes, a day of having to sit at a desk and pretend to pay attention to spelling and arithmetic lessons would be torture. She'd agreed readily that perhaps it would be best if he stayed home with her.

They'd spent the day in comfortable companionship working in her garden and greenhouse, until at last Alice had asked whether Tommy felt well enough to pay a visit up at Hawthorne Manor.

Now Alice watched a squadron of Spitfires roar across the cloudy sky. Even if one wanted to forget it, reminders of the war were never far away.

"The doctors up in London will be taking good care of your father," she told Tommy.

"I know." Tommy kicked at a clump of gravel. "That's what my mum said. But I wish I could see him."

"We'll have to see whether we can manage that very soon," Alice said. "As soon as your father wakes up, I'm sure he'll be anxious to see you, too."

She felt a devout hope that Tom Baker would survive that long— and another quick spat of anger at how broken the world was just now. But then, she could only do what she was doing here: attempting to put matters to rights in at least this one tiny corner of the world.

Tommy nodded. Alice climbed the front steps and rang the bell at the front door, which was opened a moment later by Mrs Vickers.

"Good morning. I was hoping to see Lady Gwendolyn," Alice said. "When I was last here, she asked me whether I could bring her a tincture of valerian to help her sleep better."

Lady Gwendolyn had asked no such thing, of course. But in the state she'd been during Alice's last visit, Mrs Vickers was unlikely to remember that.

"I have it here." Alice held up the small glass bottle she'd brought with her from her still room. "I could give it to her, if she's feeling up to seeing me."

"Certainly, Miss Greenleaf. I'll just go and tell Lady Hawthorne that you're here."

Mrs Vickers departed up the stairs, and Alice bent down to Tommy.

"While I'm speaking to Lady Gwendolyn," she whispered, "could you go out and see Mr Murphy, the chauffeur?"

"I suppose." Tommy looked doubtful. "But why?"

"I want to know exactly how many crates he brought up to Sotheby's in London. Do you think you can find a way to ask him that?"

Alice had slight qualms about involving the boy in the investigation. But a spark of excitement came instantly into Tommy's downcast face, and he nodded eagerly. "Just like Sherlock Holmes! The bloke that Basil Rathbone plays in the films. I'll ask him, don't worry."

Before Alice could utter another word, he'd turned and raced out the front door. At least she'd managed to distract him from worrying about his father.

A footstep on the stairs announced Mrs Vickers' return.

"Come right up, Miss Greenleaf," the housekeeper said. "Lady Hawthorne will be happy to see you now."

***

"Sotheby's?" Lady Gwendolyn repeated after Alice's initial question.

The lady of Hawthorne Manor was once again reclining on the chaise in her bedroom. Alice suspected that she had also once again taken a sedative of some variety, because her voice was sleepy, her expression vague.

The only striking difference between this meeting and the last was that Lady Gwendolyn's daughter Peggy was sitting beside her, a leather-bound book open in her lap.

Alice remembered Peggy as a brash, rather awkward girl, all knees and elbows and forever falling off her bicycle or letting her horse run away with her. She had certainly acquired polish during her time away. Peggy now wore a pale mint green skirt and blouse, and a flowered silk scarf tied back her smoothly curling hair.

Peering more closely at the book she'd been reading aloud to Lady Gwendolyn, Alice saw to her surprise that it was a copy of the Bible.

Perhaps Peggy had gained religion, as well as polish during the years she'd spent in London?

"Oh, yes, Sotheby's." Lady Gwendolyn nodded as though re-registering something she'd forgotten. "Yes, Walter and I decided to sell some things from around the estate."

"Mum!" Peggy shut the Bible and looked at her mother in surprise. "You never told me that!"

"Well, it costs quite a bit to keep the estate running, you see." Lady Gwendolyn spoke with a flickering return of her usual briskly efficient tone. "And of course letting go of our remaining help was out of the question. We'd simply got to raise the money some other way."

"How long has this been going on?" Peggy asked.

"Let me see." Lady Gwendolyn frowned. "It's been ever since Walter's Indonesia mining shares became worthless, on account of the war and the Japanese invading. So about three months, I suppose?"

"How much have you sold off?" Peggy asked.

Lady Gwendolyn bristled a little at that. "Three crates' worth of books and some old family silver. They were our things to sell, after all, and as I say, we have a good many dependents here on the estate. All of Crofter's Green looks to us to support any charitable endeavours, too."

"Oh, of course, Mum, of course." Peggy spoke hastily. "I didn't mean you'd done anything wrong. Just that I wished you'd told me sooner. Charles and I could have helped."

"Yes, Charles." A slight shadow crossed Lady Gwendolyn's expression that made Alice wonder what she really thought of her son-in-law. But she said, only, "Thank you for reading to me, dear. I believe I'll try to take a nap, now."

Since it was a clear dismissal, Alice stood along with Peggy. "I'll leave the valerian tincture here by your bedside," she told Lady Gwendolyn. "Take three drops if you're having trouble falling asleep."

Lady Gwendolyn had been drooping, leaning back against the cushions, but at that she sat up straighter. "No!"

"What's that?" Alice was startled by the strength of the refusal.

"I don't want to sleep at night. That's when the dreams come."

"Dreams?" Alice repeated. "What sort of dreams?"

"Shadows—strange figures hanging over my bed. Reaching for me." Lady Gwendolyn shivered. "Dreadful."

Alice felt a chill, as well, although not for the same reason as Lady Gwendolyn. "You're certain that they're dreams?"

"What do you mean?" It was Peggy who spoke, giving Alice a swift, startled look. "What else could they be?"

Alice debated momentarily, but there was nothing to be gained— aside from possible danger to Lady Gwendolyn— by sharing her fears out loud. "Will you let me know whether you have any more bad dreams tonight?" she asked. "I've a blend of tea that might be able to help."

"Yes, if you like." Lady Gwendolyn gave an indifferent shrug.

"Rest well, mum," Peggy said. She dropped a kiss on her mother's cheek before turning to join Alice in walking to the bedroom door. "Poor mum," she added as the door shut behind them. "Walter's death has hit her quite hard."

Walter, rather than Father, Alice noted.

"I'm sure it's a great comfort to have you back home again," she said.

"I hope so." Peggy gave Alice a swift, sidelong look as they walked together towards the stairs. "You haven't asked me why I left home all those years ago, but I'm sure you must be wondering."

"I'm sure all of Crofter's Green has wondered that," Alice said. "But that is your own business, not mine."

Peggy nodded without speaking, her expression turning darker. She was silent as they walked together down the stairs, then she said, "Let's just say that Walter wasn't at all the man whom my mother believed him to be. She should never have married him."

***

Five minutes later, Alice emerged from the manor onto the gravel drive. She couldn't help but feel a sense of relief at having escaped the Hawthorne family's ancestral home. Perhaps it was only her imagination, but the place had a tense, heavily expectant feeling, like the air just before the first flash of lightning from a summer thunderstorm.

How long would it be before something in Hawthorne Manor broke?

A bush to her right rustled, the branches shaking suspiciously, and Alice smiled a bit despite herself.

"If you're trying to stalk me, I'm afraid you could use some more practice."

Sighing, Tommy emerged from the bush, a few stray leaves and twigs clinging to his red hair. "All the American cowboy movies make it look easy to creep up on someone without them noticing, but it's jolly hard, I can tell you."

"Very," Alice agreed. "Did you manage to talk to Mr Muphy?"

"Yes, I did." Tommy nodded. "He said he brought six crates to London when he drove my mum up."

"That's what your mother said, as well," Alice said. But Lady Gwendolyn had only admitted to three. "Did Mr Murphy say who had given him the crates?" she asked. Someone must have packed them up and brought them out to be loaded into the boot of the car.

"No, he didn't." Tommy looked up at her. "Is that important?"

Alice looked out across the twilight-shadowed landscape: the newly-ploughed fields, the fens, the spire of the Crofter's Green church off in the distance.

"Yes," she said. "I believe it might be very important."

She cut off abruptly as the bushes that lined the drive rustled again, and Alfred emerged carrying a garden rake over his shoulder.

"Good evening, Miss." He tipped his head in a civil nod.

"Good evening, Alfred." Alice smiled, although she was mentally trying to calculate just how much of the conversation Alfred might have overheard. "You startled me."

"Sorry about that, Miss. Just putting my things away in the potting shed."

Alfred nodded in the direction of the back of the house, but his attention seemed caught by something else entirely. Looking in the direction he was staring, Alice saw Peggy and Charles just emerging from the front door.

"We're going for a walk down to the King's Arms, Mrs Vickers," Peggy called back over her shoulder. "Don't bother to wait supper for us, we may be late."

The housekeeper must have responded from inside the house, although Alice was too far away for the words to reach her.

"We're off, then," Peggy called back.

They started down the drive. Alice turned to Alfred, about to make some remark about Peggy's return. But Alfred was gone. Only the rake, lying on the side of the drive where the gravel met the lawn, showed where he'd been standing.

Chapter Forty-Three

Evie

"I 'm sorry." Sally Roe blinked at them with wide, troubled-looking eyes, looking from Evie to Nigel and then back again. "Do I know the two of you? Are you doctors?"

Their covert entrance into the nursing home had gone off without a hitch; so smoothly, in fact, that Evie felt almost uneasy. Too much good luck early on in a mission meant that something was bound to go wrong later.

But she had picked the lock on the side door in under a minute— not her best time, but also not her worst— and together she and Nigel had carried their mop and bucket and ladder straight down a long hallway and past a dining room where a group of the sanitorium's residents were seated at the evening meal.

They had even passed a nurse in a starched white cap and a man in a white coat whom Evie took to be a doctor, and neither had given them a second glance or questioned their right to be here.

Nigel, fortunately, already knew where Sally's room was from his previous visit, and had led the way to the chamber on an upper floor where they were now. Some efforts had been made to add a homey touch to the place. There was a hooked woollen rug on the floor and a faded picture of Queen Victoria at her diamond jubilee on the wall. But Evie still found the place chillingly bleak and depressing. The air smelled of carbolic and harsh soap, and the whole place had a stuffy, claustrophobic feel as though windows and doors were almost never opened.

Sally was a thin, faded-looking woman with pale brown hair beginning to turn to grey. She wore a print dress and bedroom slippers and had a woollen shawl wrapped around her shoulders.

She had been reading— or rather, she had been sitting in the room's single faded armchair with a book open on her lap— when they'd entered. She hadn't batted an eye at having two visitors dressed in workman's clothes burst abruptly into her room. But neither did she seem to be able to remember who they were and what they were doing here, despite Evie having already explained it three times.

Evie took a breath, about to see whether explaining for a fourth time would stick. But before she could say anything, Nigel stepped forward and crouched down beside Sally's chair.

"Miss Roe." His voice was so gentle that Evie blinked. She was almost tempted to check whether he was the same man with whom she'd snuck in here or had somehow been instantaneously and miraculously replaced by a lookalike. "I had the honour of meeting you once before. My name is Nigel Brewster. I'm an inspector with the local police, and I was here with my uncle. Do you remember?"

"Police?" Sally's brow furrowed, and then she drew in a sharp breath. "Police! But I haven't done anything wrong! I mean— I wouldn't! I promised I'd never tell a single soul."

Her voice rose, shaking with agitation.

"No, no, I'm sure you would have kept any promise that you made." Nigel's tone was still warmly reassuring, but Sally didn't appear to hear him.

"I haven't told! I'd never tell— never!" Her breath quickened, coming in harsh, wheezing gasps. Her hands shook with spasms.

"Miss Roe—" Nigel began.

Evie stepped forward and knelt down beside the older woman's chair. "Sally, it's all right," she said softly. "Just focus on the sound of my voice, can you do that?"

As she spoke, she reached to gently close the gasping woman's mouth with the palm of her hand, and with her fingers sealed off one of Sally's nostrils.

Slowly, Sally's breathing slowed down. She shuddered, a little of the panic leaving her eyes.

Nigel glanced at Evie. She couldn't entirely interpret the look, but she chose to believe it was questioning rather than disapproving.

"Hyperventilation," she said quietly, as she dropped her hand away from Sally's face. "Brought on by panic. I was an air raid warden in London before I moved to Crofter's Green. I can't even count the number of times I've had to use that trick on a civilian who panicked during an air raid. A doctor showed it to me. You're trying to raise the carbon dioxide levels in the victim's body by making their breathing less efficient."

Nigel frowned, but in the end only turned back to Sally, clearing his throat.

"I'm sorry, Miss Roe. I didn't mean to upset you. No one thinks you've done anything wrong. We just want to talk about when you telephoned to the police station because you were feeling frightened. Do you remember?"

"I—maybe I do." Sally rubbed her forehead as though it were aching. "But it was silly to try to escape."

"Oh?" Nigel's expression remained calmly conversational. "Why was that?"

"Because it's a judgment— a punishment!" Sally's voice rose again. "There are some sins that can never be forgiven!"

"What sin would that be?" Nigel asked.

Sally squeezed her eyes shut, beginning to rock back and forth in her chair. "What God has joined together, 'let no man put asunder.'"

"Sally?" Evie asked. "Are you speaking of Lord and Lady Hawthorne? Of Lady Hawthorne's first marriage?"

Sally didn't answer, only rocked harder, pressing her hands hard against her temples. "Lord Hawthorne . . . he's dead. I'm sure I heard that he was dead. He must be in torment. What God has joined—"

"Sally?" Evie placed a gentle hand on the thin woman's shoulder, trying to stop her, but Sally kept on as though she didn't even feel the touch.

"It's all in the diary. I set it all down there. Why can't I find it, though? Why?" She looked from Nigel back to Evie once more, her gaze despairing. "I've looked and I've looked and it's gone!"

Nigel opened his mouth, clearly about to ask another question, but at that moment, a footstep sounded in the hall outside.

In a flash, Evie was up and across the room, seizing hold of the small, cheaply-made dresser in which Sally kept her clothes and other belongings.

For obvious reasons, there were no locks on the insides of the doors here at Greenview. The best Evie could do was to slide the dresser away from its place by the bed and into position to block the door from swinging open.

Then again, maybe it wasn't necessary, and whoever was out in the hallway would simply pass by . . .

No such luck. The footsteps slowed and then came to a stop, and the handle of the door turned.

Whoever it was didn't bother to knock first, Evie noticed. No wonder Sally hadn't found their unannounced entrance disconcerting.

The edge of the door bumped against the back of the dresser once, then again as though the person out in the hall was checking why the door hadn't opened and had decided to try again.

"Sally?" a voice called. It was a woman's voice, stern and uncompromising. "Sally? Open this door at once!"

Chapter Forty-Four

Harry

"I'm worried about Lady Gwendolyn," Alice said.

Harry nodded, sitting across from her in the small, tidy parlour of Alice's cottage. The room was filled with the quiet comforts of Crofter's Green—a place where everything seemed close, contained. He appreciated that about the village. In London, everything was a world apart; even if something was nearby, the constant press of people and dust and noise made the city feel relentless. Sitting here, with the faint scent of chamomile tea in the air and the coziness of Alice's easy chair, Harry wondered if he'd gone soft.

Or maybe he was just relieved to be back from London.

Alice handed him a cup of tea, and Harry took a sip, letting the calm of the room settle over him. His trip home with Nigel had been smooth enough. Nigel had driven, and the little Ford, while bumpy, had held up. Yet the memory of seeing Barkley

Robbins back at the station, sliding into Nigel's old Wolseley like he'd already earned the place, gnawed at Harry. Nigel hadn't seemed perturbed—credit to him—but Harry couldn't shake his own irritation.

Alice was watching him thoughtfully, waiting, her gaze calm, steady. "So," Harry prompted, "why the worry?"

"She's selling off parts of the family collection. Not everything, mind you. But she mentioned offhand that they'd started with the 'least valuable' items, as she put it. Talked about investment accounts and needing to make some adjustments."

Harry raised a brow. He'd known Alice to be unflappable—calm, not out of naïveté but out of hard-won experience. She had the presence of someone who'd seen the worst and didn't flinch. But he saw now, in the set of her jaw, that this was different. Lady Gwendolyn was in trouble, and Alice wasn't brushing it off.

"Tell me what happened."

Alice folded her hands around her teacup. "Well, I asked about the crates—whether she was aware that things from the estate had been taken up to London to sell at Sotheby's."

"And?"

"Turns out Lady Gwendolyn had sent Mr Murphy off with three crates, officially," Alice replied, her voice as steady as her gaze. "The problem is, Dorothy had told us she'd seen six crates packed into the Daimler. I had Tommy Baker speak to Mr

Murphy, and he agreed with Dorothy: he brought six crates up to London to deliver to the auction house."

Harry took another sip of his tea, thinking back to Sotheby's. He'd seen crates and wrapped parcels on those shelves, all meticulously arranged. "So where did the extra crates come from? Or is it possible that Lady Gwendolyn is mistaken? According to what she told you, this has been going on for about three months now. Maybe she was mixing this latest trip up with another, earlier one. You said she didn't seem to be thinking entirely clearly."

"Possibly," Alice conceded, though the crease between her brows remained. "But we also have to take into account the possibility that this mysterious Italian woman Dorothy mentioned was telling the truth, and that someone is stealing from the estate."

Harry leaned forward. "Ah, well about this Italian woman—there's something off there, too. You remember Dorothy said she was Rosco's wife?"

Alice nodded, puzzled. "That's what Dorothy was led to believe."

Harry shook his head. "We spoke to Rosco's mother in London. She said Rosco's wife left him months ago."

Alice's frown deepened. "This just gets curiouser and curiouser."

"We told Dorothy at the hospital. At least she'll know to be on her guard if the woman comes by again."

"How's Dorothy's husband?"

"No news on that front."

"At least he's stable, then."

Harry paused, weighing his next words. "So at the manor. As far as we know, nothing's missing?"

"Nothing obvious," Alice replied. "There's a list of Hawthorne's collectibles, maintained by the housekeeper, Mrs Vickers. Lady Gwendolyn has given me permission to inspect the items myself, with Mrs Vickers and that list by my side."

Harry gave her a steady look. "And you're worried about Lady Gwendolyn."

"Yes." Alice's voice dropped, and she hesitated before speaking again. "Lady Gwendolyn's been... seeing things. Shadows, she said. Looming over her in bed and reaching for her. She chalked them up to nightmares, and maybe they were. She promised she'd let me know after tonight if there were more visions."

"But if they're not just visions," Harry said, "that would be a real threat."

Alice spoke carefully, "I think she's under considerable strain. And I worry that she's being made to feel unbalanced for reasons that suit someone else."

Harry nodded, absorbing her words. "Maybe we can both have a chat with her. I'll come by tomorrow when you do the inventory. Nigel and I will be there, too; we've got a visit planned with Alfred."

Alice's expression shifted. "Alfred... well, I did see him today. I must say, he seemed a bit odd."

Harry's attention sharpened. "How do you mean?"

Alice looked off toward the window, as if replaying the scene in her mind. "We were discussing the crates, Tommy and I, as we were walking away from the manor. Alfred was outside working, and I'm sure he was listening, but there was something... "

"What was it?"

"We were interrupted in our conversation. Peggy and her husband were behind us, in the hall, going out. Peggy said, 'We'll be off now,' or something like that. We looked at her, and then I looked back in the direction of the garden."

"And was Alfred still there?"

"Yes, but as soon as I turned toward him, he put down his rake and walked off. Almost hurried, actually."

"Interesting," Harry murmured. "Sounds like Alfred might know more than he's letting on."

Alice set her teacup down, her gaze unwavering. "Then let's get to the bottom of it."

Chapter Forty-Five

Evie

E vie's gaze met Nigel's.

"We could try to bluff it out," Nigel murmured. His voice was so low that it was barely audible. "Say that we're changing the light bulbs in here or making sure the blackout curtains on the window are up to code."

Evie, her pulse skipping, ran quickly through that scenario in her mind. There was a chance it would work. They had abandoned the stepladder and other tools of the maintenance trade in a supply closet at the end of the hall. But they were still dressed for the part of maintenance workers, after all. She'd be recognized as a woman, but then women were taking on all sorts of manual-labour jobs these days with the men off at war.

But she shook her head. "If someone finds out no actual work was done on either the lightbulbs or the curtains— we'd have potentially put Sally in danger. We can't do that to her."

Nigel didn't argue, at least, although he did give Evie another long, hard stare. "So our other options are what?"

"Option," Evie whispered back. "As far as I can see, we have only one."

She tipped her head towards the window, which thankfully had no bars covering it.

"Wonderful," Nigel muttered. "Lucky for me I woke up this morning hoping to climb out a third-storey window without a ladder."

The doorknob rattled again. "Sally?" the woman's voice called out. "What's going on in there?"

Sally had been following the hurried conversation with wide, frightened eyes. "That's Matron," she whispered.

Evie nodded and crouched down in front of Sally again. "We're going to climb out through the window. After we're gone, count to twenty, and then unblock the door. Tell Matron that you were looking for something you misplaced and thought that it might have fallen back behind your dresser, so you had to move it."

She couldn't tell how much of the instructions Sally actually understood, but there was no time for any more.

Nigel, to give him credit for efficiency, had already thrown up the sash on the window and had swung one leg over the sill. He leaned out, craning his neck to peer upwards. "There's no drainpipe here. We'll climb up to the roof and wait till we can get down without being seen. Can you do it?"

Evie swallowed. "I told you I was games mistress at a girls' school in France, I also taught them rock climbing. I'll be fine. You go first."

Nigel opened his mouth, but the door bumped against the back of the dresser once again. Clearly they were out of time.

He swung himself out of the room, holding onto the window ledge. He must have been able to find purchase with his feet on the rough stones of the outer wall, because he stayed momentarily where he was with the dusky blue evening sky behind him. Night was falling by now, and the light from Sally's lamp cast his features into harsh relief.

Then he started to climb with a measured, steady pace, pulling himself upwards until he was out of her field of view.

Evie swallowed again. *Right. How hard could it be?*

She paused briefly to touch Sally's shoulder and look into her eyes. "We're going to keep you safe," she whispered. "I promise."

Then she followed Nigel out the window and was immediately hit by a head-spinning wave of vertigo. The shadowy bushes and trees below her appeared to be miles away.

Don't look down.

She tilted her head to look up, instead, and saw Nigel, about three quarters of the way to the roof. Evie's hands didn't want to let go of their grip on the window ledge, but she forced her fingers to unclench and tried to copy Nigel's movements as she worked her way upwards, pressing her body as closely as she could against the rough stone wall.

Step, shift her weight, reach up to grasp another handhold. Step . . .

At every moment, Evie expected to hear the matron's voice shouting after her. Her fingers cramped, perspiration made her palms slick, and the heavy boots that had gone with her disguise made it almost impossible to find footholds in between the stones. Evie would have kicked them off if there hadn't been the danger of the Greenview Matron seeing them flash past the window.

She risked tilting her head just a fraction to look up. Almost there.

Evie reached for another handhold, but somehow this time her hand slipped on the rock before she could get a solid grip. For a second, she was one-hundred-percent certain that she was going to plummet three storeys down to her death. Then her fingers managed to close on an outcropping of stone— and Nigel's head appeared just above her.

He was stretching out his hand. Evie took a long breath, grabbed hold, and held tight as he helped her scramble the last few feet up and onto the rooftop.

Greenview had been built in the style of a Tudor manor house, with a flat roof in the centre framed by twin turrets on either end and the whole surrounded by a low stone parapet that was shaped to resemble the crenellations of a castle.

Nigel released her hand and sat with his back against the parapet. "I thought for a second there you were going to refuse all offers of help."

He looked irritatingly unaffected by the climb. Evie's heart still hammered and her muscles burned as though someone had doused them in petrol and set them on fire.

She sat down a short distance away. "I was tempted. But I also didn't want my last earthly thought to be, *Well, that was a stupid thing to do.*"

She would have sworn that there was a brief glint of humour in Nigel's gaze and that his mouth twitched in what might have been a smile. But it was difficult to tell in the semi-darkness.

"As I was saying back there in Sally's room, I think our safest bet is to stay here until it's fully dark and then find a way down," he said.

"Agreed."

Evie tipped her head back against the cool stones behind her and tried to catch her breath. Her pulse had finally started to slow down to normal when Nigel broke the silence to say, "Your husband was in the RAF?"

She might have known that the brief moment of truce between them wouldn't last.

"If you're still trying to verify whether I'm actually Evelyn Harris or an impostor, I'll spare you the trouble by telling you right now that I know very little about Paul's background or family history. We were married after knowing each other for exactly three weeks, and then six months later his plane was shot down while on a bombing raid over Germany. The entire time we were married, he was being sent on flying missions. If I was lucky, I got to see him once a week, sometimes not even that often."

All they'd had were fleeting, stolen moments. That was one of the losses that Evie had grieved: she had never shared the simple, ordinary moments of life with Paul: cooking meals, planting a garden, doing the weekly marketing . . .

"So if you start quizzing me on where he went to preparatory school and who his second cousins are, you're wasting your time," Evie said. "Because I don't know. His parents are still alive, I do know that much, although I've never met them. They live in Greenwich in the same house where Paul grew up. His mother wrote to me after Paul was killed, asking me to come and visit them." She drew her feet up, hugging her raised knees. "But I never answered."

"Why not?" Nigel asked.

The obvious answer was that it was none of his business. Evie opened her mouth to tell him that, but maybe the lingering effects of almost dying had loosened her tongue. What she heard herself say instead was, "I felt like a fraud. Grieving Paul, I mean. His parents had him for nearly forty years and I didn't even have him for one. How could I think of comparing my pain to theirs?"

"I doubt they'd have thought of it that way," Nigel said.

Evie shrugged, one-sided. "Maybe not. Look, it's surely dark enough now that we can risk trying to get down from here. She stood up. "Shall we find a drainpipe? Unless you've got a better idea."

Nigel didn't have any alternative ideas, but they did find a sturdy metal drainpipe running from the side of the roof all the way down to the ground. Even better, it was located at the join between Greenview's central wing and one of the turrets, such that they could brace their feet against the side of the turret while climbing down.

Evie managed to get nearly the whole way down without losing her grip and falling, though she landed with a force that sent a jolt of pain knifing through her weak ankle. At least they were on the ground, though.

"All right?" Nigel asked.

Evie gritted her teeth. "Fine."

Her ankle continued to throb as they worked their way around the building and back towards the copse of trees where they had originally met, but she forced herself not to limp. One admission of weakness for tonight was enough.

When they reached the deeper shadow of the trees, Nigel paused. "I parked my car just down the road. Do you need a lift back to Crofter's Green?"

Evie shook her head, although it was a wasted gesture. It was so dark here that Nigel was little more than a vague shadow and a disembodied voice in the black. "No. I hid my bicycle behind a clump of bushes not far from here. I'll cycle back."

Even with her weak ankle, the ride would be considerably easier now that she was unencumbered with the mop, bucket, and ladder.

She expected Nigel to turn and stride off, but instead he lingered, seeming to hesitate. Then he said, his voice gruff, almost awkward, "My older brother Henry was killed at Dunkirk. Nearly a year ago, now."

Evie stared, although that was also wasted effort. She couldn't make out a single detail of Nigel's expression. "I'm sorry," she finally said.

Nigel ignored that. "I haven't been back home since. My mother keeps telephoning, asking me to come to Sunday dinner. But—"

He stopped. Evie had the impression that he was trying to find the right words.

"I wanted to enlist, early on. I was told I was needed right where I am. That if I went into the army, Crofter's Green would be left without police protection. Maybe that's true, but it doesn't change the fact that Henry's dead and I'm still here, safe at home."

"Considering the way we've just spent the past half hour, I think you and I have differing definitions of safe," Evie said.

Nigel made a sound that might have been a brief half-laugh. But then he said, "I think you should go and see your husband's parents. That's all."

He turned, and Evie heard the soft rustlings of his footsteps as he walked away towards the road.

Chapter Forty-Six

Harry

From the grand foyer of Hawthorne Manor, Harry and Nigel could see through to the library.

Alice was deep in conversation with Mrs Vickers, the housekeeper. The two were standing at the well-dusted library shelves. Alice had a large ledger book opened on a little pedestal, and a pencil in one hand. The shelves brimmed with leather-bound books, most of them dark and faded with age. Mrs Vickers stood by Alice's side in her starched black dress, hands folded, watching Alice's pencil dart from the ledger to tap the spine of a book, and then back to the ledger.

"Quite the collection," Harry remarked, joining them by the tall shelves

Alice nodded. "It's extensive. More than I expected, actually." She stood on tiptoe to reach her pencil to the books on a higher shelf. "We have all these books to check, and then we're going downstairs to the wine cellar. There's a separate ledger for the bottles."

"How are you checking the books?"

"The ledger says what ought to be on each shelf in each cabinet. I compare the title and author listed in the ledger with what's actually on the spine on the shelf."

"You just look at what's on the spine?"

"Later I'll come back and look inside."

"All the books?"

"Probably not. Just the ones with the higher initial cost." She held up the ledger. "You can see the column here, just at the edge."

There was another column just to the right of the initial cost. But nothing had been written between any of the lines, at least not on the page Harry was looking at.

Harry tapped the blank column.

Alice said, "So far, nothing's been sold."

"According to this ledger anyway," Harry said.

"Some things were sold," Mrs Vickers said. She looked far more composed than the last time Harry had seen her, when she'd been recovering from a mysterious attacker. Now her grey hair was back in its neat bun, and her features were pallid, not flushed.

She continued, "Towards the back of the ledger you'll find sections for chinaware and glassware and the gun collection.

Those sections have some rows with lines ruled through and the price the item fetched in that far-right column. But not the books."

"Did he make a profit on those sales?"

"It's hard to say. I really don't pay attention to those things."

"His Lordship was fond of the books?"

Mrs Vickers shrugged. "I suppose. And I don't think anything's gone missing since I did my last inventory."

"Which was?"

"The week after Christmas. Year-end. Every year." Mrs Vickers said. "By the way," she went on, turning to Nigel, "has there been any progress in finding the man who attacked me?"

"I'm afraid not, Mrs Vickers. We'll keep trying though."

Harry glanced at Nigel, then motioned toward the French windows that opened to the garden. "Let's take a walk outside."

***

They stepped into the crisp morning air, sunlight casting long shadows over the meticulously tended garden beds. They walked along the flagstone path until they reached the bed where Alfred, the gardener, had been working just two days earlier. The soil, freshly prepared for primroses, had been disturbed.

Written in large, rough letters across the soil was a single word:

SORRY.

Harry frowned, studying the ground. "Two-foot-square letters. Impossible to miss." His gaze drifted over the bed, noting footprints pressed deep into the moist soil. "Footprints here... and more leading that way," he said, nodding toward the direction of Alfred's cottage.

The footprints trailed through the garden, accompanied by faint wheelbarrow tracks that seemed to lead them toward Alfred's small cottage. When they reached the cottage door, Harry noticed the wheelbarrow track had made a right-angle turn to the adjacent garden shed. The shed door was ajar, and inside he could see the empty wheelbarrow.

He shared a glance with Nigel before knocking firmly on the cottage door.

No answer.

Nigel tried the handle, and the door creaked open, revealing a dim interior.

In the shadows, a wooden chair lay on its side, and mud-caked boots dangled inches above the floor. Above the boots Alfred's body hung motionless, suspended from a length of rope tied to a ceiling rafter.

They entered carefully, taking in the grim scene.

Harry turned to Nigel. "The chair. No mud on the seat."

Nigel frowned. "Or on the chair back."

They moved slowly, inspecting every detail without disturbing anything. Harry noticed mud on the first three fingers of Alfred's right hand, as well as the dry mud on his boots, but there was no trace of mud in the small kitchen nearby. A trail of faint mud specks led from the front door to the spot where Alfred hung, but none beyond that.

"No footprints between here and the kitchen," Harry noted, brow furrowed.

His gaze sharpened as he spotted faint bruises on either side of Alfred's forehead. "Let's get Dr. Haggerty over here and call for the police wagon," he said. Nigel found the telephone and made the call, his voice steady.

As they waited for the doctor and the police, Nigel used his pocket handkerchief to bring the chair upright, climbed up, and took out his pocket knife. Harry held the body as Nigel cut the rope. They carefully lowered Alfred's body to the floor. Harry knelt beside him, studying Alfred's neck closely, piecing together the story hidden in the details.

"The mud on his boots is dry... and none in the kitchen," Harry mused. "But there's mud on the rug between the front door and here."

Nigel nodded, narrowing his eyes. "Meaning?"

"Meaning Alfred didn't die here," Harry replied. He gestured toward the garden. "Someone broke his neck out there, probably in that primrose bed, used his dead fingers to write 'sorry' in the dirt, then brought him back here in a wheelbar-row."

He traced the sequence with his hand, imagining each step. "They likely wore Alfred's boots while they were moving his body back to the cottage. Then they dumped the body inside the doorway and returned the wheelbarrow to the shed. After that, they came back, put his boots back on him, and hauled him up."

Nigel glanced at the clean chair. "Then they brought the chair in from the kitchen, hung up the body, and left the chair overturned as a final touch."

"As if he'd climbed up and kicked it over at the last. Only they didn't notice the chair was spotless."

"And the bruises?" Nigel asked.

"Let's see what Dr. Haggerty makes of them," Harry replied. "I'd wager he'll say there's no bruising on the neck from the rope. Someone wanted this to look like suicide, but it's more staged than a theatre production."

"Made to look that way on purpose?"

"Or just stupid. Arrogant and stupid."

Chapter Forty-Seven

Alice

"Watch your step there, Miss," Mrs Vickers said. "Those stone steps'll catch you off guard if you're not paying mind."

Alice moved carefully down the narrow, grey stone stairs, one hand on the rough whitewashed wall as they descended. The faint smell of mildew and earth hung in the air.

The steps were well-worn, polished by years of boots descending to fetch one of Lord Hawthorne's treasured bottles. Above them, a string of bare bulbs cast harsh pools of light on the walls, creating long shadows in the damp stone.

"No one came down here much," Mrs Vickers said. "Not unless his lordship requested it." She gave a small, prideful nod. "He kept this cellar as his own—a personal store, you might say. I had one of the maids sweep up since I knew you'd be coming, but I leave things as they are for the most part. His lordship wanted it that way."

"How long have you been at the manor, Mrs Vickers?" Alice asked.

"Twenty-eight years now." Mrs Vickers had a note of pride in her voice. "Lord Hawthorne took me on not long after he married Lady Gwendolyn. She wasn't prepared for the upkeep of a place like this, what with Miss Peggy on the way. His lordship wanted a proper home, and I helped make it one." Her voice softened slightly. "Lost my own husband in the first war. This manor's been my life since."

They reached the bottom of the stairs. The wine cellar was isolated, with its own heavy oak door separating it from the rest of the basement. Mrs Vickers unlocked it with a well-worn key and pushed the door open, flicking on a light that revealed rows of neatly stacked bottles lining wooden shelves.

The room was colder here, the air holding a hint of aged wood and faint mustiness, the smell of years. Each bottle sat in its appointed place, some wrapped in burlap, others bare, with labels faded over time. Dust had settled thickly over many of them.

"Which bottles did Lord Hawthorne prize most?" Alice asked, glancing over the silent rows.

Mrs Vickers gestured to a row in the far corner. "These here," she said, with an air of reverence. "Rare vintages, they are. His lordship often came down to look at them, just for the satisfaction of knowing they were his. He'd take them off the shelves, look them over, then put them back. Said they were to be kept exactly as he set them."

Alice stepped closer. The bottles looked as old as she'd expected, but something about the dust caught her eye. Some bottles had a perfect, undisturbed layer of dust, while others appeared to have a cleaner, fresher look that seemed too tidy for a place so untouched. She ran her finger gently along one of the dusty bottles, the grime thick under her fingertip.

"He must have been particular about these," she murmured.

Mrs Vickers gave a quick, approving nod. "Oh, very particular, miss. The special occasion wines are on the next shelf, but I didn't let anyone touch them. Not unless his lordship himself requested it. He liked them all to remain just so."

"Who else would have been in here?" Alice asked. "Other than you and His Lordship?"

"Well, Alfred would. And Mr Murphy. But not often."

"You give them the key when they need it?"

"Alfred has his own set of keys to everywhere in the manor. Same as I do."

Alice's gaze returned to the set of bottles with noticeably cleaner labels, and again thought they seemed out of place amidst the more aged bottles. She couldn't say she was any expert, but even her untrained eye sensed an inconsistency.

"Did His Lordship entertain much?" Alice asked.

Mrs Vickers pursed her lips. "No, not him. Lady Gwendolyn did, of course, over the years. But His Lordship liked to keep the rare ones for himself."

Then Alice noticed a row of bottles arranged upright, unlike the rest. "Odd way to store those, isn't it?" she commented, tilting her head.

"Just how his lordship liked them," Mrs Vickers replied with finality. Her tone held a slight edge, as though challenging Alice to question the arrangement further.

Alice nodded, but the arrangement seemed distinctly off. "Let's do the inventory," she said.

Mrs Vickers hesitated but finally pulled a small, leather notebook from her apron, opening it with slightly trembling fingers. "Every bottle is accounted for here," she said, her voice tense. She handed the notebook to Alice.

Mrs Vickers moved along the shelves, calling out names and dates. Alice checked them off in the notebook. As they continued, Alice pointed to a bottle with a noticeably newer label.

"This one doesn't seem to be on the list," Alice said carefully.

Mrs Vickers's hand froze, her eyes darting to the bottle. "Must be a simple oversight," she said quickly. "Maybe his lordship forgot to write it in."

Alice nodded, though she wasn't convinced. They continued, and by the end, they'd found two more bottles with fresher labels, also without entries in the ledger. As they tallied the final count, Alice compared it with the list. "We've got fifty-three bottles here," she said quietly. "But only fifty listed."

Mrs Vickers's face tightened, her smile forced. "Oh, well, at least there aren't any that are missing."

Alice glanced up, meeting Mrs Vickers's gaze with a steady look. "Thank you for going through this with me," she said evenly. "I'll go back to the library to check inside some of the high-value books."

Mrs Vickers's nod was curt, her lips pressed together. As Alice climbed the stairs, her mind was already whirring with questions.

Chapter Forty-Eight

Harry

The light through Alfred's small cottage window was muted, softened by the lingering morning mist as the clock ticked toward noon. Dr. Haggerty had been bent over Alfred's body for several minutes, muttering to himself. Harry and Nigel watched, hands in their coat pockets. Outside, the birdsong was calm, as if the natural world were unaware of the violence that had played out here.

"The bruises tell the story," Dr. Haggerty said at last, straightening with a sigh and adjusting his spectacles. He nudged Alfred's head gently. Harry could see the unnatural angle of the neck, the clear sign of a broken spine.

"Rigor's started to ease," Dr. Haggerty said, giving the body a closer look. "Temperature places the death likely around ten o'clock last night. The skull's fractured at the right temple." He gave a little nod. "Looks like a hammer blow—angled. I'd say your killer's right-handed, likely took him from behind. An attacker wouldn't have come face-on. A man like Alfred would have dodged."

Harry exchanged a quick look with Nigel, who was watching the doctor closely. Dr. Haggerty was steady, assured—a man who'd spent enough time around death to read its details without flinching. Harry admired that.

"And the fracture," Nigel asked, "would have knocked him out?"

"Definitely. Likely before he hit the ground. The broken neck came next, quick and precise. Easier when the man's already out cold." Dr. Haggerty demonstrated the grip he believed the killer had used, thumbs at the temples, fingers clamped behind. "With Alfred unconscious, it wouldn't have taken a professional to finish the job."

Harry nodded slowly. It was a brutal act, but clearly methodical. Not something done in the heat of passion. "Someone he knew, then," he said, his tone low. "To get close enough to swing a hammer from behind."

"Indeed." Dr. Haggerty stepped back, pulling off his gloves. "My work's done here for now. I'll bring him back to the examining room, see what else I find on closer inspection, though I suspect you have the main story. Skull impact, neck break, then the rope for effect." He paused, eyeing the lifeless face. "You'll note the rope left no livid bruising. No circulation—he was already gone when it was tied."

Harry glanced over at Nigel, whose gaze flickered with grudging respect. "So, someone strong enough to pull all this off. Not a weakling, not an elderly woman either, though not necessarily a heavyweight," Nigel remarked, clearly thinking aloud.

"Strong enough to get him in a wheelbarrow and trundle him downhill here to the cottage," Dr. Haggerty replied. "But if you're looking for clues in the strength department, best start with someone familiar to him. Someone he'd meet at night in the garden, maybe for money or other... arrangements."

Dr. Haggerty nodded to Harry and Nigel, gesturing towards Alfred's neat row of belongings by the window. "Saw this on his writing pad," he added, a slight frown on his face. "Hard to miss."

Harry stepped over and picked up the pad, feeling the faint impression on the top sheet where a note had been torn away. He squinted, making out three faint words: *I know you.*

He held it out to Nigel, who frowned, tracing the words with a finger. "Reckon that's Alfred's hand?"

"We should check," Harry murmured. "Maybe our gardener was sending a message to someone."

Dr. Haggerty cleared his throat. "I'll be in touch once I've had a better look."

They watched the doctor leave the cottage, followed by the driver of the police wagon and his assistant, carrying Alfred's body on a stretcher. They loaded the body into the wagon.

The cottage seemed quiet. Harry glanced down at the over-turned kitchen chair, its varnished wood free of mud. Nothing about this scene was adding up in a neat way.

Nigel stepped out the door first, heading for the garden. Harry followed, and they moved together back to the primrose bed where Alfred had last worked, the soil freshly turned and raked. Written in two-foot letters, the word SORRY was still undisturbed.

"A confession?" Nigel murmured.

Harry shook his head, kneeling to examine the disturbed earth. "The killer did, using Alfred's hand. Look at these wheelbarrow tracks. Shallow leading up to the flower bed, but now, going back to the cottage, they're deep."

Nigel nodded. "Heavy from Alfred's body."

"Ties in with the mud on the cottage floor."

"And that notepad message ... what if Alfred wrote that? *I know you.*"

Harry straightened, dusting his hands off. "If he did, he was trying to get leverage over someone."

"Blackmail? Hush money?"

Harry nodded, considering the possibilities. Then his gaze returned to the flowerbed. "But 'SORRY'... doesn't seem like a professional's touch."

Chapter Forty-Nine

Blake

Alone in his boarding-house room, Blake Collins sat at his desk, his pencil hovering over the police report spread before him. The official account of Gerald Wentworth's death read like a puzzle with too many missing pieces, each detail both illuminating and obscuring the truth. Thirty-three years ago, the death had been declared a suicide, but now, with Lord Hawthorne's murder, the old questions had re-emerged.

And Blake needed to find answers.

He scanned the report again, trying to read between the lines:

"The deceased, Gerald Wentworth, aged 39, was found lying on his bed at the King's Head Inn, Crofter's Green. A whisky flask, drained of its contents and later found to contain cyanide, was discovered beside the body. A note on hotel stationery read: 'Going to make it easy for the two of you to be together, my

dear. A sip of Dutch courage and then I'll make all the arrange-
ments.' Inside the deceased's suitcase, a loaded pistol and a vial
of cyanide were found."

The juxtaposition gnawed at Blake. The flask and the
note—both indicated Wentworth had chosen to end his life.
Yet the vial of cyanide, hidden away in the suitcase alongside
the pistol, hinted at something more deliberate. Why keep the
poison separate if he'd already mixed it in the flask? And why
ring for his car moments before his death, as the desk clerk had
noted?

Blake jotted a note in the margin: *Flask = staged? Returning*
to manor with gun?

He flipped to the statement of the reporting constable:

"Desk clerk reports Mr Wentworth requested his car at 9:10
p.m., stating he had urgent business to attend to. Time of death
estimated at 9:30 p.m. Suitcase contents indicate intent to travel,
not self-harm. No signs of struggle at the scene."—Miles Sedg-
wick, Constable.

No signs of struggle, Blake thought, except for the evidence
itself struggling to tell a coherent story. The pistol in the suitcase suggested Wentworth might have been preparing for a
confrontation, not a quiet death. And the cyanide in the suitcase—noted in the official report, but omitted by the constable—didn't that indicate self-harm? And then there was the

car. The clerk's testimony pointed to a man with unfinished business—someone who intended to leave, not to die.

Blake set the police report aside and reached for the *Crofter's Gazette* clippings. The local newspaper had eagerly chronicled the scandal in 1908, its coverage thick with innuendo:

"The untimely death of American millionaire Gerald Wentworth, whose body was found at the King's Head Inn with a cryptic note and a flask of whisky, has been ruled a suicide. The death has left Crofter's Green buzzing with speculation. Mr Wentworth's passing follows reports of tensions between himself and Lord Hawthorne. Was this the final act of a man consumed by rivalry, or something more sinister?"

The rivalry. The feud between Wentworth and Hawthorne had simmered for years, ignited during their days at Cambridge and reignited by Gwendolyn. The *Gazette* had been quick to seize on this angle:

"Eyewitnesses describe heated exchanges between Wentworth and Lord Hawthorne in the days leading up to the tragedy. Yet Lady Gwendolyn, now Lady Hawthorne, insists her late husband's intentions were noble, stating, 'Gerald sought only to end our misery. His death was a final act of kindness.'"

Noble intentions. Kindness. Blake frowned, tapping his pencil against the desk. The narrative felt too tidy, too polished, as if carefully curated to absolve Hawthorne. And the "act of kindness" phrase—a convenient way to explain away inconvenient questions.

One villager had written a scathing letter to the editor at the time, preserved in the archives Blake had uncovered:

"The coroner's ruling is too quick to accept suicide. Wentworth's note is ambiguous, his actions that night contradictory. And who benefits most from his death? Surely not the man lying in the ground."

Blake scribbled *beneficiary = Hawthorne? Ghost = guilt?* into his notebook.

He turned back to the police report, focusing on Lord Hawthorne's own statement:

"Mr Wentworth and I had resolved our differences earlier that day. He expressed his desire to free Gwendolyn from their unhappy marriage, a decision that, while tragic, was selfless. I believe that his note, though cryptic, reflects his intent to make peace."

A model of calm, collected detachment. Too collected, Blake thought. If Hawthorne had killed Wentworth, this was the statement of a man carefully distancing himself.

But why would Wentworth's death haunt Hawthorne all these years later? Blake's pencil stilled as a chilling thought crept in: *Someone else knows the truth.* The ghostly messages

sent to Hawthorne before his own death might not be mani-
festations of guilt, but warnings—or threats.

A knock at the door jolted him from his thoughts. Blake
glanced toward the sound, then at the photograph on the
bedside table. Katherine's image offered no answers, only the
reminder that clarity often came at a cost.

The knock again. And Harry Jenkins' voice: "Are you ready,
Blake?"

Chapter Fifty

Harry

"So, Alfred's dead. And Mrs Vickers is gone."

Harry looked around the kitchen table at Evie's tea shop. The early evening scene was familiar—an assortment of mugs, a teapot with a mismatched lid, and the faint aroma of Evie's fresh scones filling the room. But Dorothy was away, and the tension in the air felt as if the mystery surrounding Hawthorne Manor had turned darker.

As indeed it had.

"Gone?" Evie asked.

"Station master at Ashford says she took the train to London just after noon," Nigel said.

"She left just after we were in the wine cellar," Alice said. "She was probably on her way to the train while I was examining the interiors of the rare books." She paused to take a sip of her tea.

"Up till then, we'd only checked the titles against the inventory list."

"But she knew she'd been found out?" Evie asked.

Alice nodded. "She knew that was about to happen. The wine bottles didn't look right, and I told her I was going back to the library. Probably a mistake on my part. Probably gave it away that I suspected her."

"The books you checked were fakes?"

"Reproductions. With old covers stitched on, from old books that were in such bad condition as to have little or no value."

"How could you tell?" Blake asked.

"The words 'reproduction edition' were printed directly on the title pages. And the paper was new, stained to look old."

"But if no one opened the books, if they just sat on the shelves, no one would notice," Harry said.

Alice nodded. "The same trick had been worked in the wine cellar. New bottles with forged labels, dusted and smeared with dirt to look old."

"So you told Lady Gwendolyn?"

"And she rang for Mrs Vickers. And we learned that Mrs Vickers had already gone."

Nigel tapped a finger on the table. "There's something amiss there. Mrs Vickers doesn't have any family. So where does she go now? Where's her support coming from?"

Alice nodded. "If she's involved with the Iron Dukes, they may want to see her disappear. She's been found out, so they'd have no further use for her."

Harry gave a brief nod. "Do you think she knew that Alfred was dead?"

Alice shook her head. "I doubt it. I don't think anybody at the house knew."

"There's Mr Murphy, to consider as well," Harry added. "He claims he was just the delivery man, swears he didn't know what was in the crates, thought it was all legitimate business being handled by Sotheby's."

"And we've no evidence to prove differently," said Nigel.

Blake, who had been silent up to this point, spoke up. "Co-ordinating at Sotheby's would be Rosco's role, wouldn't it? He watches for a stolen crate, sets it aside, waits for the right moment, then sends it along to the fence."

"Seems likely." Nigel looked at Harry, a question in his eyes. "But why kill Alfred?"

Harry leaned forward, elbows on the table. "It's just odd, the timing. He was killed the night before Alice and Mrs Vickers were due to meet. Did someone else know about the meeting? Did they think the thefts were about to be exposed, and kill him so he couldn't talk?"

Evie's expression tightened. "And that notepad found in his cottage—'I know you'—had been written on it, though the note itself wasn't there. But who was that message for, exactly? Did Alfred write it, angry and ready to confront someone? Or was it left by someone else, as a warning, and then found by Alfred and destroyed?"

They fell silent, each lost in thought, until Evie said, "What about Lady Gwendolyn? How has she reacted to all this?"

"Fearful. Shivery, even," Alice said. "It's as if she's living in her own haunted house. Can't say if it's guilt or just nerves, though. And now she's got a legitimate reason to worry—her finances aren't what she thought they were."

"What about Sally Roe?" Harry asked.

"She's terrified for Lord Hawthorne," Evie said, "—or rather, for his spirit, as if he could be trapped in some sort of eternal punishment."

Nigel leaned forward, his brows knitting. "She spoke of some terrible sin, almost as if she believed she was responsible."

"A sin?" Blake leaned in, intrigued.

"Something about driving the American, Wentworth, to his death all those years ago. Said that God wouldn't forgive her. She hinted it had something to do with splitting up their marriage, violating that 'let no man put asunder' business."

"But wouldn't breaking up a marriage just have been between Lady Gwendolyn and Lord Hawthorne? How would Sally Roe be involved?"

"She did mention a diary, but she still can't find it, she says," Nigel said.

Alice's eyes widened. "If she has a diary, it could contain things that could get her killed."

Harry nodded. "Just like Alfred. Sins of the past, sins of the present. And someone's trying to keep those sins all buried."

"So who?" Nigel's gaze swept the table. "Let's start with Alfred. Who had reason to kill him?"

Alice sighed. "Peggy and Charles had the clearest motive if they wanted to stop him from stealing any more. But why kill him when they could have just turned him over to the police?"

"Maybe he knew too much about the Iron Dukes." Harry leaned back, staring into his teacup.

There were too many clues—the glowing chemicals found with Lord Hawthorne, the mushrooms gone missing, the lost diary, Alfred's crumpled note—

He pulled himself out of the fog that swirled in his imagination. "Then we go back to basics, right? Who among the household staff could've had the means and motive to kill Alfred?"

Silent faces all around.

"All right then. Motive and means to kill Lord Hawthorne?"

"Lady Gwendolyn's the one who benefits." Alice sounded reluctant. "But is she truly capable of murder? All her nerves could come from guilt... or they could come from fear."

"Fear that she's going to be the next victim?" Evie asked.

Blake cleared his throat. "Then there's that note from Sally Roe, talking about a threat against her life."

"Whoever was threatening her could've had ties to Lord Hawthorne," Nigel said. "Might have wanted to protect Lord Hawthorne from whatever Sally knew."

Evie's expression brightened. "And what about the sins of the past and present colliding, Harry? You said earlier, what if the past and the present are somehow... overlapping?"

Harry nodded. "Exactly. Two worlds, two types of crimes, but one shadow over the estate."

"So," Nigel said, steepling his fingers, "who's the common link?"

Harry was about to respond when Evie broke in. "Well, if we're all lost in theories, perhaps it's time to consider... more unconventional methods."

Everyone stared at her.

Chapter Fifty-One

Dorothy

E ver since Tom's army unit had been sent overseas— ever since the start of the war, really— Dorothy had spent so much time being worried and afraid that she would have thought she knew everything about being scared that it was possible to know. Today, though, she'd learned something else: the only thing worse than being afraid was being bored and afraid.

She was sitting in the hospital ward beside Tom's bedside. He didn't look any worse than he had yesterday morning, but he didn't look any better, either. His cheeks were still flushed with fever, and occasionally he twisted and turned his head against the pillow as if he were trying to get away from something. But in the three or so hours since Dorothy had arrived, Tom hadn't woken up or responded any of the times that she'd held his hand or tried to talk to him.

Dorothy had also thought she'd learned everything there was to know about missing her husband. But somehow, she missed him more when she was sitting right here next to him than she had when he'd been off fighting overseas. She'd give anything for him just to open his eyes and look as though he knew who she was.

The squeak of metallic wheels made her turn with a jolt to see Viola approaching with her cart full of books.

"Hello." Viola was wearing another dress that had definitely been made for someone else. It was yellow with a pattern that looked like sunny-side-up eggs printed all over the material. But her smile was warm. "How is he today?"

"All right." At least, Dorothy hoped that was true. "Do you have anything else to read?" she asked.

"Did you finish *A Study in Scarlet*?" Viola asked.

"I did. I read it out loud during the bombing raid. Here, you can have it back, now." Dorothy pulled the book out from her purse. "I liked it, and so did everyone who was listening. But—"

"But a story about murder isn't quite what you're hoping for today," Viola finished. "Of course. Hmmm." She frowned down at the books on her cart, ticking off the spines one by one with her fingers. "Let me see . . . yes, here we are. Try this one."

She selected a book and handed it over to Dorothy.

Dorothy read the title on the well-worn cover. "*The Secret Garden*?"

"You'll love it, I promise," Viola said. "It's one of my favourites. I pick it up and read a chapter or two every time I'm feeling worried or out of sorts . . . which means I've read it approximately fifty-three times in the past six months." She smiled a little sadly, then straightened as someone called to her from the opposite side of the ward. "I have to go finish my rounds now; I have three more wards to do. But I'll tell you what—after I've finished, I'll come back here and sit with you a bit and you can tell me if you like the story."

"All right."

Dorothy watched Viola push her cart down the aisle. Then she opened up the book.

She hadn't been expecting to enjoy it much. She hadn't felt as though she were in the mood to enjoy anything right now; it was really just desperation that had made her ask Viola for something to read. But almost from the first page, she found herself caught right up.

It was easier going than the Sherlock Holmes book had been, maybe because it seemed to have been written for children. And then, too, the description of the wild moor and the gardens at Misselthwaite Manor reminded her a bit of the countryside and the farm where she'd grown up with her mum and dad. She was just reading about Mary's first meeting with Ben

Weatherstaff, the gardener, when a footstep beside her made her jump and look up.

Dorothy had been expecting Viola, and gaped in surprise to find the Italian woman standing beside her.

"I have found you," the Italian woman said. She no longer wore the grey wig that had turned her into an old woman. Instead, she was dressed in deep, old-fashioned mourning today: a long black silk dress and a black hat with a veil that could be turned down to conceal her face. "I was not sure that I would."

She looked nervous, Dorothy thought, her breath coming quickly as though she'd been running.

Good. Maybe if she was nervous enough, she'd fail to notice Dorothy's own nervousness. Dorothy suddenly felt as though her tongue had been glued to the roof of her mouth and her heart had just skipped several beats.

She cleared her throat. "Has something happened?" she asked.

The Italian woman nodded. "Yes. I think—" she lowered her voice. "I think that Rosco and his men are planning to kill someone. I overheard them speaking of it last night."

"Kill—" Dorothy's heart went from skipping to trying to jump up into her throat. "Who are they going to kill? Lady Hawthorne?"

"I don't know." The other woman shook her head. "But you must warn those back at Hawthorne Manor. As soon as you can."

"I will." Dorothy nodded.

The Italian woman stared at her a long moment as though trying to make sure that she was speaking the truth. Then finally she said, "See that you do."

She cast one last quick look around the ward and then turned away, pulling the veil over her face as she sailed down the ward's central aisle towards the door. Dorothy looked down at Tom, but he seemed to have fallen into a more peaceful sleep, his breathing deep and slow and his face relaxed. She could leave without having to worry— at least, she wouldn't be worrying about Tom.

Dorothy shut her eyes for a second. Her offer to follow the Italian woman had seemed much less reckless when she'd made it back in Crofter's Green. But a promise was a promise, and her reasoning still held true. She wanted to be the kind of wife Tom would be proud of.

Luck was with her, too, because just as the woman in black was about to leave the ward, Viola came back, nearly colliding with the Italian woman in the doorway.

Dorothy waited until the Italian woman had manoeuvred herself around and out into the hall before she ran to join Viola.

"That woman," she said breathlessly. "I have to follow her. Can you come with me? Are you allowed to leave the hospital?"

Viola blinked and turned automatically to look in the direction the woman in black had gone. "Of course I'm allowed to leave; I'm not a prisoner here. And it's my memory that's not working, not my legs or my eyes. But who was that woman? Why would you want to follow—"

"I know it sounds completely mad, but she's someone who has ties to a dangerous criminal organisation," Dorothy said in a rush. "I need to see where she goes when she leaves here."

Viola stared, but at least she didn't say that worrying about Tom had clearly sent Dorothy off her head. Dorothy took that as a good sign.

"I'll explain everything else on the way," Dorothy said. "But if you're willing to come along with me, we have to leave straight away, before she's too far ahead for us to catch her."

Chapter Fifty-Two

Dorothy

"I think she's going to turn up there onto Upper Marsh Street . . . no, false alarm." Dorothy released a breath, keeping her eyes fixed on the black-veiled figure who was about twenty yards ahead of them, threading her way through the sandbags, barricades, and makeshift shelters that lined the street as part of the city's air raid precautions.

She and Viola had been in luck. They'd reached the exit to St. Thomas' just a half minute or so behind the Italian woman and had hung back on the steps, watching as she started on her way down Royal Street, her black silk skirts sweeping the ground.

Dorothy had taken the chance to explain as much as she could to Viola about the Italian woman's earlier visit to her and the Iron Dukes and about the death of Lord Hawthorne back in Crofter's Green. She wasn't sure whether she'd been clear enough to make much sense, but at least Viola was here, walking beside her.

The sky was overcast, and the air smelled faintly of smoke and damp concrete, a reminder of the nightly bombings. Many of the buildings they were passing had their windows boarded up with plywood or else were scarred by shrapnel. But there were still plenty of people out and about. Men in military uniforms were walking alongside civilians in work clothes. A lot of the workers were women, dressed in overalls and on their way to or from a shift at a factory or a munitions plant.

The big red double-decker buses still trundled along, both upper and lower levels packed with people. But there must have been damage to the rail lines in this area, because Dorothy hadn't yet seen a single tram go past. Maybe that was lucky for them. The Italian woman was easier to follow so long as she was on foot.

As Dorothy watched now, she paused, then turned and ducked into a small tea shop that was still open, despite the heavy bombing damage to the building next door.

"Now, what?" Dorothy murmured. "We can't follow her inside; she'd see us."

"Then we'll just have to wait until she comes back out again," Viola said.

Dorothy frowned. "That'll look a bit strange, won't it? If we're just out here standing on the pavement with nothing to do?"

"So we won't just stand here. Look, there are a couple of shops open across the street." Viola gestured to a row of three stores that had somehow gotten off relatively unscathed by the bombings: a dressmaker's shop, a greengrocer's, and a shoemaker's. "We can pretend to be looking in the windows."

Dorothy's heart was still beating hard and fast as they crossed the street, and she had to fight the urge to look over her shoulder to see whether the Italian woman had come out yet or, still worse, was watching them from the front window of the tea room. She and Viola established themselves in front of the dressmaker's shop. The bay storefront window was crisscrossed with scrim tape, but two mannequins dressed in the latest spring fashions were still visible, along with a display of ladies' gloves and handkerchiefs.

"Now we look at all the clothes and pretend to be counting up coupons as though we're wondering whether we have enough for a new coat or pair of gloves," Viola directed.

Dorothy smiled faintly. "I think you're better at this than I am. Maybe you were a spy before you lost your memory."

Viola smiled, too, although her smile was tinged with sadness. "Goodness, I hope not."

They stood in silence for a few moments. Dorothy discovered that by staring at the reflection in the glass, she could keep an eye on the tea room across the street, although so far she couldn't see the Italian woman.

"How are you enjoying the book?" Viola asked.

Dorothy gave her a startled glance, and Viola added, "We'll look more natural standing here if we're chatting about something."

"Oh. I like it," Dorothy said. "It reminds me a bit of Crofter's Green."

"That's the village where you live?"

"That's right. It's an entirely different part of the world from Yorkshire, of course," Dorothy said. "I've never been up North to see it for myself, but all the same . . ." She struggled for the right words. "The way Mary Lennox sees all the birds and the gardens and the growing things . . . it gives me the same feeling that I used to have on the farm, when my dad went out to do the spring planting. Everything green and hopeful. And Martha, the maid? When she talks about her mother, it reminds me of my mum. I haven't read far enough to know, but I hope Mary Lennox gets to meet her in person sometime."

Viola smiled, this time a little wistfully. "Well, I won't spoil the story for you by telling you what happens to Mary and Martha and Mrs Sowerby. But I wish I could meet your mother. And see Crofter's Green sometime, too." Then she stopped and stiffened, peering more intently into the window's reflected version of the tea room. "Don't look around, but isn't that the woman we've been following just sitting down at the table near the window?"

Dorothy drew in a sharp breath and stared, too. She could just make out a figure in a black dress and hat sweeping up to sit down at one of the tea shop's front tables.

"It's her! And look— someone's with her." Dorothy couldn't make out the second figure seated opposite the Italian woman; the reflection wasn't clear enough for that. She could tell it was a man, but that was about all. "I wish I could get a look at whoever that is with her. But I can't get close enough; she'd recognise me and know that I've been spying on her."

"You can't get close," Viola said. "But I can. She's only seen me for about a half second in the hospital ward. I doubt she'll remember me. And even if she did recognise me, she'd probably think it was just a coincidence. We're near enough to the hospital that lots of people probably come here for a cup of tea or a meal after they've been to see someone in St. Thomas'."

Dorothy could see the sense in what Viola said, but she still had to ask, "Are you sure? We don't know anything about this woman, only what she's told us. And whoever she's meeting with could be dangerous."

"I'll be all right." Viola turned around. "One of the advantages of not having any memories of who I am is that I don't know whether I'm a nervous, cowardly sort of person or not. So I'm going to assume not and do something bold and brave myself for a change, instead of only reading about it in books. I'll be back."

She marched across the street, and a moment or two later, Dorothy saw her push open the door to the tea room and step inside.

Dorothy turned back around, staring into the dressmaker's window as though her life depended on which pair of gloves she was going to buy. She opened her purse and looked through the contents as though she were searching for her booklet of clothing coupons. But really her entire attention was fixed on the reflection of the tea shop.

Cars and ambulances passed by, and once a bulldozer rumbled down the street no doubt on its way to clear a bomb site.

Finally, after what seemed like an hour, Dorothy saw Viola's slim form walking quickly towards her across the street. She opened her mouth, but Viola shook her head quickly and took hold of Dorothy's arm, propelling her down the street back in the direction of St. Thomas'. Only when they'd come to the next street did she say, "I was trying to get as close to their table as I could so that I might be able to hear what they were talking about. So I pretended that I'd got a broken shoelace and needed to tie it. But then when I stood up, the man— the one the Italian woman was sitting with— was staring at me.

I didn't dare stay or try to spy on them any more after that." She bit her lip. "I'm sorry."

"Don't be sorry," Dorothy said. "I'm glad you didn't take the chance of staying. Did you hear anything?"

"The man was saying something about . . ." Viola's brow furrowed as she tried to remember. "Something about Green-fields, was it? No, Greenview, that's right. He was asking whether the woman in black knew a certain patient at Green-view."

"How strange." Dorothy frowned. "What did he look like? Can you describe him?"

"Dark brown hair. About thirty, maybe a little younger. Very handsome, if you like that type— which apparently I don't— and knows it. Oh, and he has his left arm in a sling. Do you know him?"

Dorothy shook her head. "No. But I think we'd better find a public telephone box. I need to make a call back to Crofter's Green."

Chapter Fifty-Three

Harry

At the scarred wooden desk in the cramped Crofter's Green police station, Harry flipped through the case file on the Hawthorne murders, hoping to notice something new, or at least useful. The faint smell of damp paper and ink lingered in the air, though the late spring breeze drifting through the open window was beginning to chase it away.

The deaths of Lord Hawthorne and Alfred, the groundskeeper, had left the village shaken—and Harry restless. Something didn't sit right. Two men dead, and yet the motive remained murky. Were the two deaths even related? Harry had a nagging sense that the real story was far more complicated.

He leaned back in his chair, rubbing a hand over his chin as he reviewed the notes. Behind him, Nigel sat at the second desk, absently tapping a pen against the edge of his notebook.

The only other sounds in the station were the ticking of the clock and the occasional creak of the old wooden floorboards.

The sudden, shrill ring of the telephone cut through the quiet, making them both start. Harry set the file aside and reached for the black receiver.

"Crofter's Green police," he said briskly.

"Harry, it's Dorothy!" Dorothy's voice, sharp with urgency, snapped him to attention. "I'm in London with a friend, and we've just seen Rosco's wife!"

Harry sat up straighter, gripping the phone tighter. "Where did you see her?"

"She was in a tea shop near Marylebone," Dorothy replied quickly. "She was meeting with a man—dark hair, very self-assured, and with his arm in a sling. I've seen him around Crofter's Green, but I couldn't place him at first. Viola heard him mention Greenview."

Harry frowned. "Greenview? The asylum here?"

"Yes," Dorothy confirmed.

Harry's instincts flared. "Hold on. Who's Viola?"

There was a pause, long enough that Harry felt the silence settle in his gut. Then Dorothy said, with measured calm, "A friend. But it's not important right now."

Harry filed the name away for later, his focus narrowing on the description of the man. "You say you've seen this fellow before?"

"I think so," Dorothy said, her tone uncertain. "He looks familiar, but I can't quite place him."

Harry thought back to his own unease in recent weeks, the way Superintendent Sedgwick had taken such a shine to a particular young recruit with all the right connections and an easy charm. And an arm in a sling. "Could it be Barkley Robbins?"

Dorothy hesitated. "The mayor's son? Now that you mention it... yes, it could be him."

Harry's jaw tightened. Barkley had been the subject of more than one sleepless night for Harry. The lad's ambition and privileged upbringing had set him on a rising path within the local force, but Harry had seen types like Barkley before. In his view, they were men who cared more about career climbing than upholding justice. If Barkley was tied to Greenview, Rosco, and the Italian woman, this was no coincidence.

"Anything else?" Harry asked.

"Yes," Dorothy said. "Viola's just telling me. She overheard something about a warehouse." She paused, and then said, "Viola thinks it's something about a stag and a crown."

The Stag & Crown.

The name sent a chill down Harry's spine. "That's in London, near the docks. Smuggling, black-market dealings—it's a hive of trouble." He paused. "Dorothy, you've done well, but listen to me. Stay out of this. The Stag & Crown is no place for you or... Viola."

"We'll keep away," Dorothy promised. "But, Harry... be careful."

"I will," Harry replied firmly.

As the line went dead, Harry hung up the receiver and turned to Nigel, who had been watching him intently.

"What is it?" Nigel asked, already reaching for his hat.

Harry stood, pulling on his coat. "Rosco. Barkley Robbins. Greenview. And the Stag & Crown Warehouse. Everything's coming together, Nigel, and it's uglier than I'd like."

Nigel frowned. "And you're thinking we go to London to poke the hornet's nest?"

Harry gave him a small, tight smile. "Something like that. Come on, lad. We've got work to do."

Chapter Fifty-Four

Harry

Harry stepped out of the cab, his boots sliding slightly on the uneven cobblestones of the docklands pavement. The salty, sour scent of the Thames at high tide hung in the air, mingling with the faint odour of coal smoke from the nearby factories. Around them, the narrow streets were lined with warehouses, their brick walls scorched and pitted from shrapnel, their windows either boarded up or jagged with broken glass. The Luftwaffe's bombs had left gaps where entire buildings had once stood. Piles of rubble still littered the edges of the streets, and scaffolding leaned precariously against damaged facades.

Faded signs swung in the breeze, creaking faintly, and the murmur of distant voices carried over the occasional clang of metal and the hollow echo of footsteps on wood. A gaping crater nearby, half-filled with rainwater, served as a stark re-minder of the chaos that had rained down only months before.

"This is it, then?" Nigel asked, adjusting his bowler hat as he climbed out beside Harry. His eyes flicked warily to the warehouse in front of them, its shadowed entrance like the maw of some huge beast waiting to swallow them whole.

"This is it," Harry replied grimly, pulling his coat tighter.

Nigel squinted at the building. "I don't suppose they've got an afternoon tea service inside."

"No tea. Only trouble," Harry said. "Come on. Keep close."

They slipped into the narrow alley that ran alongside the warehouse, passing a stack of broken crates that reeked of mildew. At the back of the building, they found a pair of double doors, one of them left slightly ajar. Harry motioned for Nigel to stop as he eased the door open just enough to peer inside.

The first thing that struck him was the stillness. The interior of the warehouse was dim, lit only by the thin shafts of sunlight that pierced through cracks in the boarded windows. The air was thick and stale, carrying the faint metallic tang of old machinery.

Rows of shelves stretched toward the far wall, each one packed with crates of varying sizes. Most were marked only with numbers or vague identifiers like *Estate*, but others bore fresher shipping labels. Harry's sharp eyes swept over the markings, and his stomach tightened when he spotted a pile of crates stacked on a wheeled cart, near the centre of the room.

"On the cart, the two crates near the middle," he murmured, pointing.

"What about them?" Nigel whispered.

"They're just like the ones we saw at Sotheby's a few days ago," Harry said. "The ones marked with the initials of Hawthorne Manor."

Nigel's brow furrowed. "You think they're the same crates?"

"The same writing, anyway," Harry clarified, his voice low but tense. "Look how they're stencilled. Just the initials."

"Vague enough to slip past most inspectors."

"But enough to identify the origin if you know what you're looking for." Harry's voice hardened. "It's no coincidence."

As they crept further into the room, Harry's eyes swept the scene, noting other stolen treasures hidden among the chaos. Ornate furniture, half-covered in sheets, glinted faintly in the dim light. A cabinet built to display chinaware sat precariously on one shelf. He even spotted a painting in one corner, the edge of the frame peeking through the burlap wrapping.

"Den of thieves," he muttered.

Before Nigel could respond, the faint sound of voices reached them from deeper within the warehouse. Harry motioned for him to stay low as they crept closer, weaving between the shelves and crates.

At the far end of the warehouse, in a cleared space near a flickering lantern, four figures stood clustered together.

Harry recognized Rosco immediately—the scarred face matched the photograph he'd seen in Rosco's mother's house. Beside Rosco was a sharp-featured woman with an air of icy confidence—Rosco's wife, no doubt, for she, too, matched Harry's recollection of that same photograph.

The two were speaking to an older woman clutching a handbag tightly to her chest.

"Mrs Vickers," Harry muttered.

"And that," Nigel said under his breath, gesturing toward the fourth figure, "has to be Barkley."

Harry's jaw tightened as he looked at the young man with his left arm in a sling. Barkley stood stiffly, his face pale but set, as though he were bracing himself for what was to come.

"... no use to me now," Rosco was saying as they drew closer. His voice carried a slick, almost amused tone. He gestured toward Mrs Vickers, who was trembling visibly. "With Alfred gone, you've got no one left to sneak things out of Hawthorne Manor. You're just a liability."

Mrs Vickers shook her head frantically, her knuckles white as she clutched her bag. "Please, Mr Rosco, I didn't mean for any of this—"

"Didn't mean for it?" Rosco interrupted, his smile widening. "You and that old groundskeeper were perfectly happy to pocket your share when the goods were flowing. But now, your usefulness is at an end."

He reached into his coat and pulled out a revolver, handing it to Barkley. "Go on, then. Prove yourself."

Nigel stiffened beside Harry. "He's not actually going to—"

"Quiet," Harry hissed, his eyes locked on Barkley.

Barkley hesitated, his hand trembling as he took the weapon. For a long moment, he simply stared at it, as though weighing his options. Then, with a sharp breath, he raised the gun—

—and pointed it at Rosco.

"You're under arrest," Barkley said, his voice shaking but resolute. "I am Detective Sergeant Barkley Robbins, Ashford Metropolitan Police. Rosco Leonato, your operation is over."

For a moment, the warehouse was silent. Then Rosco's lips curled into a slow, mocking smile.

"Thought so," he said softly. Then he made a beckoning gesture with his right arm.

From behind the crates, five men stepped into view.

Chapter Fifty-Five

Evie

"You're sure you don't want to try searching the bed-rooms first?" Diana asked.

They were in what had once been Lord Hawthorne's private study, a chamber on the ground floor with tufted leather couches and a big mahogany desk. Framed paintings of red-jacketed horseback riders galloping in pursuit of unlucky foxes lined the walls and the air smelled faintly of brandy and tobacco. And yet what struck Evie most was how ordinary the room felt: no sense of emptiness or abandonment, no eerie reminders that the hands that had held the pens arranged on the desk were now buried in the churchyard. Bright morning sunlight streamed cheerfully in through the windows, and firewood had been neatly stacked in the big old-fashioned fireplace, giving the room a cozy feel.

Only a few short days after Lord Hawthorne's death, and already his home seemed to have forgotten that he had ever lived here.

Evie shook her head in response to Diana's question. "No. I'll search the bedrooms if we can't find anything in the rest of the house. But I doubt our suspect— or if we're wrong, whoever the guilty party really is— would be stupid enough to hide the missing diary in his or her own bedroom. Too much chance that a well-meaning housemaid would find it while changing the bed linens or dusting. No."

Evie stepped back a little towards the study doorway, casting a look around the room. "If the missing diary really is here— and it's always possible that Sally herself misplaced it, she's in a very fragile mental state— then I think we're most likely to find it in one of the common rooms."

She had talked the matter over with Harry before cycling up to the manor house this morning, and they had agreed on a strategy for the search. Although Harry still didn't know that she could enlist Diana for assistance. He was intelligent enough that Evie wouldn't be surprised if at some point he realised for himself that Diana had an alternate purpose in being here than simply paying a visit to an old school friend.

But for the time being, enlisting Diana's help had been Evie's own private idea, one she hadn't shared.

Diana wore red today: red espadrilles with ribbons that crisscrossed up her ankles, paired with a red and white candy-striped dress belted with another red ribbon and a large red bow at her waist. She also carried Bonzo in her arms. But her gaze as she, too, surveyed the desk and the twin bookcases behind it was keen. "And since Walter's dead and practically no one comes in here now, it would make for a good hiding place," she said.

"Exactly."

Evie was about to go on when a step sounded just outside the study door. She startled, but before she could make any move to intercept whoever it was, Diana had already stepped nimbly to the door and flung it wide.

"Oh, Mr Murphy," she said. "Hello there."

Evie considered herself fairly proficient at playing a part, but she had to admit that Diana's ability to instantly transform into a new character was masterful. As though someone had just thrown a switch, her voice, her expression, even the way she moved were all those of the vapid, brainless nit-wit she had played since coming here to stay with Lady Hawthorne.

The Hawthorne Manor chauffeur stood on the threshold, looking at her with a startled expression. "Sorry to interrupt, Miss Lovecraft, but Miss Peggy, she thinks she might have left a pair of her gloves in here. I was just about to take her for a drive and she sent me back, asked me to look for them."

"Oh, I see." Diana opened her eyes very wide. "How unlucky, though. I'm afraid my poor sweet Bonzo must have eaten something that upset his little tummy, the naughty boy." She dropped a kiss on the top of Bonzo's head and then leaned forward to add in a confiding tone, "He's just been sick all over the carpet in here. We were just waiting for the housemaid to come and clean up the mess."

"Oh—ah— I'll just tell Miss Peggy I couldn't find the gloves after all," Mr Murphy said hastily.

He turned and fled without another word.

"Well done," Evie said, as Diana shut the door once more. "You've probably just ensured that no one will venture near this room for the remainder of the day."

Bonzo had started to squirm in Diana's arms, so she bent, letting him hop down onto the floor.

"What do we think of Mr Murphy's story?" she asked.

"It might be true," Evie said.

"You sound sceptical."

"No more than usual. He really might have been telling the truth. Look, there's even a pair of gloves there on top of the mantle."

She pointed to a pair of white ladies' gloves with lacy cuffs that had been laid down beside the mantle clock.

Diana murmured agreement, but Evie scarcely heard. Now that she was looking in the direction of the room's fireplace, her attention had been caught by something else.

"Why are there logs in the hearth now, in the middle of May? It's too warm these days for a fire to be lighted."

Diana tapped her finger against her upper lip. "Maybe Walter liked to light a fire in case it got chilly in the evenings?"

"Did you ever see him do that?"

"Now that you mention it, no."

Bonzo had started to sniff around the hearth rug. Diana picked him up again while Evie knelt down and lifted the logs one by one out of the grate, stacking them beside her.

"Aha. What have we here?" A small leather-bound book was nestled under the spot where the logs had been. The word Diary was stamped in gold on the cover.

"It looks as though your instincts were exactly right," Diana said. "Provided it's the right diary."

"It is— look." Evie held open the flyleaf so that Diana could read the name printed there: *Sally Jemima Roe.*

Then she turned the pages, scanning the earliest entries. "It seems to begin before Sally came to work at the manor, when she was ladies' maid to Lady Gwendolyn and Lady Gwendolyn hadn't yet married Lord Hawthorne."

"That sounds promising," Diana said. "Any sign of the motive we were looking for?"

"Oh, yes." Evie had landed on a page about a third of the way through the diary and been struck by the words at the top of the page: The master is dead. She read the remaining words on the page once, then again to make sure. "Yes, I think this makes the motive quite clear. Now we just have to go about proving it."

Chapter Fifty-Six

Harry

H arry's breath hitched as his eyes swept the group in the warehouse. One of the men had a sawed-off shotgun cradled in his arms, its barrel gleaming faintly in the dim light. Two others carried revolvers, and two more were holding truncheons. These weren't ordinary street thugs—they moved with the confidence of men who'd handled this kind of violence before.

Rosco pointed toward the wheeled cart stacked with crates. "You three. Get those onto the wagon—we're already late," Rosco barked.

Harry, crouched behind a row of crates, kept his eyes fixed on the scene, his breath slow and steady. The three men Rosco had addressed leapt to action, wheeling the cart across the uneven warehouse floor toward the front doors. The crates jostled with every bump, but the men moved quickly, clearly accustomed to moving stolen goods under pressure.

Rosco gestured toward the two remaining guards. One was stocky, with a scar that cut across his left eyebrow, a heavy truncheon resting casually on his shoulder. The other was wiry, his restless fingers wrapped around the grip of a revolver. The guards advanced to Barkley and Mrs Vickers. In a minute or two, Barkley and Mrs Vickers sat tied to chairs just a few feet from where Rosco stood.

Barkley's face was pale and tight with controlled anger, though he hadn't said a word since his failed attempt to arrest Rosco. Mrs Vickers, by contrast, looked ready to burst into tears, her trembling hands clutching at the edges of the chair. Her discarded handbag lay on the floor near her feet.

Harry's eyes narrowed as Rosco's wife stepped forward, a sharp-edged smirk curving her lips. She crouched beside Barkley, reaching out to pat his cheek in a gesture that was both mocking and oddly intimate.

"*Ciao, bello,*" she purred.

Barkley flinched, his jaw tightening, but he kept his mouth shut.

Harry couldn't help but feel a grudging flicker of respect for the lad. Barkley's youth and entitlement grated on Harry, but the boy had backbone—he'd give him that much.

"Get the crates and barrels ready," Rosco ordered. He jerked his head toward the prisoners. "And keep an eye on our guests.

Don't let them cause any trouble. About an hour, and we'll be back with the wagon."

The two men nodded silently.

Rosco adjusted his bowler hat and turned toward the doors, his wife following. The heavy doors creaked open, letting in a gust of cooler air that swept through the warehouse before slamming shut again with a hollow thud.

Harry waited, ears straining as the sound of footsteps faded into the distance. Only when the silence settled fully did he lean closer to Nigel.

"Now," Harry murmured.

The stocky guard was pacing back and forth, the truncheon balanced loosely on his shoulder. The wiry guard had drifted toward the shelves, leaning against a stack of crates with his revolver held low.

"Flank the wiry one," Harry whispered to Nigel. "Grab something to use as a weapon. I'll deal with the big lad."

Nigel gave a tight nod and began edging along the shadows, his movements careful but quick. Harry turned his attention to the stocky guard, waiting for the right moment to strike.

The man's pacing took him closer to Harry's hiding spot, his boots crunching on the dusty floorboards. Harry crouched lower, his muscles tensed, a wooden crate lid already in hand. As the man turned his back, Harry surged forward—but his foot caught on a loose plank, sending a small stack of boxes clattering to the floor.

The stocky guard spun around, his scarred face twisting into a snarl. "Oi!" he shouted, raising his truncheon.

Harry cursed under his breath, abandoning stealth for speed. He swung the crate lid in a wide arc, aiming for the man's midsection. It connected with a dull *thud*, and the man staggered, but he recovered quickly. He swung the truncheon in a vicious arc, forcing Harry to duck low.

The weapon grazed Harry's forearm. A sharp jolt of pain shot up to his shoulder.

Harry muttered a few choice words to himself, gritting his teeth.

The guard smirked and stepped forward, confident now. He swung again, but Harry was ready this time. He sidestepped the blow and spun into the man's outstretched arm, grabbing the wrist that held the truncheon. With a sharp twist, he forced the weapon aside and delivered a hard elbow jab to the guard's ribs.

The man grunted, his balance faltering, but he still held the truncheon. He shoved Harry backward, nearly toppling him into a stack of crates.

Harry caught himself just in time, then surged forward again. Before the guard could react, Harry brought the edge of the crate lid down hard onto the man's wrist. The truncheon clattered to the ground, and Harry finished him with a swift elbow to the temple.

The stocky man slumped to the ground, unconscious.

Harry looked up just in time to see Nigel facing off against the other guard.

"Well, what do we have here?" the wiry man sneered, his voice dripping with contempt.

From Harry's vantage point, he saw Nigel hefting a wooden rod—a broken broom handle, perhaps—and squaring up against the guard, who was now raising his revolver.

But before the guard could take aim, Nigel darted forward, feinting left before jabbing the end of the rod upward into the man's throat.

The guard gagged and staggered back, clutching at his neck, trying to breathe. He dropped the revolver, which clattered to the ground and spun out of reach.

Nigel pressed the advantage, stepping forward to shove the guard into a stack of crates. The heavy wooden boxes swayed dangerously, and Harry's eyes flicked upward, calculating the inevitable.

With a groaning creak, the topmost crate toppled loose, its full weight crashing down onto the wiry man's shoulders. He crumpled to the ground with a wheeze, pinned beneath the edge of the fallen crate.

Nigel didn't hesitate. He grabbed a length of rope from a nearby shelf and quickly tied the man's wrists and ankles, his hands trembling slightly but steady enough to finish the job.

"You all right?" Nigel asked as Harry approached, rubbing his arm where the truncheon had struck him.

Harry flexed his hand, wincing slightly. "Been worse," he said, glancing at the unconscious stocky man before giving Nigel a faint nod of approval. "You did well, lad."

Together, they tied up Harry's still-unconscious opponent, and then dragged both guards behind a stack of crates, out of sight of the front doors. Only then did they turn their attention to Barkley and Mrs Vickers.

Barkley's shoulders sagged with visible relief as Harry approached, while Mrs Vickers let out a quiet sob of gratitude.

"You're safe now," Harry said gruffly, cutting Barkley's bonds. "But you've got some explaining to do."

Chapter Fifty-Seven

Harry

Harry crouched beside Mrs Vickers, cutting through the ropes binding her wrists while keeping one ear attuned to the warehouse's eerie stillness. Her hands trembled as they came free, and she clutched them tightly together, as though trying to stop them from shaking.

"Thank you," she whispered, her voice hoarse. "But please... you've got to get me out of here. Rosco—he said I was a liability. If he comes back—"

"He's not laying another finger on you," Harry said firmly. "You're safe now, Mrs Vickers. But if we're going to put a stop to this, I need to know everything. What's Rosco been having you do?"

She hesitated, her fingers twisting in the fabric of her skirt. "It was Alfred," she said finally, her voice breaking. "He dragged me into it. Alfred said we could make some money—good money—selling things off piecemeal. Furniture, silver, artwork. He knew this man, this Rosco, who had buyers for all of it. Alfred said no one would notice."

Harry nodded grimly, his mind racing to connect the threads. "And when Alfred was killed?"

Mrs Vickers shuddered, her shoulders crumpling inward. "I didn't want to keep doing it, but Rosco said I didn't have a choice. He said he'd tell the police I was the one who killed Alfred, and I'd hang for it." Tears spilled down her cheeks. "I didn't kill him! I swear it! Alfred was dead when I got there—I found him in the shed..."

Her voice cracked, and she dissolved into quiet sobs.

Harry exchanged a look with Nigel, who stood nearby with his arms folded, a grim expression on his face. Nigel gave a subtle nod, silently urging Harry to press on.

"We'll get the truth sorted, Mrs Vickers," Harry said, his tone softening. "But first, you need to tell me—what's Rosco planning? These crates... they're not just stolen goods, are they?"

Mrs Vickers shook her head, her voice trembling. "No... they're smuggling other things. Contraband from Europe, things they said were worth more than gold. I don't know what exactly—Rosco didn't trust me with the details. But he's working with someone higher up. A man in London... they call him the Broker."

Harry's jaw tightened. The Broker. That name stirred up old memories he'd rather not revisit—whispers of a shadowy figure who orchestrated smuggling, blackmail, and worse, always staying a step ahead of the law.

Barkley, who had been watching silently from where Nigel had freed him, cleared his throat. "Rosco's operation is bigger than I realised," he said quietly. "I knew he was smuggling, but if the Broker's involved... this isn't just a local racket. It's part of something much larger."

Harry turned to him, his sharp gaze narrowing. "And you've been working undercover in the middle of it."

Barkley nodded, looking weary but resolute. "For six months now. I was brought in to track the smuggling rings tied to Greenview and Crofter's Green and find out who's pulling the strings."

Harry frowned. "Greenview? The asylum?"

"That's right," Barkley said grimly. "I know you and Nigel helped shut down the Black Briars' silo operation in Crofter's Green in February. That was a big blow to their network. But while you were dealing with that, the Iron Dukes were expanding under the Broker's orders. They've been using Greenview as a hub—not for stolen goods this time, but contraband drugs. Morphine, opium, cocaine—the kind of things that can bankroll an empire on the black market."

Harry exchanged a grim look with Nigel, his jaw tightening. "And you're saying they're moving it through the asylum?"

Barkley sighed, rubbing his injured shoulder. "They've got an inside man—a senior orderly who's being paid off to stash shipments in one of the storage facilities on the grounds. It's a perfect cover. No one's going to question supply deliveries to an asylum."

Nigel folded his arms, his expression darkening. "That's bold. And despicable."

Harry's eyes narrowed. "Are the patients involved in this? Are they in any danger?"

Barkley hesitated, then shook his head. "Not directly. But there was one incident last November—a patient saw something they weren't supposed to. It was late at night, and they spotted crates being unloaded by men who clearly didn't belong there. It upset them enough that they made a complaint to one of the nurses. That was when I was brought in to investigate."

"What happened to the patient?" Harry asked sharply.

Barkley's tone turned cautious. "I was told they were... 'relocated.' Likely transferred to another ward, maybe even another facility. But given how the Iron Dukes operate, I wouldn't be surprised if they did something worse to keep them quiet."

Nigel's voice broke in, his tone clipped but steady. "There was another call recently—a patient at Greenview phoning the station. That one came to me, though the department didn't take it seriously. I brought Harry in to help. It wasn't about smugglers, though. She claimed to be seeing ghosts, but... it's more than that. She knows something."

Barkley frowned. "You think it ties back to the smuggling?"

"It just might," Nigel said slowly.

Harry's thoughts were churning. "But if Rosco's been bribing staff and moving shipments under their noses, it's not hard to imagine someone like Sally Roe seeing something she shouldn't have. The question is whether it's connected to the murders back in Crofter's Green."

Nigel glanced at Barkley. "You mentioned Rosco, but Mrs Vickers said he's working for the Broker. What can you tell us about him?"

Barkley nodded grimly. "She's right. Rosco's just the middleman. The Broker's the one running the show—the drugs, the smuggling routes, even the bribes to keep it all quiet. He's got operatives like Rosco all over. No one knows his real identity, but he's smart—never gets his hands dirty. Everything traces back to someone else."

Nigel let out a low whistle. "Ties in with what we learned in February. The local Iron Dukes operative was supposedly the sister of the gang leader."

Harry nodded grimly. "So we've got Rosco, the smuggling ring, this Broker... and the murders back in Crofter's Green to untangle. That's quite the mess."

"Too right," Barkley said. "I've been trying to get enough evidence to shut down the drug end of things, but now..." He hesitated, glancing toward Mrs Vickers. "Now that Rosco knows who I am, he'll come back to kill me. Then he'll move the operation before the police can catch him."

Chapter Fifty-Eight

Harry

Harry folded his arms, his mind working quickly. "Right. Here's what we're going to do—once we've secured the prisoners. Is there a telephone?"

Barkley nodded towards the front of the building.

"Good I've got a man in the Metropolitan Police who can help us move fast."

Barkley raised an eyebrow. "You trust him?"

"With my life," Harry replied. "Now, let's get moving."

Within minutes, the unconscious guards, still tied securely behind a stack of crates, were gagged with burlap sacking, and covered with more burlap sacks draped over them, just in case anyone happened to peek inside before help arrived. Mrs Vickers, still pale and shaken, insisted on staying out of sight, so she was behind more crates at the back of the large warehouse.

In the front office, Harry lifted the black receiver and dialed a number from memory.

The line rang twice before a familiar voice answered, gruff and no-nonsense. "Inspector Crosswell speaking."

"Jim, it's Harry," he said, keeping his voice low but urgent.

There was a pause on the other end. "Well, well. Thought you'd retired," Crosswell said, his tone light but edged with curiosity.

"Retired, not buried," Harry shot back. "Listen, I've got a situation. How fast can you get to the Stag & Crown Warehouse in the docklands?"

"How bad is it?"

"Rosco," Harry said simply.

There was a beat of silence. Then Crosswell said, "I can be there in twenty minutes. Maybe less."

"Make it less," Harry replied. "And bring backup. It's the Iron Dukes. We've got stolen goods, and we've got witnesses that Rosco wants to silence."

"I'll be there," Crosswell said firmly. They retraced their steps to the shadowy heart of the warehouse. Nigel was still in the cleared space near the tied-up guards, standing watch with a calm that belied the tension thrumming in the air. Mrs Vickers sat cross-legged on the floor behind him, clutching her handbag as if it were her last lifeline.

"Any trouble?" Harry asked as he stepped into view.

Nigel shook his head. "Quiet as the grave so far. But Rosco won't be gone much longer."

"Good," Harry said. "We need to make sure he walks straight into a trap."

Barkley frowned, glancing at the bound guards hidden behind a stack of crates. "What exactly is our plan?"

Harry folded his arms, his mind already working through the possibilities. "First, we leave enough crates out to make Rosco think everything's under control, like the job's halfway done. If he sees things in motion, he won't hesitate to come in and finish what he started."

Barkley nodded slowly. "And the guards?"

Harry glanced toward the two unconscious men. "We'll leave them hidden. If Rosco sees them trussed up, he'll bolt. We'll deal with them once we've got Rosco and his crew pinned."

Nigel stepped forward. "What about blocking the doors? Once Rosco's inside, we can keep him bottled up."

"Exactly," Harry said. "Find something heavy to move into place once they're in. We'll box them in and take them before they realise what's happening."

Nigel nodded, already scanning the room for suitable materials.

Harry turned back to Barkley. "While Nigel handles that, you and I need to get these crates positioned near the front.

We'll make it look like they've been staged for loading, the way Rosco ordered. That'll buy us a few seconds." He paused, noticing Barkley's sling. "Can you manage?"

Barkley grimaced. "Not sure how much lifting I can do with this shoulder," he admitted. "But I'll use my good arm—and I can push as well as anyone."

Harry studied him for a moment, noting the lines of strain around the younger man's mouth. Barkley was clearly in pain, but the determined set of his jaw told Harry there was no point arguing.

"Fine," Harry said, his tone gruff but approving. "Just don't push yourself too hard. We need you sharp when Rosco shows his face."

The next twenty minutes passed in tense silence. Harry and Barkley worked quickly, moving the crates into position near the front doors. Barkley used his good arm to help nudge the crates into place, grimacing occasionally but not once complaining.

"Rosco will recognise these," Harry muttered as he hefted one of the lighter crates into position. "It'll look like his men were just about to finish the job when they ran out of time. Perfect bait."

Barkley nodded, breathing heavily. "He'll walk straight into it."

Meanwhile, Nigel dragged a pair of heavy barrels toward the doors, standing them on end where they could be slid into position to block the entrance once Rosco's men stepped inside.

Finally, Harry walked back to the still-unconscious guards. He crouched beside them, checking their bonds and gags one last time before covering them again with the burlap sacks.

Nigel straightened, brushing dust from his hands. "Everything's set. What now?"

Harry glanced toward the side door, his jaw tightening. "Now we wait for Crosswell."

Just as Harry spoke, the faint sound of footsteps reached his ears, followed by a low creak as the side door eased open. He tensed, motioning for Nigel and Barkley to stay low.

A familiar figure stepped inside, his silhouette sharp against the dim light. "Jenkins?" a gruff voice called softly.

Harry straightened, relief flooding through him as he recognized the man. "Crosswell. Took your time, didn't you?"

Crosswell, a solidly built man with silver streaking his dark hair, smirked faintly as he stepped further inside. "You said twenty minutes. I made it in eighteen."

"You can pat yourself on the back later," Harry replied dryly. "Did you bring backup?"

Crosswell jerked his thumb toward the shadows behind him, where two uniformed constables emerged, both armed and alert.

"Good," Harry said, his tone firm. "Here's the situation: Rosco's crew will be back any minute. We've staged the warehouse to look like the job's still underway. Once they step inside, we'll block the doors and pin them in."

Crosswell nodded, his expression grim. "Understood." He turned to his two men, his gaze taking in both Nigel and Barkley as well. "This is it. Everyone get in position. Take them alive if you can, but don't hesitate if they make it ugly."

Chapter Fifty-Nine

Dorothy

Dorothy jumped and almost dropped the book she'd been holding. She was sitting by Tom's bedside again and had been deep in the midst of *The Secret Garden*, just about to learn who it was that Mary Lennox heard crying in the middle of the night. But she forgot about that entirely when she saw that Tom's eyes were open, and not only that, he was staring at her with a gaze that was shadowed but finally aware.

"Dorothy?" His voice was hoarse, barely more than a whisper. "Are you really here? I thought . . . I remembered seeing you, but then I thought . . . it must have been a dream . . ."

"Shhh." Dorothy smoothed the hair back from Tom's forehead, trying to blink back the sudden rush of tears to her eyes. Relief felt like an unlocked door inside her chest. Tom's skin was a little clammy, but cool to the touch. Cool. The fever must have broken. "Yes, I'm here."

"Where's here, then?" Tom craned his neck as though he were trying to look around.

"We're in a hospital. In London," Dorothy told him.

Tom's brow furrowed. "Hospital. Was I hurt, then?"

"Yes." Dorothy's pulse quickened and her eyes stung, though this time for another reason. She took a breath. "You were shot in the leg. Do you remember?"

"I—" Tom's face screwed up in an effort of remembrance. "Who shot me?"

"The Germans!" Dorothy stared at him. "Don't you remember the war? You've been away fighting for nearly a year, now."

Tom looked at her for a moment, his brow still knotted up. Then he gave her a shadow of his old grin. He was unshaven and too thin, his eyes hollow, but for this moment he looked just like the Tom that Dorothy remembered.

"Just . . . pulling your leg," he said. "If you could see the look on your face."

"You were—" Dorothy shook her head. She was trying not to smile, but she couldn't quite manage it. Her lips curved all the same. "You're just lucky you're lying there in a hospital bed looking like a dog's dinner, that's all."

Tom winked at her. "Sorry. You looked . . . sad."

"So you decided to cheer me up by making me think you were losing your marbles? Thanks a lot!" Dorothy felt herself smiling again, though, even as she was still perilously on the verge of tears.

Tom sank back on the pillows. Even these few minutes of talking had tired him out, Dorothy could see it. But he asked, "Is Tommy all right?"

"Oh, Tommy's doing grand. He's grown so tall you'll hardly believe it," Dorothy said. "He'll be turning cartwheels to hear you're better. He's been begging me to bring him up to London so that he can see you."

Tom nodded, his eyes sliding half shut. "Missed him. Missed both of you."

"I know."

Dorothy thought Tom would drift off to sleep, but he opened his eyes again, searching her face. "Dorothy? Is everything all right?"

She'd never been any good at keeping secrets from Tom. He'd have to be told about his amputated leg. He'd realise it for himself, probably the next time he woke up enough to really be aware. But for now the words stuck in her throat.

"Of course everything's all right." She leaned forward and kissed Tom's cheek. "You're home in England, and soon we'll have you back in Crofter's Green."

Chapter Sixty

Harry

The warehouse felt colder now, though Harry suspected it had less to do with the temperature and more to do with the tension crackling in the air. The team had split into their respective positions, each man blending into the shadows. Harry crouched behind a stack of crates with Nigel, close enough to the front doors to keep them in sight but far enough to remain hidden.

On the other side of the warehouse, Barkley had positioned himself behind a row of barrels near the centre aisle, his injured arm cradled protectively against his chest. Crosswell and his two constables had taken up spots closer to the rear entrance, ensuring they could cut off any potential escape.

"Quiet," Harry murmured to Nigel, though the lad hadn't made a sound. He could see the faint sheen of sweat on Nigel's brow, the rigid line of his shoulders. This wasn't like chasing poachers in the countryside—this was the kind of danger that got men killed.

"Steady, lad," Harry added, keeping his voice low. "We'll have them before they know what hit them."

Nigel nodded, swallowing hard.

From his vantage point, Harry could see the crates they'd staged as bait near the front doors, stacked just unevenly enough to look hastily prepared. It was a subtle touch, but—as Harry had learned from years of policing—it was the details that counted.

And then, at last, they heard it: the low creak of the warehouse door as it swung open.

Rosco's voice was the first thing Harry recognised, gruff and impatient. "Get a move on, you lot. We're already behind."

The clatter of boots followed, echoing off the walls as Rosco and his men filed inside. Harry counted them quickly: Rosco, his wife, and three thugs—just as Barkley had predicted. Each man was armed, though they carried their weapons casually, as if confident they'd find no trouble.

"Where are Stan and Greaves?" Rosco asked, his sharp gaze sweeping the warehouse.

One of the thugs, a broad-shouldered brute with a scar running down his cheek, shrugged. "I'll check. At least they got the crates ready."

"No," Rosco snapped. "We don't have time. Get the crates onto the wagon—now."

Harry's jaw tightened. They'd timed this perfectly. Rosco's men were already scattering, two of them heading toward the baited crates while the others lingered near the entrance. Rosco himself stood near the centre of the room, his eyes narrowed as if something wasn't sitting quite right. His wife, standing beside him, seemed equally suspicious, her sharp gaze darting around the space.

Harry glanced toward Crosswell's position, catching the faintest flicker of movement as the inspector signaled. They had seconds to act before Rosco or his wife caught on.

"Now!" Harry barked, his voice knifing through the tension.

Nigel was already moving, shoving the pre-positioned barrels into place to block the front doors. The barrels toppled with a deafening crash, slamming into the floor and creating a temporary barricade.

At the same time, Crosswell and his constables stepped out from the shadows, revolvers drawn and aimed. "Police! Drop your weapons!" Crosswell's voice rang out, sharp and commanding.

Rosco's reaction was immediate. His hand darted toward his coat, but Harry was faster. He stepped into the open, his revolver levelled squarely at Rosco's chest.

"Don't even think about it," Harry growled, his tone ice-cold.

Rosco froze, his eyes darting between Harry and Crosswell. "Well, well," he said, his voice laced with mockery. "The great Harry Jenkins, still playing copper even in retirement. Didn't think you had it in you."

"Drop the weapon, Rosco," Harry said, ignoring the jab. "Or do you want your wife to be a widow?"

Rosco's lips curled into a sneer, but he didn't move. Behind him, his men hesitated, their hands hovering near their weapons as they assessed the situation.

"Do as he says," Crosswell barked. "You're surrounded, and there's nowhere to run."

For a moment, it seemed as if Rosco might comply. His hand twitched, moving away from his coat. But then his wife, standing just behind him, let out a low, humourless laugh.

"*Cretino*," she said softly. "You think they'll take us alive?"

And with that, chaos erupted.

One of Rosco's men lunged for the crates, shoving them toward Crosswell in a desperate attempt to create a diversion. The constables fired a warning shot into the air, their voices lost in the sudden clamour as Rosco and his crew scrambled for cover.

Harry ducked as a shot whizzed past his head, his heart pounding. He fired once, aiming low, and caught one of the thugs in the leg. The man let out a howl, dropping to the floor clutching his knee.

"Barkley!" Harry shouted, glancing toward the younger man. "Get down!"

Barkley didn't need to be told twice. He dived behind the barrels, his injured arm cradled protectively against his chest. From his position, he managed to grab a loose plank of wood, swinging it hard at a thug who got too close. The man went down with a grunt, sprawling across the floor.

Meanwhile, Nigel had positioned himself near the back wall, his makeshift weapon—a rusted crowbar—clutched tightly in his hands. He swung it with surprising force, catching another thug in the ribs and sending him staggering backward.

Rosco's wife made a break for the side door, her shoe heels clattering on the floorboards. But Harry spotted her movement out of the corner of his eye and reacted instinctively.

"Crosswell! The side door!"

Chapter Sixty-One

Harry

Harry watched as Crosswell's constables moved in perfect sync, cutting off the woman's escape before she
even made it halfway to the side door. Her heels skidded on
the warehouse's concrete floor, and her hand darted toward
her handbag.

Harry's grip tightened on his revolver. *Is she going for a
weapon?* he wondered, his gaze focusing on the slim bag.

"Don't," one of the constables warned, his revolver held
steady.

The woman froze, her dark eyes darting between the constable and her bag. For a split second, Harry thought she might
test her luck, but instead, she let the bag slip from her fingers.
It hit the ground with a dull thud, and she scowled, lips curling
in disdain.

"Smart choice," Crosswell muttered, stepping in to cuff her
wrists.

Meanwhile, Rosco, seeing his crew faltering, let out a furious roar. "You think you've won? You've got no idea!"

Harry levelled his revolver at Rosco once more, his voice cutting through the chaos. "It's over, Rosco. Call off your men, or I swear I'll put you down myself."

For a moment, Rosco hesitated, his chest heaving with exertion. Then, slowly, he raised his hands, his revolver clattering to the floor.

"Stand down!" he barked at his men. "Stand down, all of you!"

The remaining thugs froze, their weapons dropping one by one as the fight drained out of them.

Within minutes, Rosco, his wife, and their crew were disarmed and handcuffed, their expressions ranging from fury to defeat. Crosswell's constables worked quickly, securing the prisoners while Crosswell himself inspected the crates.

"Well, Jenkins," Crosswell said, his tone grudgingly approving. "Looks like you haven't lost your touch."

Harry snorted, lowering his revolver. "Let's just say I've had a bit of practice."

Nigel stepped up beside him, his face pale but steady. "What happens now?"

"Now," Harry said, his gaze sweeping over the subdued prisoners, "we make sure every piece of this operation is accounted for. Crosswell, you'll want to get your men to inventory those crates before Rosco's organisation decides to try their luck again." He pointed to the crates near the centre. "And there are two more fine specimens tied up over there, under burlap. You may need to wake them up a little."

Crosswell nodded, already signaling to his constables. "Consider it done. I'll have your sleeping beauties shipped off to the station for questioning, along with"—he gestured to Rosco, his wife, and their captured crew— "along with these fine folks."

As the constables began their work, Harry turned his attention to Mrs Vickers, who was still seated near the stack of crates where Nigel had hidden her earlier. Her face was pale, and her hands trembled as she clutched her handbag, but she managed to meet Harry's gaze with a faint, flickering sense of gratitude.

"It's over now, Mrs Vickers," Harry said, crouching beside her. His voice softened as he added, "Rosco won't hurt you—or anyone else—again."

She gave a small, shaky nod, her voice barely above a whisper. "Thank you, Mr Jenkins. I—I never wanted to be part of this. I just didn't know how to get out."

"You'll need to give a statement, and you may have to face some charges back in Crofter's Green, but I'll make sure they treat you fairly," Harry assured her. "Now, I'll have Crosswell's men escort you somewhere safe."

Mrs Vickers hesitated, then reached out to squeeze his hand. "You're a good man," she said quietly.

Harry straightened and gestured to one of Crosswell's constables. "Take her to the station. Get her a cup of tea and see she's looked after."

The constable nodded, helping Mrs Vickers to her feet and leading her toward the exit.

As the team began securing the scene—Rosco and his wife hauled to their feet, the remaining thugs marched out or carried out—Harry allowed himself a brief moment to exhale. The trap had sprung, the fight was won, but the case was far from over.

Nigel stepped up beside him, brushing dust from his coat. He still looked shaken, but there was a glimmer of pride in his expression.

"Now," Harry said, clapping Nigel on the shoulder, "we head back to Crofter's Green." He glanced over to Barkley, who had just finished re-tightening the sling on his injured arm. "You're coming too, lad. You'll need to give us everything you've got on Rosco and the Broker."

Barkley nodded, his expression resolute. "I owe you both for getting me out of this mess. Count me in."

Harry gave a faint smile, his gaze drifting toward the now-silent warehouse. "Then let's finish this properly."

Crosswell approached, shaking Harry's hand firmly. "Good work, Jenkins. And Nigel," he added, nodding toward the younger man. "You're a sharp one—I can see where you get it from."

"Thanks, sir," Nigel said, his cheeks colouring slightly.

"Keep me updated on anything you find in Crofter's Green," Crosswell said to Harry. "And if this 'Broker' makes a move, I want to know about it."

"You'll be the first to hear," Harry promised.

With that, Harry, Nigel, and Barkley made their way out of the warehouse, stepping into the brisk evening air. The faint hum of activity from the docks surrounded them as Harry hailed a cab.

"Liverpool Street Station," he told the driver.

As the cab trundled away from the shadowy docklands, Harry allowed himself a rare moment of pride. They'd done it. Against all odds, they'd taken down Rosco and disrupted his smuggling operation right here in London—his old battle-field, a city that still carried the echoes of his decades of service. For a brief moment, he felt the thrill of returning to his old ways, the satisfaction of a fight well won.

But as the cab rattled closer to the station, his thoughts turned to Crofter's Green. That quiet little village, with its country lanes and windswept moors, had become his home—and more importantly, it was where his future lay. His friends were there.

He thought of them now: Dorothy, young and emotional but steadfast in her loyalty, juggling far too much for someone her age; Evie, calm and collected, the kind of person people naturally looked to in a crisis; Alice, a sharp mind paired with a deep knowledge of the village's traditions; Blake, the wounded teacher, whose keen intellect sometimes outpaced his social graces; and Nigel, his nephew, solid and steady, though Harry suspected there was more bubbling beneath the surface than Nigel let on.

Harry smiled faintly, picturing the group gathered around the tea shop table where so many of their plans had been hatched. Unlikely allies, all of them, but together they'd become something stronger than the sum of their parts.

And yet, whoever had killed Lord Hawthorne and Alfred was still out there.

Chapter Sixty-Two

Alice

"Is there anything else you need?" Alice asked.

She and Evie were standing at the front door of her cottage and speaking in low voices in deference to Tommy, who after a day of playing and working with her in the garden had finally succumbed to exhaustion and fallen asleep on Alice's sofa a short while ago. He lay curled up now with his cheek pillowed on his clasped hands. Alice had covered him over with a crocheted afghan her mother had worked years ago, and decided to let him sleep for as long as he could.

"No, I think that's everything." Evie shifted the bundle of fabric in her arms. "Thank you for the loan of your gauze curtains. They ought to do splendidly."

"They're not of much use to me at the moment with the blackout regulations in place," Alice said. "But are you certain you're prepared for this?"

"Oh yes. Really, it's not likely that there'll be much in the way of danger," Evie said.

If Alice hadn't known better, she would have sworn there was a hint of regret in Evie's voice. "You're a rather unusual tea shop owner, dear."

Evie gave her a crooked smile. "Don't imagine that same thought hasn't also occurred to me. Now, have you spoken to Lady Gwendolyn so that she understands what we need from her?"

As the one best acquainted with Lady Gwendolyn, Alice had agreed to be the one to speak with her about tonight.

"She knows as much as is safe for her to know," Alice said. "For obvious reasons, I couldn't tell her everything. But the important thing is that she has agreed to do everything we've asked."

"And have we decided what to do about Sally Roe and the Greenview end of this plan?" Evie asked. "Harry thinks that we can make do with just a pillow and bunched-up blankets, but I'm not so sure. Nothing about this affair says to me that our suspects are stupid or easily fooled."

Alice was about to agree when the trilling of the telephone in her front hall interrupted her. She crossed to lift the receiver quickly, before it could wake up Tommy. "Hello?"

"Hello, Alice?" Dorothy's voice came on the other end of the line. Even before she spoke again, Alice could hear the difference in her tone. She sounded lighter, more buoyed up than she had in days. "I was just calling to tell you that Tom is better! His fever is gone and he was able to talk to me a bit."

"That's wonderful news, dear," Alice said. "Your Tommy's asleep at present, but I'll tell him the moment he wakes up."

"Thank you. I'm going to take the next train home, so I should be in Crofter's Green by supper time," Dorothy said. "Tom's very weak, still, and they're giving him morphine for the pain. The nurse said that he'll likely sleep all night tonight, so I thought I might as well come home so that I can see Tommy and Mum and give them the good news." She paused. "And help with the plans for tonight, if we're still going through with it all," she added.

"We are." Alice glanced at Evie. "But are you certain, dear, that you really want to be involved? You've been through a dreadful strain—"

"No more than countless others these days," Dorothy said. "I want to help. I'm sure."

Alice thought back to her and Evie's conversation of just moments ago. "In that case," she said. "I believe we can use you."

Chapter Sixty-Three

Evie

Evie had just finished lighting the candles on the parlour's mantle when Harry and Nigel entered, accompanied by Lady Gwendolyn, Peggy, and Charles.

Evie had already extinguished all the electric lights, leaving the room crowded with shadows that turned even ordinary objects like tables and chairs eerie and somehow menacing. Peggy wore an electric blue skirt and blouse that were bright even in the semi-gloom of the candlelit room, and had her dark brown hair pinned up in a high chignon. She was already speaking as they came in.

"Of course we're only too glad to help, Mother. But I don't understand. What is this all about?"

"Please." Lady Gwendolyn looked careworn and years older than she had just a few days ago, her eyes shadowed as though she'd not been sleeping well and her shoulders slumped with fatigue. "Let's all sit down and I can explain."

She gestured to the small card table that Evie had set up in the centre of the room and surrounded by a ring of chairs.

"Certainly," Charles said. He looked around the room. "But there's no reason we need to sit in the dark, is there? Let me put the light on—"

"No!" Lady Gwendolyn turned to him sharply as he approached the switch on the wall. "No. Too much light would disturb the spirits."

Evie saw Peggy and Charles exchange a brief glance. Then Peggy said, carefully, "Mother, I know you've been under a terrible strain—"

"I'm not going mad!" Lady Gwendolyn's voice was still sharp. "So you needn't speak to me as though I were a child. But I told you earlier that your father was haunted before his death by what he believed to be a spirit from beyond the grave."

"Well, yes." Again, Peggy glanced at her husband before saying, "But I thought we'd agreed that he must have been imagining things."

"He wasn't!" Lady Gwendolyn's voice shook a little. "He wasn't, because I've also been receiving visits from a restless spirit."

"But mother—" Peggy began.

"Sit down!" Frail and tired-looking or not, Lady Gwendolyn still had the commanding air of the lady of the manor as part of her repertoire. Both Peggy and Charles immediately dropped into seats at the table. Lady Gwendolyn did the same. So did Harry, although Nigel remained standing, taking up a place by the door and effectively fading into the background. He was very good at that, Evie thought. She doubted whether anyone besides herself and Harry even remembered that he was in the room.

"Thank you," Lady Gwendolyn said, when everyone had settled themselves. "Now. I told you a moment ago that I have been troubled by spectral visits, just as poor Walter was before he died. I intend to ask for his help in contacting whatever restless spirit has been attempting to reach me."

She spoke as matter-of-factly as though she'd just announced her intent to add a raffle to a planned charity luncheon. So much so that it seemed to take Peggy and Charles a moment to absorb the meaning of her words.

Then Peggy said, "Mother, are you speaking of . . . of a seance?" she made a sweeping gesture that incorporated the candles, the table, and the ring of chairs. "You surely can't be serious!"

"I am quite serious," Lady Gwendolyn said. "I have just discovered that Evelyn here is a gifted medium." She nodded to Evie, who took it as her cue to slip into the empty chair at the end of the card table. "I want the energy of my family around me to lend support to our effort to contact your father."

"You?" Peggy stared at Evie. "A medium?"

"I prefer the term sensitive," Evie said calmly. "But yes. There are spirits all around us. And I think one"— she closed her eyes as though concentrating deeply. "Yes, I believe there is one here who is struggling to reach out to someone in the room."

As she spoke, she tugged lightly on the length of fishing line that she'd secured under the table. Even in bright light, it was nearly invisible, but in the darkness it completely vanished. Her tug had the effect, though, of making something white and spectral-looking flutter at the far corner of the room.

Alice's gauze curtains, being put to good use.

Charles startled. Even Lady Gwendolyn gasped, one hand flying up to her mouth.

Peggy, though, crossed her arms on her chest. "Nonsense."

Chapter Sixty-Four

Harry

Harry's eyes followed Peggy as she rose abruptly from her chair, her face set in an expression of stone-cold defiance.

"I won't sit here and be part of this nonsense," she said. Without waiting for a response, she turned and stormed out, her heels striking the floor like a hammer driving nails into wood.

Harry watched her go, his sharp gaze narrowing slightly. The sound of a door slamming upstairs echoed through the manor.

"She's always been that way," Lady Gwendolyn said, breaking the silence. "Stubborn as a mule, with the temperament to match. But she forgets, Mr. Jenkins: I've spent a lifetime dealing with the unruly and the ungrateful."

Harry didn't reply. Across the room, he saw Nigel's eyes flick to him, a silent exchange passing between them. Go, Harry's look said, and without a word, Nigel slipped quietly out of the room.

Charles shifted in his chair, smoothing the lapels of his jacket. "I'm sorry about that. Returning here has been difficult for Peggy. Would you like me to bring her back?"

"No, no, that's all right," Harry told him. "Better let her go."

"This will still work, won't it?" Lady Gwendolyn asked, her voice wavering as she turned to Evie. "Without her, I mean?"

"It will work," Evie replied gently, her tone steady and reassuring. "All we need is the energy of those present—and your willingness to hear the truth."

Charles shifted again, crossing his arms as he leaned back in his chair. "I'm not trying to be a naysayer, but do we really believe that this tomfoolery—"

"That's enough, Charles," Lady Gwendolyn snapped. "You agreed to this. If you're going to sit there and sneer, you may as well leave now."

Charles held up his hands in surrender. "Sorry. I'll keep quiet—and attempt to keep an open mind."

Evie moved smoothly into action, adjusting the lights and rearranging the candles arranged on the table. The flickering flames cast long, wavering shadows on the walls, adding an eerie ambiance to the already tense atmosphere.

Harry adjusted his position slightly, his boots scraping softly against the polished floor. His years on the force had taught him patience, and he was using every ounce of it now.

"Everyone, place your hands on the table," Evie said softly as she took her seat. "Close your eyes and focus your energy on Lady Gwendolyn's question." She spoke with the calm authority of someone used to commanding attention without raising her voice. "Spirits, if you are present, we ask for your guidance. Lady Gwendolyn seeks the truth. Please, if you are here, make yourself known."

Harry complied, placing his hands on the polished surface of the table. He didn't close his eyes, though.

The room fell silent, save for the faint crackle of the candle flames. For a moment, Harry thought he heard something—a creak, perhaps, or a whisper—but it was impossible to tell whether it was coming from the room itself or somewhere deeper in the house.

"Lord Hawthorne," Evie said, her voice taking on a more commanding tone, "if you are here, speak to us. Reveal the truth of what happened on the night you died."

Harry's grip on the table tightened slightly. He could feel the tension in the room thickening, the air heavy with anticipation. Lady Gwendolyn's eyes were closed, her lips moving in what might be a silent prayer. Charles's expression was harder to read, but his muscles were tense.

When no answer came, Evie leaned forward slightly, her hands pressing more firmly against the table. "Is there anyone there who can help us?" she asked, her voice quieter now, but no less resolute.

At that moment, Harry thought he heard it again. A faint sound, like the whisper of a breath. It could have been the house settling, or the wind against the windows, but it was enough to make him glance toward the door.

Charles shifted again, his fingers tapping lightly against the table before he caught himself.

"Shh," Evie said firmly, her focus unbroken. "The spirits are near. We must remain still. I ask again, Is there anyone out there who can help us?"

Chapter Sixty-Five

Dorothy

Pretending to be asleep was harder than Dorothy would have expected. The blankets were itchy and too hot, but she didn't want to risk moving to throw them off, and every small night time creak of the old building settling around her, every rustle of the wind in the trees outside, make her want to jump out of her skin. She lay in the pitch dark, ramrod stiff under the blankets in Sally Roe's bed, trying to remember how she held her arms and legs when she was actually asleep and not waiting for someone to come in and try to kill her.

Sally was safe, secretly moved by Alice and Evie to an empty room on one of the lower floors of the asylum for the night. Not even the matron had been told. Given what Harry had uncovered about the staff at Greenview while he'd been in London, no one was willing to trust that there wasn't another traitor or two who hadn't yet been identified.

Dorothy stared up at the darkened ceiling and worked on convincing her lungs to breathe slowly and deeply rather than letting the breath hitch up in her throat. She just had to hope that the secret about Sally hadn't gotten out.

She also had to hope that the police officer who was supposed to be waiting just down the hall really was loyal to Harry and Nigel.

She hadn't had time to get the story about Barkley Robbins entirely clear. According to what Harry had said during their hurried conversation on the drive here, they'd thought he was a traitor and in the pay of the Iron Dukes, but then he'd turned out not to be one after all. Good for Barkley, but it left Dorothy with the nasty, tickling doubt in her mind as to whether there were any other traitors— any actual traitors— on the police force.

She let out her breath and forced herself for the hundredth time to close her eyes and try to relax.

All she had to do was think about Tom to feel determined that any risk she was taking tonight was worth it.

Tom would get better, but he'd never get his leg back, never be fully the same again. After that, there was no chance that Dorothy was going to let Britain lose this war, not if there was anything she could do to prevent it.

When the door to the room clicked open, Dorothy thought for a second that she'd imagined the tiny sound. But then soft footsteps approached the bed and stopped. Dorothy squeezed her eyes more tightly shut and fought the urge to hold her breath. The seconds ticked by, marked by the thud of her own heart.

One. Two. Three.

When she got to fifteen, Dorothy started to worry that maybe this was just an innocent visitor after all. Then a soft hand patted the pillow in an exploratory way, brushing against her shoulder and cheek.

Dorothy had to channel every bit of her will into holding still and not recoiling. She'd never have believed how skin-crawlingly repellent the simple brush of unseen fingertips against her skin could be. But whoever stood by her bed was trying to gauge her position in the dark. Not wanting to risk a light, they were feeling around and trying to decide just where her head was.

Dorothy heard a soft rustle, as though the secret visitor had just taken something out of a cloth bag. Then a pillow was clamped firmly over her face, smothering her nose and mouth.

Instinctive panic shot through Dorothy, and she thrashed, struggling to twist away. She couldn't help it, but surely that didn't matter. Even if she really had been Sally Roe, she might be expected to fight. But her feet and legs were hopelessly tangled in the blankets, and the invisible hands pinned her down with an iron grip. Try as she would, she couldn't manage to get the pillow away from her face. Her lungs burned like fire. Her heart hammered as though it were going to burst.

Where was the officer who was supposed to have been watching the door to this room from down the hall?

Maybe he really was a traitor.

Maybe he'd just gotten tired and dozed off.

Bright spots danced in front of the blackness that covered Dorothy's vision. No one was coming to save her, though.

She kicked desperately, finally freeing her legs from the tangle of sheets and blankets. With the roar of her pulse loud in her own ears, Dorothy swung her foot up in a wide arc at where she judged her attacker's torso must be. Her foot connected with a jolt that reverberated all the way up to her hip, but she heard her invisible opponent let out a grunt of mingled pain and surprise. The pressure of the pillow against her face slackened.

Dorothy gritted her teeth and kicked again, harder, sinking every last ounce of her strength into the vicious swipe.

Her attacker cried out and fell to the floor with a solid thud. Dorothy shoved the pillow off her face and sat up, panting and trying to see into the shadowy darkness so that she'd know from where the next attack might come.

But before she could do more than brace herself, the door to the room swung open and the overhead light clicked on.

The young man she'd seen in London— the one with dark hair and his arm in a sling—gave Dorothy a brief nod. Then with his good hand, he levelled a gun at the figure in dark clothes who lay sprawled on the floor. He smiled a bit grimly. "Don't do anything stupid," he said. "We're going to go up to Hawthorne Manor and have a talk about what's been going on."

Chapter Sixty-Six

Harry

The parlour had gone so quiet that Harry could hear the faint hiss of the candle flames, their flickering light casting wavering shadows along the dark-panelled walls. The air felt colder now, heavy and pressing, as though it carried the weight of something unseen. Harry sat rigidly, his hands flat on the table, his sharp eyes shifting between Lady Gwendolyn's pale face and Charles's stiff shoulders.

Then came the voice. Soft at first, quivering, like the murmur of a breeze brushing through dry leaves.

"I'm here..." the voice said, hollow and hesitant, drawing out the words as though reluctant to speak. "I'm here. I'm Miss Sally Roe..."

Lady Gwendolyn's breath hitched sharply, her trembling fingers clutching at the table's edge. "Sally?" She leaned forward slightly, her wide eyes flashing a questioning look in Evie's direction. "But Sally is alive! She's been a patient at Greenview for years--"

"No longer." The quivering, hollow voice spoke again. "Passed on. No longer on this mortal plane."

Lady Gwendolyn shook her head. "I don't understand this at all. Sally, when did you pass on? And how did you die?"

"My time . . . here is short," the haunting voice answered. "I have a message I must deliver. Otherwise I cannot pass onwards to the Great Beyond."

Alice certainly had the gift for improvisation. Harry's gaze flicked toward the speaking tube hidden near the wall. He could almost picture Alice, sitting in the kitchen with the diary in hand, her lips trembling slightly as she read aloud from Sally Roe's final, tormented words.

Harry's glance traveled first to Lady Gwendolyn, then moved to Charles, who sat with his arms folded across his chest, his fingers tapping a slow rhythm against the polished wood, his expression hovering somewhere between disbelief and unease.

Evie's voice broke the silence, smooth and coaxing. "Miss Roe," she said softly, her tone laced with calm assurance, "we hear you. Please, tell us what you need to say."

The voice cracked, trembling, as though struggling to push the words out. "I must confess... before it is too late."

"You are safe here," Evie said, her voice like a balm, steady and sure. "What is it that weighs on your soul, Sally? What do you wish to confess?"

A pause followed, and Harry could feel the room holding its collective breath. Then the voice broke through again, low and heavy with guilt.

"I saw him..." it said, trembling. "I saw him do it."

Lady Gwendolyn gasped faintly, her hand fluttering to her chest as though to steady her rapid heartbeat. Her lips moved, but no sound escaped.

"Who?" Evie asked, her tone a perfect blend of sympathy and curiosity. "Who was it that you saw, Sally?"

"Lord Hawthorne," the voice admitted, the name carrying an almost physical weight as it settled over the room. "I was there."

The tension in the room thickened, the flickering candle-light seeming to dance more erratically. Harry kept his eyes locked on Charles, whose fingers had gone still. A muscle twitched in his cheek, and his eyes were fixed on a spot just above the table, his expression tightly controlled.

"Where were you, Sally?" Evie pressed gently, her voice drawing the confession forward like a slow, winding thread. "Tell us what you saw."

The voice sighed, long and unsteady, as though the memory it carried was almost too much to bear. "It was... on the lawn.

The men and my Lady Gwendolyn were playing croquet. It was so hot... the sun beating down. They'd left their jackets inside. I was in the conservatory... watching."

Harry's mind conjured the scene as the voice described it. He could almost see the vivid green of the lawn, the croquet hoops pressed into the grass, and the lazy drone of bees drifting through the air.

"Lady Gwendolyn had a parasol," the voice continued, faltering slightly. "She couldn't swing her mallet with it in one hand, so he—Lord Hawthorne—was holding it for her. I remember Mr Wentworth..." The voice paused, and Harry imagined Alice's fingers tightening on the pages of the diary. "His belly stretched his shirt tight. He looked... so fat, the buttons strained against the fabric."

"And then?" Evie's voice was calm, measured.

"Lord Hawthorne said he'd forgotten his cigarettes," the voice murmured, trembling. "He left the lawn... came up to the conservatory..." The voice hitched. "I didn't want him to see me, so I hid. But I saw him... I saw him take a silver flask from Mr Wentworth's jacket pocket."

Lady Gwendolyn's knuckles were white as she gripped the table. Her breathing had grown rapid and shallow, her eyes locked on the table as though she couldn't bear to look at anyone else.

"And what did he do with the flask, Sally?" Evie asked gently.

The voice quivered as it replied. "He took a small bottle... from his own jacket. It had... dark liquid inside. I saw him... I saw him drip the liquid into the flask."

Lady Gwendolyn made a small, strangled sound, her lips trembling. But the voice continued, unwavering now.

"He put the flask back into Mr Wentworth's jacket pocket," it said. "Then he ran upstairs. To the suite where Lady Gwendolyn was staying. He didn't see me... I followed him."

"Why did you follow him, Sally?" Evie pressed, her voice gentle but persistent.

"I don't know," the voice admitted, breaking on the words. "Curiosity, maybe. Or fear. He was holding the bottle, and I... I wanted to know what he was doing. I saw him go into Lady Gwendolyn's room. Then I heard him... in Mr Wentworth's room."

"Go on," Evie coaxed softly. "What did you see?"

"I followed him," the voice whispered, the tone growing fainter. "He didn't see me then. He was crouched over Mr Wentworth's open suitcase... It was on the stand at the foot of the bed. He put the bottle inside... buried it beneath the clothes. The clothes weren't hung up yet—they were still folded."

Lady Gwendolyn's shoulders shook with silent sobs, her face pale and anguished. Harry's sharp eyes flicked to Charles again. The man's hands had curled into tight fists, his knuckles white against the table.

"Did Lord Hawthorne see you at any point, Sally?" Evie asked gently.

"I thought he did," the voice replied, trembling. "He looked around as he left the room... but he didn't say anything. I was too afraid to speak. Too afraid to tell anyone."

"Why were you afraid?" Evie pressed, her voice laced with a soft urgency.

The voice hitched again, breaking. "Because I knew what he was doing. I knew... and I failed to stop him. I failed you, my lady."

Lady Gwendolyn's sob broke through, raw and anguished. Harry felt a pang of sympathy for her, but his focus remained on Charles, whose composure was beginning to crack.

"This is absurd," Charles snapped suddenly, his voice harsh and defensive. "You can't arrest a dead man!"

Harry leaned back slightly, his sharp gaze pinning Charles. His voice was calm, deliberate, and cold as steel.

"No," he said, the weight of his words settling over the room. "But we can arrest a dead man's murderer."

Chapter Sixty-Seven

Evie

"What are you talking about?" Charles was on his feet, staring across the table at Harry with a challenge in his gaze. "I never—"

He broke off abruptly, looking down at the ground. Bonzo was at his ankles, standing on his hind legs with his tail wagging and his front legs planted on Charles' knee.

"What the dickens— what's the dog doing in here?" Charles demanded.

Evie doubted that anyone else had seen Nigel quietly open the parlour door, just enough to allow Bonzo to slip through. Diana, as per their previous arrangement, had been holding him outside in the hall.

The little dog's arrival should have been an almost absurd anti-climax to Harry's accusation of murder, but instead the tension in the room was palpably thicker. Evie could almost feel it crisscrossing the air like arcs of electricity.

Charles was still blustering, trying to shove Bonzo off. "Why Diana can't keep a closer eye on the blasted animal—"

"The dog seems to know you," Harry said, his voice mild.

"Know me?" Charles glanced up. "Of course he knows me; I've been staying in the house the past few days."

"He knew you rather before that, though, I think," Harry said. "I believe your acquaintance began when you played the part of Willis, the gardener's assistant."

"What? That's madness." Charles' voice was a little too loud, too forceful, though. "Why should I have wanted to be a gardener?"

"Because of the opportunity it gave you, first to haunt Lord Hawthorne with apparent visits from beyond the grave, and then to kill him." Harry's voice was still calm.

Charles' mouth opened and shut. He swallowed. "Why should I have wanted to do anything of the kind? You were here when my father-in-law's will was read. My wife got nothing except the offer to live here on the estate."

"That's true," Harry said. "You and your wife don't appear to have profited from Lord Hawthorne's death, at least not immediately. But you were playing a rather longer game than that, weren't you? Kill Lord Hawthorne, ensuring that the estate passes to Lady Gwendolyn. Then kill Lady Gwendolyn, which would allow your wife Peggy to collect on the hefty life insurance policy that Lord Hawthorne took out on her."

Lady Gwendolyn had been listening in silence, her face ashen and her lips slightly parted in shock. At that, she made a small, strangled sound.

Charles licked his lips. "You've no proof of any of this." He gave a harsh laugh. "Unless you count the dog."

"We've a little more than that." Nigel stepped forward, speaking for the first time. "For one thing, there's your background in chemistry. You read chemistry and botany at Oxford, didn't you? And took firsts in both."

"Well, what of it?" Charles demanded. The flickering glow of candlelight showed how the veins in his forehead were standing out.

"Nothing." Nigel's tone was as measured and calm as his uncle's had been. "Except that the knowledge allowed you to formulate the solution that you used to fabricate glowing apparitions. Like this one."

With a sudden, swift movement, he jerked a length of glowing green— what looked like a long, gauzy scarf— out of his inner coat pocket.

Charles startled. Bonzo let out a yelp and dived under the table, his tail between his legs.

"I'd say the dog recognizes that, too," Harry said with satisfaction. "You used it the night that you got Bonzo to lure Lord Hawthorne to the staircase. Tied it around Bonzo's neck. Unluckily for you, the glowing chemicals irritated the dog's skin, which led us to suspect how the trick was done. Knowing Lord Hawthorne's fondness for Bonzo, you used the dog to lead his lordship out of his room and to the top of the stairs. Then you broke his neck and sent him toppling."

Lady Gwendolyn made another small, wordless sound. Charles said nothing.

"The only trouble was Alfred," Harry went on. "He recognised you as Willis. Recognised you and tried to cash in on his knowledge with a spot of blackmail. Which meant that he, too, had to be silenced."

"You killed Alfred two nights ago," Nigel said. His expression had turned hard, now, remorseless as he took a step forward. Evie almost shivered. "Then you staged the scene as a suicide."

"It's not true!" Charles burst out. He was breathing hard, his voice ragged. "Ask Peggy. She'll tell you I was in our room all night two nights ago. I never left."

Chapter Sixty-Eight

Harry

The parlour door creaked open, then slammed hard against the wall, startling everyone inside.

Peggy entered.

She wore a nurse's uniform—a rumpled white apron over a pale blue dress, with her dark brown hair spilling out from beneath a starched cap. Her face was pale, her jaw tight, and her dark eyes burned with a volatile mixture of defiance and dread.

Her hands were shackled in front of her.

Barkley Robbins, in his Ashford Police uniform, held her firmly by the arm.

Lady Gwendolyn rose abruptly from her chair, her voice filled with alarm and disbelief. "Peggy! What on earth are you doing here —and dressed like that? We thought you were up-stairs in your room!"

Peggy's sharp gaze flicked to her husband, Charles, who stood rigid near the table. She said nothing, but her lips curled into the faintest sneer.

Dorothy entered next, pale but composed. She closed the door behind her with trembling hands and stepped into the room. Though her movements were measured, Harry could see the strain etched in her face.

Evie stood from her seat, her voice tinged with concern. "Dorothy, what happened? Are you all right?"

"I'm fine," Dorothy said, though her voice carried the weight of her ordeal. She gripped the back of a chair for support, steadying herself. "Peggy tried to smother me at the nursing home," she continued, her tone calm but cutting. "She thought I was Sally Roe. But thanks to Officer Robbins, she didn't succeed."

A gasp escaped Lady Gwendolyn's lips as she clutched the edge of the table. "Smother you? Peggy, how could you?

Peggy's composure cracked further. Her voice wavered as she snapped, "It wasn't real! I just wanted to scare her, that's all."

Barkley tightened his grip on Peggy's arm, his voice sharp. "Not a chance," he said. "If we hadn't dragged her off, she'd have gone through with it. She fought us every step of the way. This was about silencing Sally Roe, plain and simple."

The weight of his words hung heavily in the air.

Nigel moved to stand beside Harry, his sharp gaze fixed on Peggy. "And you helped with this, too, didn't you?" he asked, his tone biting as he held the green scarf aloft. "You and Charles were planning to use the same trick on Lady Gwendolyn, weren't you?"

"Already had done, I'd say," Harry said. To Peggy, he added, "We found that scarf in your husband's room."

Peggy's eyes darted to Charles, who remained stiff and silent, his face pale and his jaw clenched. Her sneer turned venomous as she hissed under her breath, "You fool."

Lady Gwendolyn's trembling hand went to her mouth, her wide eyes shifting between Peggy and Charles. "This... this can't be true," she murmured, her voice fragile and strained.

Harry kept his voice level. "It's true enough," he said firmly. "But there's more to it, isn't there, Peggy?"

The room fell into tense silence, broken only by the creak of the door as it opened again. Alice entered, clutching Sally Roe's diary tightly against her chest. She paused for a moment, her knuckles white where they gripped the leather cover, then stepped into the room with quiet determination.

Harry turned to her and nodded. "Miss Greenleaf," he said, his tone softening slightly, "would you read us that entry you found earlier? The one about Lady Gwendolyn, when she was still Mrs Wentworth."

Alice hesitated briefly, then flipped through the diary with trembling fingers. When she reached the marked page, she drew a deep breath and began to read aloud.

"June 14th, 1908," she began. "Mrs Wentworth is ill again with her morning sickness. She hopes it will be gone before we travel to Hawthorne Manor. She begged me not to tell a soul—not even Mr Wentworth."

The silence that followed was suffocating. Lady Gwendolyn's face flushed crimson, her lips parting as though to speak, but no words came.

Finally, she whispered, "It's true. I was already pregnant with Peggy when I married Walter. He knew—or at least, he suspected. He told me he accounted for it in his will, but we never spoke of it again." Her tear-filled gaze locked onto Peggy. "And you knew, too, didn't you? That's why you left Hawthorne Manor ten years ago."

Peggy's sneer returned, though it was weaker now, her bravado slipping. "Of course I knew," she spat. "I read that diary."

Evie stepped forward, her voice sharp and deliberate. "You stole it from Sally Roe, didn't you?" she said. "We found it where you'd hidden it in your father's study. You tried to cast suspicion on Mr Murphy by sending him there to fetch a pair of gloves you'd accidentally left while you were placing the diary in the fireplace. He's entirely innocent, but you knew the police would have to be looking at him closely since he was the one to drive the crates of stolen goods up to Sotheby's.

"Then tonight, you tried to kill Sally to stop her from revealing the truth. She's the only one who could reveal the motive you had for wanting the man everyone else thought was your father dead."

The room seemed to hold its collective breath. Lady Gwendolyn let out a muffled sob, her hand trembling against her mouth.

But Charles reacted differently. His composure shattered like glass, and his face twisted in fury. "You stupid cow!" he bellowed, his voice splitting the silence. He turned on Peggy, his fists clenched tightly.

Nigel moved swiftly, stepping in front of Charles, but Peggy ignored the attempt to intervene.

"Me?" Her voice rose. "This was all your idea! Your genius plan that couldn't possibly go wrong!"

"Quiet!" Charles roared.

Despite the shackles on her wrists, Peggy managed to wrench herself out of Barkley's grasp and threw herself at her husband, her own face contorted with rage.

Nigel caught her. "That's enough!"

Peggy didn't heed the warning; she was too far gone in fury. She kicked out, struggling and thrashing in Nigel's grasp like a hissing wildcat. Barkley tried to help, but his arm was still in a sling, and he staggered back as Peggy tried to claw his face with her painted nails.

Charles's eyes darted to the door, wild desperation flashing across his face. He made a dash for it, but Harry was ready. Harry stepped into his path, his arm blocking the escape route … and realized his miscalculation just a fraction of a second too late.

Quick as a striking snake, Charles' hand slid into his jacket pocket and came out with a pistol, which he jabbed hard into Harry's ribs.

"Unless you want to die today, step aside," he snarled.

Harry ran swiftly through possible options: one, try to wrestle the gun away. Two, hope that Nigel and Barkley could rid themselves of Peggy and get across the room before Charles could get off a shot.

He frankly didn't like his odds with either option. But in the split second before he could make a move, Evie jumped up from the table, seized hold of her chair, and brought it down with a ringing crack on the back of Charles' head.

The chair was a cheaply made, gimcrack affair and shattered on impact so that the blow didn't do more than momentarily stun Charles. But it did cause him to swing the gun around on Evie and squeeze off a shot.

Harry looked on in horror as the deafening echo of the gunfire rang in his ears. He fully expected to see Evie collapse on the ground, a bloody wound in her chest. But she didn't flinch. She stood without moving, entirely unwounded, and looked with contempt at the weapon in Charles' hand.

"Next time you decide to devote yourself to a life of crime, either learn to shoot better or bring a friend who does."

Charles was still gaping at her as she knocked his gun hand up, seizing hold of his wrist. She spun the gun away from her, twisting Charles' arm to the right, then using the momentum to flip Charles to the ground.

He landed flat on his back with a solid thud. Evie stepped over him, planting her foot on his wrist so that she could yank the pistol out of his grasp. She was so fast that Harry doubted that Charles had time to register what was happening until it was all over.

"Much obliged," Harry told Evie.

"Don't mention it." She straightened, handing the gun over to Barkley.

Harry cleared his throat and then hauled Charles to his feet. "Charles Brentwood, you're under arrest for the murders of Lord Hawthorne and Alfred Travers. Mrs Brentwood, you're under arrest as an accessory in those murders, and for the attempted murder of Sally Roe."

Chapter Sixty-Nine

Harry

Harry Jenkins sat at his now-favourite table by the window in the King's Arms. His plate held the remnants of shepherd's pie and a few stray crumbs from the thick slice of bread he'd been using to mop up the gravy. Voices of the lunchtime crowd were a distant hum behind him.

He nursed his pint of bitter, savouring the fleeting stillness after the storm of recent days. Through the window, the town green at the heart of the village basked in the late May sunshine, the new leaves golden and rustling in the breeze.

The bell over the pub door jingled, and Harry glanced up out of habit.

Nigel and Barkley strode in, both looking purposeful, though Nigel's pace was more deliberate while Barkley's steps carried a touch of youthful energy. They spotted Harry immediately, making a beeline for his table.

"Thought we'd find you here," Nigel said, his tone warm as he shrugged off his coat. "Mind if we join you?"

Harry waved at the empty chairs across from him. "Not at all. Just finished my lunch."

Barkley sat down with a slight wince, shifting to adjust his arm in its sling. "Could do with a bite myself," he muttered. "We've had a busy morning."

Harry raised an eyebrow, waiting. Nigel gestured to the barmaid to bring two more pints, then leaned forward, lowering his voice.

"We've just come back from Ashford," Nigel began. "Had a meeting with Superintendent Sedgwick. Thought you'd like to hear how things turned out."

Harry's eyes sharpened, his hand cradling his pint. "Go on, then."

Nigel glanced at Barkley, who took up the thread. "Rosco's spilling everything he knows," Barkley said. "Not just about the smuggling ring or the racket at Greenview, but his connections to the Broker. He's given enough to confirm what Crosswell suspected—this operation is bigger than we thought."

Harry grunted, his fingers tapping lightly against the table. "Bigger how?"

Barkley leaned in, his expression serious. "The Broker's got a hand in operations all over the country. Smuggling, forgery, contraband drugs—you name it. But Rosco's never met the man in person. Says orders always came through intermediaries."

"Convenient," Harry muttered. "Anything we can use?"

Nigel nodded. "Rosco's hints line up with what we already know about Clara Woodhouse and how she tried to blow up the Black Briars' warehouse a few months ago to make way for the Iron Dukes." He hesitated, then added, "The Broker could very well be Clara's brother."

Harry let out a slow breath, his thoughts turning over this possibility. "That'd explain a lot," he said. "We'll need more than Rosco's word to nail him, though."

Barkley leaned back slightly, adjusting his injured arm in its sling. "Rosco's wife might help," he began. "She's not exactly off the hook, but her situation's... complicated. Turns out, she's been playing both sides. She claims she only stuck by Rosco because it kept her alive—and, apparently, she was collecting evidence on him the whole time."

Harry raised an eyebrow. "Collecting evidence, was she? Sounds convenient."

Nigel nodded. "I thought the same at first, but Crosswell confirmed some of what she said. The notes she handed over included details even Rosco's own men didn't know about—like payout schedules, smuggling routes, and meetings she wasn't even supposed to be privy to. She was keeping records quietly for months."

ANNA ELLIOTT AND CHARLES VELEY

Harry's expression hardened. "Doesn't make her a saint, though. Let's not forget she was about to pull a gun on us at the warehouse."

"She says that was for Rosco's benefit," Nigel added, his tone sceptical. "According to her, she had to look loyal in the moment to avoid being shot herself. She claims she wasn't planning to use it."

Harry let out a dry chuckle. "That's an awfully fine line to walk. So what's happening to her now?"

Barkley sighed. "She's been offered limited immunity—strictly conditional. I'd say she's lucky she's not sharing a cell with Rosco."

Nigel shrugged. "To be fair, her notes have already led to two major warehouse raids."

Harry considered this, his jaw tightening as he mulled over the details. "Still smells a bit fishy to me," he muttered. "But if it leads to shutting down the Broker's operations, I suppose we'll take what we can get."

Barkley nodded. "Crosswell's optimistic."

Harry was about to speak, but the pub door jingled again. He turned to see Alice Greenleaf step inside, her satchel slung over one shoulder. She caught his eye immediately and gave a nod before making her way to their table.

"Afternoon, gentlemen," she said briskly, setting her satchel down with a quiet thud. "Eleanor Piggot's been complaining about her back again. Thought I'd bring her some comfrey and willow bark." She glanced between them, her sharp gaze lingering on Barkley's sling. "And what about you, Officer Robbins? Is your shoulder healing up? You're based in Ashford, aren't you?"

Barkley managed a faint smile. "I'm fine ma'am. Yes, I'm based in Ashford—but looking to keep working in London if I can. Superintendent Sedgwick said Crosswell might be able to put in a word for me with the Met."

"I was just about to suggest that," Harry said. "I'll put in a word myself."

Barkley nodded, a hint of gratitude softening his usually brash demeanour. "Understood. And thank you. Both of you." He grimaced slightly. "I'll still need the Wolseley, though. For getting to and from London."

Nigel chuckled, sitting back in his chair. "Fine with me." He turned to Alice. "The Prefect fits Crofter's Green nicely, don't you think?"

Alice smirked, her tone arch. "You mean that little sardine can you're driving now? At least it won't block the lane outside the tea shop."

Harry snorted into his pint, shaking his head. "It's got its uses, Alice. Doesn't waste petrol, and it keeps young Nigel here humble."

Nigel rolled his eyes good-naturedly but said nothing, his smile faint.

The table fell into an easy silence, the weight of recent events settling comfortably now that the immediate dangers had passed. Through the window, the hum of village life carried on—a reminder that while the world outside was at war, Crofter's Green remained a small but steady refuge.

For now.

Harry allowed himself to savour the moment. The shadows of the past lingered, but with allies like Nigel, Alice, Evie, Dorothy, and Blake, he knew they'd face whatever came next together.

And that, he decided, was enough for him.

Chapter Seventy

Dorothy

Balancing a tray with two teacups on it, Dorothy pushed open the door of the hospital ward. Then she stopped at the sight of Tommy and his father. Mr Murphy had driven her and Tommy up to London first thing this morning. Dorothy wasn't sure at first which had excited Tommy more: the prospect of seeing his father again or the ride in the fancy car. But the second they set foot inside the hospital, all thoughts of the Daimler dropped away, and Tommy had hugged his dad so hard that Dorothy hadn't been certain whether he'd ever let go.

She'd gone a few minutes ago to fetch them a couple of cups of hot tea from the canteen. Now she watched as Tommy and his father tried to set up a game of draughts on top of Tom's bed. The playing board kept tilting, though, which sent the draughts sliding in all directions, and after a minute Tom and Tommy decided that it was more fun to flick the draughts at each other like artillery fire anyway. They were both laughing, Tom pretending to duck and cover his head every time Tommy sent a red or black checker spinning his way.

"Does he know yet?" a voice behind her asked.

Turning, Dorothy found that Viola had come up to join her in the doorway.

"Yes," Dorothy said. Tom had had to be told about his leg this morning. He'd taken the news very quietly, his first thoughts seeming to be only of her and Tommy. "He asked me if I minded," she told Viola. "I said I wouldn't care if he came back with both legs and his arms gone, just so long as he was home again. And you can see for yourself that Tommy feels the same."

"So he's all right then?" Viola said.

Dorothy studied Tom's face. He was laughing and joking with Tommy, just like old times. But his eyes were shadowed, and there was something in Tom's smile that had never been there before.

"Not quite," she said. "But I think he will be. He'll find his way. We just need to get him home to Crofter's Green for a start."

"Your village that reminds you of Misselthwaite Manor," Viola said. She smiled wistfully. "I wish I could see it sometime."

Dorothy thought of going home with her Tom and Tommy, home to her mum and to her work at the Cozy Cup, home to the place where all three of them belonged. Viola didn't belong anywhere or to anyone, not that she could remember.

"I'll tell you what," Dorothy said. "After we get Tom home and get him settled in, you ought to come for a visit."

There wasn't any room in the tiny flat she shared with Tommy and Mum— just fitting Tom in was going to be a squeeze— but she knew Alice would let Viola stay with her for a few days. Or else Evie would.

"Really?" Viola's wistful expression lit up.

Dorothy nodded. "It's a promise."

Chapter Seventy-One

Evie

E vie was in the kitchen, contemplating her nearly empty bin of flour and wondering whether the government's latest suggestion— a recipe for parsnip pudding— could possibly be turned into something appetising enough to sell when she opened the Cozy Cup tomorrow. Darkness had nearly fallen outside, so she had all of her blackout curtains drawn, but they couldn't muffle the roar of aeroplane engines passing overhead.

It must be a busy night for bombing raids.

She was about to start grating the parsnips in a fit of probably misplaced optimism when a knock sounded on her kitchen door. Mindful of the regulations, Evie switched off the kitchen light before going to open it. She'd been expecting Alice; the older woman often popped in for a cup of tea and a chat in the evenings. So Evie was all the more startled to find Nigel on her back doorstep.

He was wearing a light spring overcoat over his navy-blue uniform and the brim of a black felt homburg hat shaded his angular face. He was also holding a pasteboard carton in his arms.

"I thought you might be able to use these," he said. The carton held a bag of flour, one of sugar, and a four-ounce parcel of margarine. "I generally eat my meals at the King's Arms, so I seldom use up all my ration coupons."

"Thank you." Evie stepped back to allow him to enter, though she gave him a raised eyebrow. "This wouldn't be an apology, would it?"

Nigel set the carton down on the kitchen table. "Call it a peace offering? I appreciate what you did for my uncle today. You're remarkably adept at disarming a gunman."

Evie couldn't entirely interpret the look he was giving her, but she didn't think it was one of suspicion— which surprised her all over again.

"I admit I'm better at disarming a gunman than I am at, for example, climbing up the side of a building," she said.

"Ah. So the story about being a games mistress and teaching rock climbing courses?"

"Entirely fictional," Evie said. She picked up the parcel of margarine and put it away in the larder. "I didn't want you to have to worry about me."

"Considerate of you." Nigel's expression was level, but she'd have sworn that his eyes hid a smile.

"Not really. We both had a higher chance of survival if you weren't distracted."

This time Nigel's lips actually twitched. "At any rate, thank you," he said. "If you hadn't stepped in to get the gun away from Charles, things might have turned out very differently."

"I told you. I like your uncle," Evie said. "Although I imagine that even a foreign agent might feel the same. He's a likable man."

Nigel rubbed the back of his neck and sighed. "Several days ago, an anonymous caller telephoned to the police station and accused you of being a German spy."

"What?" Evie stared at him. "Who would have done that? And why?"

"I can answer the *who*," Nigel said. His expression turned a bit grim. "It was Charles."

"Charles accused me of spying for Hitler?" Evie stared at him.

"He admitted as much under questioning. He was trying to bargain his way to a lighter sentence by spilling as much information as he could. No self-sacrificing hero, our Charles." Nigel's mouth twisted in contempt. "He squealed like the proverbial stuck pig. Apparently he's been dabbling in a bit of espionage himself. Minor assignments— the only kind anyone would trust him with— for pay from a German agent based in London. This man apparently sent him here with instructions to stir up trouble for you. So Charles put in his phone call. And he also tried to frighten you with the same sort of setup he worked on Lord Hawthorne: a glowing mask and sheet rigged up to look like something supernatural."

"So it must have been Charles you saw the other morning, slipping away from my back garden," Evie said. She could decide whether she was relieved or made still more uneasy by that information. On the one hand, Charles was now in custody. On the other—

"That's what you saw?" Nigel asked. "A ghostly apparition? You never said as much."

"Would you have believed me if I had?"

"Probably not in that moment," Nigel admitted. He was silent a moment, then said, "As to why Charles would have been sent here to cause trouble for you . . . well, that's something I'd still like to know."

Evie debated, but only for a moment. All the reasons she'd given Diana for keeping her past life a secret still applied— for now. "Bring me another pound of two of flour and sugar and maybe I'll tell you."

She'd expected that Nigel might try to argue a better answer out of her, but instead he only nodded. "If you ever find yourself in a position where sharing a few secrets might be helpful, the offer's there."

Evie blinked, feeling oddly touched— which was surely absurd. Then Nigel cleared his throat and added, "I've been thinking about what you told me about your husband's parents. It's none of my business, of course. But I think you ought to go and see them. I think they'd be glad if you did."

He was right about it not being his concern, but Evie somehow couldn't manage to work up any resentment. "Maybe I will. If you agree to go and have dinner with your mother and father the next time you're invited."

Nigel looked at her, startled. "Me?"

"Yes. Your parents have already lost one son— your brother. They didn't get a choice about that. But you've got a choice about whether or not they have to lose a second son, as well."

Nigel didn't speak at once, only stood motionless, his hands in the pockets of his coat. "I hadn't thought of it that way," he said at last.

"So is it a bargain?" Evie asked.

"It's a bargain." Nigel looked as though he were about to offer to shake hands on it, but in taking his hand out of his coat pocket, an envelope fluttered out and onto the floor. "Oh, that's right, I'd forgotten," he said. "I met Willie Shoemaker, the postman, at the end of the lane and told him I'd save him the trouble of cycling out here to you since it was getting late. He just had the one letter."

He handed the envelope over to Evie. It was a plain white envelope, slightly grubby, with Evie's name written in block capitals and a return address in London that Evie didn't recognise.

Evie frowned. She had a few friends in London, still, but none who lived at that location—

She tore open the envelope. Then she went cold. The envelope contained a single sheet of ordinary notepaper with a single line printed at the top.

Found you.

— Siegfried.

THE END ... but only for now ...

... because you can continue your adventures with the Homefront Sleuths! Our next installment in the series, *The Spitfire Murders*, is now available. Just click here to order! https://geni.us/piK3ljC

Chapter Seventy-Two

Historical Notes

T his is a work of fiction, and the authors make no claim whatsoever that any historical locations or historical figures who appear in this story were even remotely connected with the adventures and events recounted herein.

However, we can make a few more observations that we hope you'll enjoy ...

1. Manor Houses in Decline

By the 1940s, many of Britain's once-grand manor houses were crumbling under the weight of modern realities. Wartime rationing, sky-high taxes, and a vanishing servant class left aristocrats scrambling to adapt—or abandon ship. Some sold their estates; others rented them out to government agencies or the military. For families like the Hawthornes, keeping up appearances was a Herculean task, especially with a war on.

2. Ghosts, Séances, and Wartime Spirits

Wartime families longing for lost loved ones turned to mediums, séances, and ghostly whispers to bridge the gap between the living and the dead. Add to that Britain's traditional love for haunted house tales, and you get a nation enthralled by the supernatural. Lady Gwendolyn's attempts to reach her late husband weren't unusual—whether by candlelight or creaking floorboard, every ghost has a story to tell.

3. Bombing of the Docklands

The docklands were London's lifeline during the Blitz, keeping Britain supplied with food, fuel, and munitions. Naturally, they were a favourite target of the Luftwaffe, with devastating raids in 1940–41 reducing warehouses to ashes and streets to rubble. Yet through the smoke and destruction, dock workers kept at it, shifting crates, repairing ships, and defying the odds. Their grit and determination didn't just keep the war machine moving—it became the stuff of legend.

4. Bonzo

Bonzo, the plucky Pomeranian, steals every scene he scampers into. One moment, he's charming Lord Hawthorne with a tilt of his fluffy head; the next, he's unwittingly assisting a villain's schemes—or blowing the whole case wide open. Following in the proud pawprints of the British canine cartoon character first created in 1922, and Bob, the terrier from Agatha Christie's *Dumb Witness*, Bonzo reminds us that even the fluffiest companions can have a nose for justice.

Chapter
Seventy-Three

A Note to Readers

Thank you for reading ***The Spectre of Hawthorne Manor***. We hope you've enjoyed it!

As you probably know, reviews make a big difference! So, we also hope you'll consider going back to the Amazon page where you bought the story and uploading a quick review. You can get to that page by using this link:

https://geni.us/xOePs

You can also sign up for our Sherlock and Lucy mailing list and get a FREE download of four new classic-style Sherlock Holmes adventures and audiobooks:

dl.bookfunnel.com/o56982auvp

If you continue to the next few pages, you'll see a list of all our adventures with links to order – they're all FREE if you have Kindle Unlimited.

Chapter Seventy-Four

Also by Anna Elliott and Charles Veley

(geni.us/w5n7)

The Crown Jewel Mystery

(geni.us/4Xf4JR)

The Jubilee Problem

(geni.us/KaiX)

Death at the Diogenes Club

(geni.us/BBeq)

The Return of the Ripper

(geni.us/Sqydk)

Die Again, Mr Holmes

(geni.us/SzaJS)

Watson on the Orient Express

(geni.us/txthZq)

Galahad's Castle

(geni.us/hs0Mjz)

The Loch Ness Horror

(geni.us/alZwfBr)

The Adair Murders

(geni.us/D0m6no)

The Cornwall Mermaid

(geni.us/ItWT)

Miss Nightingale's Gala

(geni.us/xZkBHK)

The Affair of the Coronation Ball

(geni.us/Fygm3iL)

THE SHERLOCK AND LUCY SHORT STORIES AND NOVELLAS

Flynn's Christmas

(geni.us/05rfH)

The Clown on the High Wire

(geni.us/wuaCNZE)

The Cobra in the Monkey Cage

(geni.us/Vww7n)

A Fancy-Dress Death

(geni.us/aupJEYh)

The Sons of Helios

(geni.us/hHmxk8)

The Vanishing Medium

(geni.us/964s6)

Christmas at Baskerville Hall

(geni.us/wkLFDTo)

Kidnapped at the Tower

(geni.us/hAhF)

Five Pink Ladies

(geni.us/65MWaN0)

The Solitary Witness

(geni.us/c8QLom)

The Body in the Bookseller's

(geni.us/8ZBD)

The Curse of Cleopatra's Needle
(geni.us/kBowMn)
The Coded Blue Envelope
(geni.us/aDhPW0h)
Christmas on the Nile
(geni.us/gHBvFG4)
The Missing Mariner
(geni.us/EptP)
Powder Island
(geni.us/8J1H)
Murder at the Royal Observatory
(geni.us/zvWXvcD)
The Bloomsbury Guru
(geni.us/sYBCW)
Holmes Takes a Holiday
(geni.us/WFvz)
Holmes Picks a Winner
(geni.us/UP9Ax)

THE COLLECTED STORIES
Season One
(geni.us/MBK65F3)
Season Two Volume I
(geni.us/Wl8q)
Season Two Volume II

(geni.us/JBHTr8)

Season Three Volume I

(geni.us/r7pGlK)

Season Three Volume II

(geni.us/B5kG)

THE BECKY & FLYNN MYSTERIES by Anna elliott

Guarded Ground

(geni.us/V68jco)

Hidden Harm

(geni.us/1HQOFo)

Watch and Ward

(geni.us/wnNkN)

Safe You Sleep

(geni.us/SvHX4)

Star-Sown Sky

(geni.us/SNAqd)

The Becky & Flynn series page at Amazon:

tinyurl.com/bdcnbhdj

AUDIOBOOKS

The Sherlock Holmes and Lucy James series (Audible):

tinyurl.com/4fnds4p2

The Becky and Flynn series (Audible):

tinyurl.com/227xeabr

FOLLOW US
AMAZON

Anna Elliott

(tinyurl.com/ys2u2m2s)

Charles Veley

(tinyurl.com/3rbap8ya)

GOODREADS

Anna Elliott

(tinyurl.com/2udr75dk)

Charles Veley

(tinyurl.com/46993kp8)

BOOKBUB

Anna Elliott

(tinyurl.com/mwh46rm5)

Charles Veley

(tinyurl.com/yc6w25c)

AUDIBLE

Anna Elliott

(tinyurl.com/227xeabr)

Charles Veley

(tinyurl.com/27aduhjj)

Chapter Seventy-Five

About the Authors

Anna Elliott

is an author of historical fiction and fantasy. She enjoys stories about strong women and loves exploring the multitude of ways women can find their unique strengths.

She was delighted to co-author the Sherlock & Lucy series, thrilled to continue with her own spin-off series featuring Becky and Flynn, and she's loving her time with the brave and heartwarming villagers of Crofter's Green.

Her first series, the Twilight of Avalon trilogy, is a retelling of the Trystan & Isolde legend. She wrote her second series, The Pride & Prejudice Chronicles, chiefly to satisfy her own curiosity about what might have happened to Elizabeth Bennet, Mr Darcy, and all the other wonderful cast of characters after the official end of Jane Austen's classic work.

She lives in Pennsylvania with her husband and five children.

Charles Veley

has been a lifelong devotee of writing fiction, and of Sherlock Holmes. Back in the day, he read the entire Holmes canon during bedtime stories to his ten-year-old daughter—who decades later became Anna Elliott, an established fiction writer on her own.

Since 2017, they've created thirty-four stories in the acclaimed Sherlock and Lucy Mystery series together, as well as the books in the current Homefront Sleuths series. Anna has also written many other historical novels, including five in the Sherlock and Lucy spinoff Becky and Flynn series, set in World War I Europe.

During the Seventies Charles taught at City University of New York and penned other novels before a transition to law and corporate real estate. He also wrote the Gilbert and Sullivan-inspired musical, "The Pirates of Finance," which earned an award at the NY Musical Theatre Festival in 2013.

Charles lives in Pennsylvania, near his daughter and her five children, and cherishes life with his wife of over five decades.